I0701667

IN
PIPES

IN PIPES

DOMINICK CHAVEZ

CITI OF BOOKS

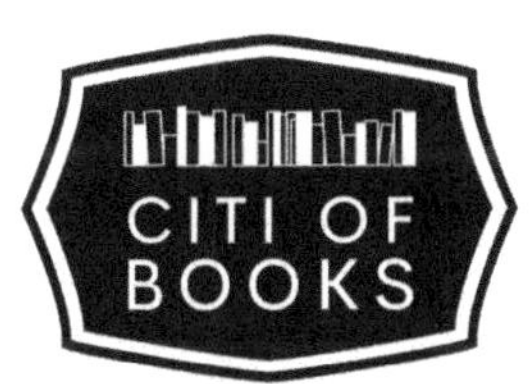

Copyright © 2024 by Dominick Chavez

All rights reserved. No part of this publication may be reproduced, distributed, or transmitted in any form or by any means, including photocopying, recording, or other electronic or mechanical methods, without the prior written permission of the copyright owner and the publisher, except in the case of brief quotations embodied in critical reviews and certain other noncommercial uses permitted by copyright law. For permission requests,write to the publisher, addressed "Attention: Permissions Coordinator," at the address below.

CITIOFBOOKS, INC.
3736 Eubank NE Suite A1
Albuquerque, NM 87111-3579
www.citiofbooks.com
Hotline: 1 (877) 389-2759
Fax: 1 (505) 930-7244

Ordering Information:
Quantity sales. Special discounts are available on quantity purchases by corporations, associations, and others. For details, contact the publisher at the address above.

Printed in the United States of America.

ISBN-13:   Softcover   979-8-89391-170-1
                   eBook   979-8-89391-171-1

Library of Congress Control Number: 2024912920

TABLE OF CONTENS

Dominick Chavez

dachavez37@gmail.com

In Pipes

By: Dominick Chavez

CHAPTER ONE

Basking in the mucky copper foundation with nowhere to go but nowhere to stay either. The spring kid, Marvin, crawls his way through the inside round path that he has lived in for some time already. Many pass through this way for one reason only, to go to The Deep. Which is why the spring kid always brings his sleeping bag along. Never is it uncommon for someone to leave behind what they bring to sleep in. Pipes always lead in many directions yet not exactly leading anywhere specific. Regardless, sometimes a creature will need to stay wherever they are at, at that moment.

It's been awhile since Marvin last saw his friends. The turns and climbs into many pipes that have been his way of getting around. As well as been ways of many answers and new housing for either a long or short time. Loosing track of his friends has never been a problem. There are many places in pipes. Regardless, if their exhibit was closer to his, The Deep would never be a priority.

Something else about getting to The Deep are the grids. Metal rusty grids that block his path most of the way getting there. One grid bothers him the most and keeps Marvin from jumping in the pool immediately. He would ask someone on the other side to take it off, but no one is there. Voices are too far down bellow to yell at anyways. He looks from left to right, wondering, why would anyone put this metal piece back? From his belt, Marvin takes out a wrench, his wrench.

Loosening a bolt or two water twists between metal with rust releasing it's tang smell. A smell all too familiar before entering The Deep. The metal grid is not a problem, but removing this barrier gets old after a while, and one time he almost dropped it. If the metal grid fell on another creature, Marvin would be frowned upon in The Deep. Last thing Marvin wants is attention from other creatures.

His fingers tighten on the grid, each finger in a separate square. Marvin feels the cold of the metal bars underneath his hands. Wet and rusty, dirty and always the same. Just as it always has been. Already he can imagine the temporary marks that will imprint his palms. With a pull, the grid completely comes out. He leaves the gate on the side where it should just stay. But again, for some reason a creature keeps putting it back on. No more worries about the door, he is in. Echos bounce from the brick walls which are held up with bolts, screws and the pipes that run and keep it together. Underneath him is the pool. He hears laughter and splashes of water. The smell is that of moisture compacted in one space, like water been closed in a jar for too long. But the moister is not that thick this time. That means, there are not a lot of creatures here. Good, makes it easier for Marvin to spot out his friends this high up.

This course, what some would call a day just not in this place, there are children splashing and jumping in the sewer pool. Marvin can see this happening from where he is but the laughter is not his concern. What is his concern is a bit more far off toward the stream from where most of the water is coming from. Like usual, Bazook is trying to keep any bulbous head from floating. The fat body pushes down with one hand inside the water. Underneath his hand, trying not to drown is one of the white round headed kids. The bulb head gets more frustrated with each breadth he has to catch. He should be more provoked with annoyance through all of this dipping but he isn't, not this time while he is trying to breath. Bazook has done this before to the same bulb boy, and hardly does the bulb boy know how to escape. The small child's voice is so high pitched that Marvin can hear screeches of it.

"Stop it!" He breaths in and has a chance to say before his head goes back inside the water. Another dip and bubbles make their way to the top. As if they had gurgled voices of their own, the bulb

boy's underwater sounds manage to reach Bazook's ears. "Don't you ever get tired of doing this?"

Bazook understanding pulls out the bulb headed kid looks at him and wonders why the child says this every time. Bazook is an odd creature. His mud like skin substitutes for fat. Both eye sockets sag as his black marble eyes look down at the child who's round head is bigger and wider than his thin stick like body. Bazook said to him plenty of times before. "You float though. Aren't you supposed to go up and down like that?" He wonders this question as the small legs of the bulb head kick rapidly as if trying to run away in the air. Bazook continues to put the boy's head in the water and watch him go up and down, wondering if he will ever stay inside the water.

Marvin climbs down the ladder. He hears the laughter and splashes get louder the further down he goes. The area is so wide, almost as vast as an entire pipe foundation housing thousands of creatures. Of course it's hollow here and every one inside can be seen. It will be a long swim to the other end to reach his bulb headed friend. Halfway down, Marvin stops and looks at the green sewage pool. The damp smell of wet sludge tinges inside his nostrils this time. He lets go for a faster landing and also to cause a splash of his own.

Inside the deep is dark and murky like ink inside water. Many lights are seen from above on the ceiling and are blurred from Marvin's view. Everyone knows about The Deep's pool, but yet other areas are difficult to reach. If Marvin had gills he would be able to swim toward any of them. At the bottom he could go and wonder inside the brick structure that looks like a maze so far down below. Enough light filters through the top, Marvin can continue looking down to see what is happening in the maze. Two black dots travel inside pathways. Like trying to see where ants are crawling to inside water, Marvin cannot help but realize how big the area gets as each dot moves further around. The light providing this sight dims. He looks up to see an elongated body passing some many feet near the top of him. The red fish-like face has large white eyes that take up almost the entire head. The serpent Leslie has a mouth that is half the size of her face. She wears her usual green drape that practically matches the muck water. Marvin always wonders why a creature like her would need one, other than to tell the serpent away from the rest of her kind. Anytime her lips move, white sharp teeth can be seen. She already knows Marvin is there and dips deeper.

With her nose so close to the spring kid, Marvin grabs next to her by the gills. Water rushes through Marvin's face. The light blocked a moment ago is familiar again and partially blinds Marvin once noticeable. Not only is the light revealed but so is the air and noises of The Deep's pool. When he lets go Leslie ignores Marvin and just swims away. As she goes, the underwater creature disappears into an opened pipe in the wall. A wall that is now nearly reaching distance that Marvin would not have to use his spring arms if he did not want to. And a wall that also ends to form a sidewalk. He swims up and feels the damp air of The Deep.

The first thing he does after collecting himself above water is swim to the now close sidewalk. He ignores everyone until he grabs hold of the side. It is wet and smells of wet dirt, even though it is made out of brick. The hard sidewalk takes little effort to get on as Marvin brings himself up letting most of the water drench through his thin layers of clothing. Bazook is still putting one of the kids in the water, trying to see when he will not float anymore. The legs on the kid now move a lot slower than before. His expression sags also. "Bazook," The big mud faced child looks at Marvin. "Can you let him go now?"

Bazook looks at Marvin with his same old confused stare. "What do you mean? Isn't that what he is for?"

"No, who wants to be dipped into water every five picks?"

Bazook scratches under his hanging chin, looking to the ceiling.

"Want to know where some of this water comes from?" Marvin changes the subject. "Water drips from the ceiling and then makes it's way down. But that's not a good thing. It can lead to overflow. Filling this place up. Then there will be no Deep. I saw water dripping from the top a while ago. Only I can stop it, and Shrub needs to help out."

Ending his confused look, Bazook drops his hand and looks at Marvin. "I don't believe you. You usually stay in the pipes."

"You should believe me." Marvin reaches toward his belt. He pulls out the same wrench that he used a while ago. Wet saggy cloths hang and he points the wrench at Bazook partially swinging it up and down. "I am one of the only creatures who can get up to the ceilings. Remember, I have the arms and legs to reach it. That means I can fix it."

Bazook knows that Marvin has spring legs and arms. If there was anyone to realize water dripping from anywhere, it would be him. "I guise you would know about something like that."

"I do know about something like that." Bringing down the wrench. "Let Shrub go. We need to make sure no water drips through any longer." Marvin smiles thinking of other things to say. "If we do not find out how to stop it, this area will flood. I don't think you can float like a bulbhead."

Bazook still holds up Shrub. Not because he wants to see if he can float again but mainly because of him thinking about the pipes that may be leaking above.

"Bazook!" Marvin reminds him that he's there as the fat creature's mind drifts.

The fat child snaps out of wonderment. "Oh, see you Shrub." Bazook let's go of Shrub. He makes his usual fall into the water with a small splash barley throwing any drops out. Only his head is seen. His skinny feet kick fast in water as if he saved all his energy just for this moment to get away.

"You better leave me alone for now on you fat slob! I don't have time for this!" Shrub says with his high pitch voice. Head above water kicking his legs and arms like little motors.

Bazook looks at Shrub hurt, as if he never did anything wrong to the bulb-head. "What did you say?"

Shrub gets up on the bricked sidewalk. Water drips off him as he walks closer to Marvin. "You heard me..." The high pitch voice is completely silenced as Marvin's hand covers the small mouth.

"Nothing, Bazook. Just, sit there and don't bother anyone." Bazook looks at both of the friends confused. Marvin forces Shrub to keep walking. "Come on let's just go. How in all these pipes do you keep getting caught by that ball of mud?"

The two friends pass where the other children are playing. Most are bulbous heads. Shrub is the smallest out of them all. "I swim next to the sidewalk and he always grabs me! I hate him, he is so damn annoying." Shrub shakes his arms to make them dry faster. His voice is not as high pitched as before but still has a shriek to it.

Marvin would tell Shrub not to float so close to the sidewalk, but he remembers when he went down a drain. Finding Shrub was no easy task. Because of his size, Shrub can fit in almost any pipe. Every pipe, no mater how big or small, needed to be searched. It did take Marvin and his friends to new areas in the exhibit, opening and entering pipes here and there. But it was the longest search any of them have done.

The small bulb head has been told not to go in the water at all. That would be too depressing for him. That would be too depressing for any creature that young. Mainly he swims to show off to all the other bulb heads that preach or make fun of him. That and Shrub is the most stubborn creature in the exhibit that Marvin has ever met.

"So where are we going?" Shrub asks with a smirk knowing that what Marvin told Bazook was a lie.

"We find Lisa. After that we go to the Wide Areas."

Shrub looks up at his friend again with a completely different expression. "You mean through Copper Tunnel? No, too many strange creatures pass through there. And never have we been to the Wide Areas before. Creations are made at that place. Who knows what those giants are capable of."

Marvin looks down at Shrub with a serious look. "Quit your worrying. There is nothing a creation can do to us unless we start messing around or something. Also, aren't you a bit curious about what is beyond this exhibit? Have you ever talked to anyone to find out how all the things we have work? We order anything from clothing to utensils from there. I want to see how that stuff is processed before it is shot out through the pipes to get to us."

"Remember when we went through the pipe Floundery?" Shrub says. "Remember that blue gilled creature who was there from the Wide Areas, and how he did not even want to talk about his job. No one from there wants to explain anything they know. Want to know why? They are all just a bunch of boring jobs that's why. Nothing special. Those creatures on the other side are no different than we are. They went the wrong way in their display of paths and created a place from nothing. Nothing but a giant working area. Not only did we meet that weirdo, but we could not find the way out of that place. Even though we never omitted that we were lost to anyone, but...we where lost!"

"Calm down already. We do not need anyone to know where we are ever going." Marvin looks around for their friend, Lisa. "I wish Lisa was never so quiet. We would find her a lot easier if she wasn't."

"Like usual her kind stays around pipes that hold plenty of water. We all know how most aquatics like misty places." Shrub says as he stretches his arms out at the same time. "Honestly, I have not seen Lisa at all. Then again, I was been dipped for a long time." Shrub says noticing Marvin looking around. "Let's see if Dodrill knows where she's at. If he's seen her, at least we will know she has been here."

Without saying anything Marvin looks for the reptilian everyone calls Dod. Luckily finding him now is not a difficult thing. Not too far away he is easy to notice with half his tail and legs inside the water as he lays back on a blanket. Eyes probably closed behind the shaded glasses he has on. The tall reptilian rests both arms behind his head slightly revealing one webbed hand. His fin that reaches from the bottom of his chin to the middle of his chest sticks out completely between his vested shirt. The two do not know if they should wake him or just ask someone else about Lisa. They walk up to Dod, quietly both lean a little closer and see if the green skinned reptilian boy wakes up. He is sound asleep. Muffled air is heard coming out slowly through his nostrils each time they shrink in and out.

"Looks like he won't be telling us anything." Marvin says, knowing that Dod is sleeping. "Let's ask someone else."

A small thump kicks Dod on his side. "Wake up you drain lizard." Shrub says as he brings back his skinny leg.

Dod twitches looking around and wonders what just happened. He sees the two who now block the light shining down upon him. Marvin with an uncomfortable kid like stare and Shrub with a mean grin. "Oh, hey creats, what's the matter. Or what should I say? Is something going wrong with me?

What's going on?" The reptile asks in his dreary state. Dod grabs a cup that's on his side and takes a drink form the straw. These are the shakes that everyone knows Dod by. Their flavor passed around all over this area. He finds different sewage drains for recipes. "You guys want to try out some of my new Sew Due?" He holds the cup closer to the two.

Shrub leans back with a cringe thinking only scaled sewer things can drink what is in the cup. Marvin practically ignores the drink. "Have you seen, Lisa?" Marvin looks around hoping to see her so he won't have to bother Dod more than he already has. Even though now it is too late. "I noticed she is not at her usual spot."

Dod takes another drink and thinks about the girl. The twist on his lips shows he doesn't know where Lisa is. If he did not see her already then everyone knows the girl is not stopping by The Deep. "I have not seen her yet. Maybe she decided to stay home." He takes another drink. The sound of the liquid filters through the straw.

"Funny because she is usually here. I'll keep looking, maybe go to her place." Marvin says still looking around for Lisa, hoping the girl will show up.

Dod leans forward to get up. His webbed feet pull out of the water dropping large amounts of it back in. The webbed feet slap the brick floor the same way a wet towel would. "I'll help you find her. None of you can go inside the pipes that have water the way I can."

Marvin would not mind the scaled guy to come along, even though there are no running water pipes to go through that he can think of where they are going. He also does not want to keep Dod from doing what Dod usually does, making new drinks. "Are you sure? We might have to go to the Wide Areas."

"That's great! I need something to do. I made this new drink and want others to check it out you see. Maybe one of those boring working creats will like what they taste. You know, lighten up their flow for once." Dod says with a laugh. Marvin does not get the humor, but he lets out a little chuckle anyway. Shrub stays quiet on purpose. "You get me. When my old pap did business with any of them on the other side. We noticed they were no different than that pile of bricks over there." He points with his reptilian snout.

"Well good. Maybe you can benefit from this. Now let's go find our friend." Shrub says. He walks toward a hanging pipe pouring water where Lisa usually stays. The ramp is wide and goes up for the water runoff but is not a problem to walk up on. It does not take the group long to get near the top. Splashes slap the ground and burst, wetting whatever is around. Shrub lifts his head trying to look behind the waterfall as he gets closer. Portions of water fall on brick as it comes out of the pipe. They smell the dreary mist as it rises. As dirty as the water looks, its vapor has a clean scent which seams undisturbed. As the three get closer to the area it is obvious no one is there. Shrub checks behind the running water anyways. The mucky wall is alone and silent. "She's gone alright."

"Well yeah." Dodrill says before taking a drink from his cup.

Before anyone has anything else to say, Marvin has another idea. "Let's go to Lisa's compartment. That's the only other place I can imagine her at." Marvin says. The two friends nod their heads, knowing how Lisa is.

"No point in staying in the deep." Shrub says. "I'm tired of seeing all my cousins and their friends and their cousins and their friends. My siblings and their friends also. A way out of this sector will be a relief actually."

Marvin smiles. "And you did not want to go."

They turn around and see families, friends, kids or whoever wants to be at the deep. Most of them are bulb heads. This is the time for families. Creatures their age will show up later. Or maybe they won't.

Regardless, the three will not be around. The search for Lisa will continue until she is found.

The laughter's volume is still loud as the three are about to make their way back down.

Back down until a creature all too familiar stands at the bottom, and he is not alone. Bazook stands underneath the wide end of the runoff ramp. He looks up at the three friends and does not say much and does not have to. There is a green thing with arms and legs standing beside him that has oval eyes and a stomach that looks like a bag filled with water. The third is something of a black beetle creature but with no wings, only shell, and has two arms and two legs. One thing that looks the same on them is their outfits.

"Yeah, they said there was a leak. I don't know guys I think that is what they are doing up there." The slow voice of Bazook says.

"Fixing leaks." A confused voice that sounds like there are shells snapping in his mouth. The beetle like creature spits seeds on the floor. He continues to chop on shells still. "Looks like a bunch of creatures just standing on top a dip trying to figure out what to do with their lives. I think they were lying to you Bazook."

"That mud ball has friends?" Shrub asks himself but also needing an answer from his own group. "I always imagined creatures just passed by him, mainly to ignore the smell."

After taking a drink from his shake, Dod crosses his arms and shakes his head. "What would bring these guys to us?"

"I think Bazook just got a few creatures concerned with a lie that would concern anyone." Marvin swallows. "Ugh…"

"I have not seen no leak." The green one with a large stomach says. "We are about to do protocol and flush this place. Not that we have done any of those things for a long time, but we find it necessary if there's leakage."

"Who named you idiots sealers of protocol." Shrub says with an angry shake of his fist. "I say you guys get out of our way. We have things to do."

The three look at each other. Beetle creature is the first to talk. "Let's go. They're just a bunch of kids."

"Wait a second." The green one says. "They pulled a false alarm. If we did follow protocol, and listened to Bazook, then this place would be flushed out and drained for no reason. That's a lot of work.

It's also not safe. Especially with all the families around. I think we need to get rid of them. They are the real problem." He presses his fingers onto his nose that then makes him sound congested. "I don't know about Bazook here. He smells like slime out of a carcass."

"We should have him to dip these guys in the drainage water. Then we can flush them to another sector. That way we can never see these idiots again."

"Whatever. We all know how much he likes to put the bulb-head in the water. How do we get his fat ass up there though?"

"What are they talking about creats?" Dod takes a drink of his shake again. "I don't know but let's bug out of here ourselves." Marvin says.

"Bazook stays here and we go up and chase 'em. You got that Bazook?" Beetle creature looks up at the large child.

"Um, ya sure."

"Good lets go."

As the two make their way up, Marvin holds back his arm as if to pitch a ball. The two stop with wide eyes and wonderment. The green one is surprised by Marvin's action. "He's got something. The spring kid is going to throw it at us."

There is a loud laugh. "That spring kid could not hit a moth the size of that pipe up there." The creature nods up. "Quit been such a sap and lets get them. It was your idea."

Marvin puts the wrench to the pipe above him. There is a reason why not too much water is allowed from the pipe above. He loosens a bolt that allows not much but little more water to come out. Shrub looks at Mavin wondering why he does not twist it fully. "Well, let it all out."

"The place will flood."

"It will get rid of these guys at least. Everyone in here can swim." Shrub's stubborn voice comes out. "I don't see what the big deal is."

"He's loosening the bolts." The two creatures quicken their pace to get to the top of the ramp. "Screw it." Marvin says.

"More like, unscrew it." Dod replies. "You know this will keep us out of here for good?"

Marvin thinks about what Dod said. "We are going to a bigger place anyways." The spring kid loosens the bolt causing more water to spill.

The steepness of the ramp intensifies with all the water coming down. "I can't make it. The green creature says and slips. His beetle friend has no time to reply and falls also. Bazook on the other hand lets the water surround his fat body and poor into the pool behind him.

"It worked." Shrub says.

Marvin's wrench is still on the bolt. Not because it's stuck, but because he cannot tighten it back to where it was. "Oh yeah. Now I can't seal it. Find something to block the pipe." Marvin looks down the ramp. Surprisingly, the water is now up to Bazook's stomach. "Great."

"Nothing around here is going to block that!" Shurb says as water pours out. Yells and laughter increases. No telling whether which are in terror or joy. "Use your arms to spring us out of here."

"I can't carry you both." Marvin puts the wrench in its place on his belt. "Dod can you swim?

I'll hold on and pull you as best I can."

"Of course, creat. But no need. The serpents are already taking creatures out of here." He takes a drink from his shake. Serpent creatures like Leslie and herself are letting other ride them as they get out of the now flooding Deep. "Just wait. They will be here soon. Looks like these two will need to drain this place after all."

"Not for us." Marvin looks at the slob of a creature Bazook. It takes two serpents to carry him. Water is now up to his chin. The spring kid looks around the ceiling for anything to grab hold of. Many rusted handles from some time never were took out. Handles where creatures hardly to never hang around on anymore. Will they hold the three friends? "Shrub find a way out. I need to pull Dod and myself up."

In the middle of the Deep are two hands flying in the air. Two springs stretch underneath. Marvins's hands reach the ceiling directly above. Dod drops his drink and grabs hold of Marvin's waste. With the water and pull he brings Dodrill and himself out and they fly up. Shrub takes hold of Dod's tail as the three fly up.

The fat creature's hands are now above water because it's Bazook's turn to make bubbles underneath. Both serpents are having problems as they float as best they can with the fat slob. All other creatures are either gone or almost out. Marvin notices this as he grabs the rusted handles moving toward the wall like a monkey. "He will definitely drown if no one helps."

"And that's a bad thing?" Shrub is able to hear his friend. Marvin is not sure if he is serious or just sarcastic.

The two workers are already on higher ground, forgetting about who brought this situation upon them in the first place. The three are able to make it to an opened pipe. As Shrub goes deeper in Dod looks at Marvin wondering why he stopped.

Marvin with both hands springs out his arms to grab hold of the fat child. Realizing there are hands above him the slob creatures own hands grab hold of Marvin. "I don't think I can do this." The body of Marvin pulls back. There is so much going on it's a bit of a hassle and it seems as though the water is rising faster for some reason. Marvin just a thing in the air for now tries his hardest to bring in his two springs. "I don't know if I can do this." He has to say again.

Dod sees as Marvin struggles to pull Bazook. "Oh crap, Marv is having a hard time." Dod turns toward what is happening with Marvin and Bazook. "Aren't you going to help?"

Rolling his eyes, Shrub does the same. "I guess." The two wrap their arms around Marvin's waste once more. With the three on ground and water lifting and two serpents. They lift the fat body as

best as they can. Shrubs legs running as fast as possible. He wonders why he's using this effort to help the same creature that caused him to swim like this in panic earlier. Kicking mud everywhere behind him.

The Deep is practically full and all the children and families are gone. The two workers are drenched but bring themselves to their own pipe elsewhere across. They look around for the children that did this.

Dod sees them as they struggle. "I'm guessing those guys will be looking for us."

The fat creature sees the roof and reaches for a bar. He grabs hold and relieves the three somewhat. All they can hope for is that the bar doesn't break. Out of all of them, Bazook breathes the heaviest in panic. "We are going to have to find another sector for sure after all this." Marvin says trying not to lose focus. The serpents are able to bring

Bazook to where the three friends are. All meet up. Two fish like heads stick out of water.

"How did this happen?" One asks.

Before Bazook has anything to say Dod gives him a drink. Marvin smiles at the two serpents. "I have no idea guys but we got to go home."

CHAPTER TWO

There is a drip somewhere. An echo in the hollow tin distance. That is about all the three friends hear. Some pipes are a way out and also a way in somewhere else. They walk past a skinny man with wide eyes and a beak that points at them. There are feathers where hair should be above his head. The rest of the creature is bald. The three pass by not saying a word and travel through the pipe. Deeper inside the tunnel a sleeping bag rests on the side with no one inside. Realizing that might be the bald feathered creature's, the three just look at the bag. Small grid gates get ignored by anyone who passes. The wet tangy smell of rust lingers inside these pipes, like it does in most. As they reach a fork leading three directions the third on their right is the path they go through. The pipe pathway gets wider. Steam leaks from a corner. Metal patches bolted to keep any more of the mist to seep out, along with vents in other parts. Many chrome doors appear on the sides. Each one looks different if not for the rusty patterns that appear overtime.

Marvin starts the first conversation since they left The Deep. "You know, I feel like we are on the run. We shouldn't bring this to Lisa."

"We are on the run and it's not like she will get blamed. Even if we are found here by anyone." Shrub walks looking at each door. "Everyone knows how quiet she is. And knows that she would not get involved with something so scheming to make her life difficult."

"That's the problem, creat." Dodrill takes a drink form his shake. "No one knows what she does.

She is such a secret creature. I'm surprised she has a job."

The friends stop at a door, Marvin knocks. No one shows up for awhile, but that is expected.

The view slit slides moments later and two black eyes appear.

"Marvin," Lisa's mother says in a wisp of a voice. She is not one for much talk just like her daughter, so she tries to make every conversation as brief as possible. "Are you looking for Lisa? Because she is not here."

Marvin looks at Shrub then at Dod confused. "Do you know where she may be, Kristy?"

"Thought she would be at The Deep like always. Or with you." The black eyes turn out of sight now reveling sleek black hair. "Ben," The three friends hear her call out to her husband from the other side of the door. "Do you know where Lisa is at?"

A faint "no" is heard. Kristy's eyes appear once more. "We don't know where she is at. Check the Plate Works room. Maybe she went to go make dishes." Marvin is about to ask Kristy why Lisa would be there at this time but she talks before he has time to ask. "Let me know if you see her. I will tell her you came by if she comes home. Wire me." The slide closes.

Marvin turns around facing his friends confused. "Lisa never goes far, and never travels to different areas alone. I doubt she will have to be wired."

"I hope she did not fall into a pipe by mistake. Maybe she is making dishes." Shrub says concerned. "Looks like her and her family are in need of some trade."

"They're probably thirsty at that shop. Now I can find more creatures to check out my new shake. I should of asked Lisa's peeps if they wanted to try some." Dod takes a big drink from out of a straw. "I don't think she would of payed much attention though."

"Is that all you think about?" Shrub goes back to been angry as he looks at Dodrill.

"Let's just go to Plate Works. Maybe she is making ceramics. Weird why she would change her routine. Or who knows, maybe she just felt like molding a plate or two." Marvin says while still thinking that bieng only one possibility.

Dod takes a huge drink from the bottle again. He wipes his mouth with his scaled arm in relief. "Plate Works it is then. We better hurry, or else she will come back here and we will still think she is

lost." He looks around the area. "You think if I leave this here in front of the door Lisa's parents will pick it up?"

"Just take it." Marvin tells Dod knowing that whoever is inside would not care.

"Yeah, better not." He takes another drink. "Well if she does show up. Will her mom wire you right away?" Dodrill asks bieng the one who knows least about the family.

"I doubt it." Shrub says irritated. "Kristy will be so concerned in wiring whoever else she communicated with, that she will forget about us. To her, we will get in contact with Lisa regardless. Right Marv?"

As much as he hates to omit it, Marvin has to agree. "Yup, that does sound like Lisa's mom. Come on. Let's just go to the shop."

***

The path to the ceramic shop is more of a bridge. As difficult as the narrow walkway is inside the Plate Works the creatures manage to withstand the thin path surrounded by muck water. Shrub slips.

Dod who is behind him holds out his webbed hand to catch the small bulb head. With his hand up, Shrub indicates he is okay.

"Why do they make it so difficult to get in here?" Shrub complains.

Marvin does not like the situation also, but knows the reason is not a bad one. "So no creatures will walk or run out with ceramics. Unless you have wings or can crawl on a wall, this so called path would be more than difficult to get away on."

"Or spring arms." Dod interrupts. For once this entire time he does not have a drink in hand. "We're just here to find someone." Marvin keeps his balance. The door up ahead is metal and looks heavy. The three can only hope it's not locked. "I guess workers have to do this all the time. That or there has to be a pipe only for them."

"I heard the owner lives here. Common for any creature that has a business." Dod says looking into the water. "I wonder what would happen if we fell in?"

"Nothing. That's why this is stupid." Shrub says looking at the door, wanting to get closer. "Creatures can swim good around here. Even if they don't have gills like you many know how to swim regardless."

"There's dye in there, guys." Marvin figures they should know better. "Once you get out, you will be crap green for who knows how long." He says judging by the color. "You will be marked for anyone to see and taken into a cell." Meaning that many businesses do this in case of robbers. Finally reaching the floor at the door that has little room. Marvin knocks not wasting any time. Nothing but a few tings and bashes are heard on the other side while no one answers. "I hope we do not need some kind of invitation."

"Shouldn't." Shrub says examining the door. "This is a public shop." He reaches for the bar which is the handle. There again is a path but this time there are creatures.

Marvin concentrates on the few workers who sit on the sides of this walkway their feet dipped in water. But different water than what they passed earlier. Other creatures stand and are stepping in the water creating mud. Pans of mud are by the sitting worker's side on the walkway as they reach inside the water with dirty hands. Placing globs of the mud in the plates. Latter on, these globs of mud will be molded into another shape. The creatures will make plates out of what they pull out. It's when a worker gets their preferred amount for the mud clay to be ready to be shaped inside the shop that takes the most time. Lisa is not among any of them. Someone gets up with a full plate of clay. Brown mud drops fall from the rim of the dish as the girl walks. She is a skinny looking girl with a beak that is almost her entire face with eyes that are too hard to notice. The girl looks at the friends for awhile with her beak pointing right at them. Not thinking much of the group the worker walks toward another door opposite from where ethe three came from.

Shrub swallows wondering if he is the only one feeling suspicious about the beaked girl.

"Let's follow her." Marvin says ignoring any kind of procedure the workers may need to follow. No one bothers the friends as they pass. The beak faced girl opens the door, revealing many small pipes in the next room. A burst of heat can be felt and the door begins to slowly close. Marvin is able to reach the knob before the door is completely shut. Spring arms have their advantages. The beaked face girl opened the door without a problem. But the three react as if the door would lock. They look at each other and walk forward. Some creatures look at them now as if wondering who this spring kid, bulb boy and reptilian guy are.

As the three enter there are large can kilns that all the small pipes lead to. There are small walls that are in front of the kilns and a small area beyond them which is hard to make out where the three stand.

There are many ceramic that are placed around the area. Not far away the girl already walks into a room that has a large table. The room the friends are in is empty. There must be a certain time when the molding starts. Once again the three friends continue to go toward the worker. "You are not allowed in there." A voice is heard. The three friends look around and see nobody. They ignore the voice and take another step closer. "I said get out!" All three stay put knowing that they are the ones been talked to. "You are distracting everyone. You have no business here." By now the three friends know the voice is coming from inside the room the girl is in. With her now gone not blocking their vier. Inside the room they see someone disturbing.

What can be a relative of Bazook stands, or holds, himself on the table with his two thick muddy arms. His face is like a slime ball with wide eye sockets, the same as Bazook but with different eyes. Instead he has huge white balls that have black pupils which now stare at the friends. There are no legs other than a tale that drags on the table. As the mud head gets closer the tail is obviously behind what is both the head and body. "Did you here what I said, leave slumps!"

The friends have to twitch. Their emotion leans back been completely uncomfortable with this guy. Marvin wants to ask about Lisa but cannot find the nerve to say a word. The mud head moves his arms fast, getting closer. His face gets angrier as the mud sockets tighten like knots. Obviously he is going to attack the three and says no more. The mud head makes sure whatever pottery is around does not get ruined.

"Lisa, Lisa." Marvin says then smiles hoping it will stop the creature who is most likely the boss of the place.

The boss does not stop but slows down. "She's off today." He holds one hand to the corner as if to grab hold of something. Perhaps a weapon to keep pesky kids out. Or it could just be the door.

Marvin opens his mouth but there is a slam that feels like something hit inside his ears. All the spring kid can see now is a closed door.

"At least we know she is not here." The high pitch voice of Shrub says. They have no choice but to walk away.

Dod takes out a glass bottle from his pocket. He places it in front of the door. "What are you doing that for? Put that stuff away. You might get Lisa in trouble once she comes back."

The reptile shakes his head. "No, this liquid is made from the frost of the cooling pipes. Maybe this guy will like it. Looks like he needs it."

The small bulb head looks at Dod as if what he says is meaningless. "Whatever." Shrub says turning around. He looks at Marvin with his usual disappointed face. "I would have assumed that she would not be here for a long time with a boss like that."

"Maybe she just needs a place to keep busy." Dod says taking his usual drink from whatever shake he has now. "That's how that creat is. I like her because she never says much. She's like a ghost that likes to chill with you guys. So if her parents and even this guy do not know where she is, then how the heck are we supposed to find her?" He takes a big drink, some of the shake comes out of the side of his long mouth. Shrub looks in disgust.

"Well," Marvin says. "I did find her one time when she sounded her flute. I told Shrub about this before. Maybe you remember." Marvin looks at Shrub to see if he remembers the time. Shrub twists his lips trying to think of the details. "It was inside a bricked room that reached maybe about twenty feet high. Various pipes ended all around inside. The place was used for water drainage a long time ago. It's pointless now that all the pipes have been connected. Anyways, I heard the sound of a low note. Then it got a little higher with maybe three more notes that looped again. When I looked down that room it was the first time I saw the girl smile. She has small eyes so it was easy to see her brows rise on top pure black eyes. Her gills all stretched as she looked up and saw me. Climbing down was not a problem with so many pipes around. Neither was jumping out of there with her in my arms because of how skinny she is."

"So what are you trying to tell us, we listen for a flute?" Dod says trying not to sound so blunt. "No, but in case we do hear one most likely it might be her. I think she was calling for help that time. Even though she told me she just wanted a place to play."

"If she is lost, that is." Shrub says as he opens the door they came in.

"Eh, ya." Marvin hoping this searching for Lisa will be an easy and fast task. "And that flute broke anyways."

Shrub stops with the door ajar. He laughs but then stops. "You think that a flute like that might be made of clay?" He looks at his friend. "We should maybe, take a look around." Both Marvin and

Dod look at each other not sure if searching the place is a good idea. Without knowing it, Shrub closes the door. The three start walking around the room as if they were allowed to. What does it matter, this is a shop anyways. Or at least supposed to be one. Getting a closer look around, there are other sections that store the pottery and whatever tools necessary.

"Look over here." Marvin says walking toward the kilns where the walls are half the size of them. On the other side, there are various objects placed on shelves some even been brass or tin. Clay bowls and other materials are waiting to be fired up. Other objects been dishes, figurines and even random objects like caring trays or certain tin handles for attaching to what may be needed of them.

"I thought this stuff would be inside the working area." Shrub says.

"No, these are finished molded pieces. All of them need to still go in a kiln. Probably need a glaze of some sort. Let's see if there are any instruments." Marvin steps forward. The other two follow him. Then they stop and see there are a lot more items then they expected.

"Aye ugh, you want to look through all these, Marvin? What are we looking for exactly?" Dod asks while staring at all the porcelain makes. "It will take forever to find a flute."

"Just maybe if we find something of hers here, it can tell us where she is at. Otherwise I have no other way of knowing."

Shrub looks over the side of the wall. "Hurry you guys. That mud ball gives me the creeps, even more than Bazook."

The three scrambles through a few things. Finally, Marvin comes across some made up whistles and a small trumpet. The trumpet shocks Marvin by how precise it is. Regardless, he moves the large piece aside and what is behind all the instruments on the counter is a small harp. The instrument is no wider than Marvin himself, and barely reaches past where his elbow should be. The spring kid grabs it and takes a good look at the piece. "I think she made..."

"Get down!" Shrub hisses. All three drop. Dod focuses on Shrub as Marvin examines the harp.

A door is slammed for the second time. The mud boss walks placing one arm in front of the other. The same skinny beak faced girl follows him to the clay area. "Man I hope he does not come this way." "What's happening?" Dod asks.

"Just stay down and do not make any noise. I'm sure he will go back inside the work area. Slime face went where all those workers were getting the clay."

Realizing the harp has a break at the bridge, Marvin wonders if he should look around for any other parts. The pillar of the instrument is rough and bumpy. Even for Marvin, who does not know too much about instruments, thinks this is too much of a rough grip.

The hiss comes out from Shrub again. "Here he comes." The boss walks with the beak face girl with a plate full of clay. The two walk toward the room they were just in, until suddenly the eyes widen of the boss. Shrub shrieks and hides behind the wall. He does not move any closer to his friends. The boss keeps walking even though his eyes do not take their attention away from the kilns. There is a door slam. Shrub is not sure if he should bring himself back in closer but does so anyway. "He's back inside. Are we finished here?"

Marvin looks for what may have broken off from the harp but finds nothing. "I think we should go."

Shrub stops his worrying and looks back at Marvin. Seen more closely at the stored pieces a certain skull catches his attention and looking at it more he realizes why. It is that of a swimming kind of creature. He knows because most swimming creatures have sharp teeth, which the skull has. "That looks cool." All three friends look at the shelf and the skull does look aquatic. The maxilla and front mandible stick out. Even with sharp teeth there are many inside the mouth. The eye sockets wide.

Where the cheek bones are they stick out along with the maxilla. The jaw bone is pointy at the ends. "This shape looks like the kind of creature Lisa is. And look at all those teeth. Maybe she made this too... for some reason."

Marvin only wanting to take anything important wonders about the skull. And this skull does seem important. "Take it." He nods to Dod, indicating for the backpack. The reptile turns slightly so

Marvin puts it in a pocket. "Now let's leave."

"You know we're stealing." Shrub finally questions what they are doing.

"We'll pay the store back." Marvin ready to leave does not worry about what any of them are doing. "We could of bargained earlier, but that mud ball tried chasing us out."

Shrub is the first to move away from the small area not questioning anything, knowing it's time to leave. The three walk down the small pathway between kilns and another blank white wall, staring at the door leading out.

"Are you stealing from me?" The friends already know who's voice that is, and a very unpleasant tone drags with it. The mud boss quickly shows himself, blocking the pathway. "Now, I can simply drown you and make you into clay. What do you think of that?" The mud boss walks closer with his tail on the floor slowly squirming side to side like a worm. The friends wonder if he is serious or not, either way they are in trouble. "Maybe I can put you in one of the kilns after and make wonderful pieces of dishes out of you. Ya!" Now his eyes seem to be getting wider like air going inside balloons. Pore's start to open and letting out a damp kind of steam the same way some of the pipes do. "No, I think I will just eat the three of you. I'm always hungry!"

"You got issues creat." Dod says in a joking manner. Even though none think this is much of a joke.

"I'll give you currency when I come back. Where we are going there is a lot of wax." Marvin says knowing the Wide Areas should have plenty of these things. Wax is very useful and used on so many occasions in this sector. Every creature needs some but it is always hard to make or get by.

"If I needed wax, I would order it. And for food well, I can just swallow worthless creatures.

Worthless creatures like you!"

Right now they do feel worthless. Taking pottery. Just barging in the place. Even though they thought the Plate Works was a shop. "What should we do?" Shrub gasps at Marvin. The spring kid stays still having no answer. By reflex he roles up his sleeves. Never doing this before he closes his fists aiming them at the boss. The springs let out.

The blob is not done talking. Fists go inside of the boss's throat. There is wetness at the knuckles. Just the feel makes Marvin quickly bring his arms back in. He has to let out the muck on the floor. "Yuck. You sick bastard." Marvin has to say.

Before the boss finishes talking his wide mouth shuts and a cough forces its way through. His face along with some of his body twists to the side trying to clear whatever kind of throat he has.

Choking in and out comes hiccups. He coughs some more sounding like an empty pipe shooting out air. "Ill get you, just hold on." Another hiccup.

Surprised, the three just caused a new problem. "He's dying." Now Dod is amused in fright. "Damn it." Marvin acts like his punch was supposed to just keep the mud ball back. With the

damage done, there is something he needs to do. He walks to the boss and hits the back of him, as if the boy knows what he is doing.

Then the tail acts on it's own, or at least it seems that way, and wraps around Marvin's stomach. There is a laugh and the mud creature opens it's nasty mouth as wide as its body allows. The spring kid can smell his breath that is no different than that of mold. Maybe this creature can swallow him whole but Marvin has another talent of his own. His right leg stretches out like the spring it is and kicks between the bosses leg-arms.

Shrub takes out the skull from Dod's backpack and runs. He hits the forehead of it onto the forehead of the boss.

Marvin drops but just because the mud boss looses focus on him. "That, now that was too far." He touches his head knowing it hurt. His tail reveals that it has more than one purpose and is used as a leg at times. As it holds the boss up. Holds him up until he brings his arm down to step back. Then the boss starts to act dreary. His body moves side to side for a bit. Then a fall. The three are confused.

"Ha, my shake did serve a purpose." All three see what made the boss fall. The almost empty glass jar of Dod's drink roles toward their feet. The tale must of knocked it when the blob fell. Dod picks it up been the only one who cares that it is not damaged. Obvious as the other two run out. Then all three make it to the door. They pass the workers who this time do pay attention to them. The door leading out of the clay area is pushed with such force some of the workers flinch.

Outside the Plate Works Marvin and Shrub look at one another with confusion on their faces. Dod gives the glass a little shake.

"Surprised he did not drink all of my Shockla."

Marvin and Shrub now stare at Dod. "You call that, Shockla?" Marvin asks not worrying about what just happened yet still thankful because of the big break they just had.

"No, all the drinks are shockla. This one is called ugh, I have not named it yet but it needs a name now. The ice must of affected the slob. Chilled him so much it put him to sleep."

"Your thinking too much. Most likely poisonous. Make sure you first test your stuff man. Let's just get out of here." Shrub says. The three start to go further from the shop, hoping no one will know about their handling with the slob boss inside.

Getting away from the area is more than a relief. Marvin sits on a pipe wondering what he should do next. Loosening pipes and then knocking out a boss at a shop is no way of feeling as if all is okay. There are tappings in other pipes elsewhere. Which are more than likely other creatures.

Splashing of water is running in a more opened pipe some other place where the friends pay no attention. Marvin asks to look at the skull and places it next to the harp.

"So what are we going to do with those? How will any of these items help find Lisa? Not like it was a risk getting them you know." Other than his sarcasm, Shrub sees as Marvin looks at the instrument. With such odd looking pieces he is curious why someone would make them.

"That boss said he throws creatures in kilns." Marvin examines the skull more than the harp.

Laughing Shrub looks at Marvin as if he was joking. "You believe that slob? One of those workers there would of reported him if that guy was throwing his workers in there."

"But the skull is so much like her kind. No doubt it is. It makes no sense why she would just make some random skull like this. And why is this harp broken?" Questions are all that Marvin has. If

the shop owner wasn't trying to attack them, maybe he could of spent the time looking and asking what everything was exactly.

"Is that harp similar to the flute she played before?" Dod asks looking down at the broken instrument.

"Hard to tell. This looks more rough. I'm not sure actually." Marvin looks at Dod, then around the small area they are in. "That was a long time ago." Marvin looks under the skull. There is a small glisten on the top under the dome. Tape? Marvin wonders, for the skull is not yet glazed. He reaches in and pulls the piece off and exactly as he thought a sticky strip of clear tape. A small paper falls out.

"What just fell?" Shrub looks at the floor hoping whatever it was does not get lost.

Marvin stands as he picks it up and starts to unfold the small square. Before he says that there is writing on it, each friend already looks over one of his shoulders. The note reads:

"Here is the first piece to my creation. It should work well with what I'm trying to make. I still need the rest, given the time and effort it should become what I intend it to be. So please do not fire this up for it's not finished."

-Lisa

Brief, Marvin thinks to himself. He still let's out a sigh of relief knowing that the skull is Lisa's. "Creation. She is in the Wide Areas then." Dod says with his eyes open. "We been on the right

track! Heck, it was a lucky pick getting that." He points. "Who knows, maybe she has other clay works in there that we may need." He takes a drink of his shake.

Shrub loughs this time it's louder than any of them heard before. Not loud but still the amusement of the situation shows. "At least we know she was not thrown in a kiln."

"Yes, and at least we know where she is, most likely. You guys read it, she is trying to make a creation. One that is her own race because this skull is her own kind after all." Marvin folds up the note putting it in his pocket. "Come on, let's get out of here. I wonder why she would never tell me." He does not mention it, but he knows Lisa is very quiet. To create another one of her species, which is called murner, would mean most likely an easy way to have someone that really understands her and can be with her. A created murner a new friend perhaps.

"That is some tough clay she is using." Shrub breaks Marvin's focus. "Knocking that guy out and not breaking it was actually pretty cool."

Dod chuckles and agrees. Marvin practically ignores Shrub and the three keep walking. "Could be a certain kind of clay. Who knows."

CHAPTER THREE

Stepping out of a chrome door, Dod leaves his home to where the group waits for him. The door creaks as it rubs on rust and closes shut. There is no other indication that other homes are there. Bumps of plastic and wiping of cloth is heard with each step Dod takes. He has on his usual backpack that has the many plastic bottles strapped on. Some straps hang and dangle from the pack which are torn and never repaired. Others that are now seen hold together by safety pins. The lizard just attached those. He knows he will need more room if he's going to hold shakes and the clay molds.

Across on the wall from the door Dod came out of are pipes. Some have water pouring out while others don't. Water is all that is heard in this section, water dropping or running. Marvin examines all of the pipes as he tries to figure out which one leads to Copper Tunnel. Beside him Shrub holds out a map that Dod brought out. The map labels multiple wide lines with wording of pipe names in them. Other lines are solid black, indicating that water constantly flows through with the names of the pipes on the top. Other lines have a thin black line in the middle and different times that begin with 1 to 30, with the pipe's name at the bottom. These pipes are called radical pipes. One to thirty are how many splits there are during one course.

Shrub brings out a mechanical button. That of a compass or a watch. It only has one needle that points at what time a current split is. The needle points at nineteen out of the thirty. "One more split till middle time is over." He says hoping Dod hears him. The numbers on the maps are to tell what the times are when water comes through and for how long. Many choose to ignore the radical pipes because the timing can be off. Usually when someone wants to go inside a radical pipe, the timing is mainly for reference, but cannot be trusted.

Dod walks closer to the two, getting his bottle-backpack adjusted. "Alright lets go." Dod looks down at Shrub. "Are you sure you do not want to go to your place and get something for you and Marvin to sleep in? I can use my bag as a pillow no big deal. Since you and Marv went half on the map and time button you might not have any trade for bags down the trails." He looks around with his fin waddle dangling almost the same way the straps do. "Which pipe are we going through anyways?"

Shrub looks at Dod mad and confused. "You live here so you tell me. And no. If someone went to my parents place and told them about what happened at Plate Works, I will never be able to leave. If I really need one I will spend what we have left. Now hurry up and tell us which pipe to go through."

With his reptilian eyes Dod looks down at Shrub a bit irritated. "I never go to Copper Tunnel." He looks up at a circular opening that is not much of a pipe anymore but still has a small amount of water coming through. A brick frame has been built around the rim. There are multiple ladders that are all attached together going under pipes horizontal and vertically. The seepage from this tunnel is very light, running down the wall beneath it. The bricks are painted with dirt and green moss from the constant runoff of water. Dod points to the opening. "That leads to Copper Tunnel. Or at least has a pipe that does. I know some of these other pipes lead there also but are radical. To be safe this is the more convenient one everybody usually goes through. It takes longer but at least we won't be sprayed out."

All three look at the wide opening. Nothing is heard for a moment other than splattering of water.

"If this leads to Copper in anyway, that should be good enough." Shrub finally says.

"Hold on." Marvin looks at the opening more closely. "We still do not know where the tunnel will take us directly. It's one way to Copper Tunnel through one of these other pipes but there are other paths or pipeways in there. If we pass the right pipe or even another that leads to the Wide Areas, we will be more lost than anyone throughout the sector."

Sipping through a straw, Dod looks down at the map. "Study that map of yours. If you guys want to go straight to Copper Tunnel, find the pipe. If not we will go through the path and follow the map from there. Does not matter to me what we do." He takes another huge drink.

"Well I just found out the reason why everyone goes through the tunnel like your saying." Shrub looks up at the two. "Shrubs right. The only pipe to Copper is a radical one." Shrub follows the map. Than looks up at the wall to the right. He points to a pipe that now has no water coming through, for now. The pipe is high, but not hard to reach as a ladder runs straight up toward it, so anyone could pass the horizontal ladders attached to the side and go straight to the pipe. "It's that one right there. The number on the map for the pipe is twenty three."

"How much more splits till then?" Dod asks.

Shrub stares at the round timer again. The needle still on nineteen. All stare at the timer. The common way to tell time is to wait. Dots are too hard to time on some timers. No one keeps track of dots to add up to a pick. That would be too hard to time. One hundred dots complete a pick. One hundred picks make a split, and there are thirty splits per course. This needle only points at what split it is. Then the needle moves to twenty. "We got three splits. Should we go?"

Marvin looks at the pipe, then at the tunnel. "Usually the times are correct, but they are sometimes inaccurate. If we get pushed out then we will have to start all over again. How long does it take until water to comes out?"

Shrub looks at the map. "Different times, Marvin. Last time water shot was actually two courses ago."

"Wow, that's a huge gap." Dod once again drinks from his bottle.

"The tunnel is the best choice. We will find our way to Copper that way. If we somehow pass it, then we will have to find another one to the Wide Areas." Marvin starts to sink into the ground. Then, his legs get longer and stretch pass his normal height. The brown shoes he wears pass Shrub's then Dod's head. Both feel the air wisp past them as Marvin leaps up. Marvin brings in his legs to normal height once he lands onto the tunnel entrance.

"That's not fair." Dod says. He takes one more drink and places the cup in one of the straps. He begins climbing the ladder. Shrub follows putting the map between his pants and waste since his pockets are too small. Above Dod turns his body in a crawling position as his stomach rubs on the ladder he climbs. Grabbing hold of an attached ladder that runs horizontal is not difficult because of his reptilian way of moving. The reptile manages pretty well on the wall ladders even as he stays climbing sideways. Shrub continues to go straight up on the ladder he's on. Although Dod went in different turns, he makes it to the tunnel before Shrub.

Shrub on the other hand falls on his ass. He rubs his nose and shakes his head. Marvin ignored how small the creature is with such a head is so wide that his skinny arms need to work extra to do certain tasks. One been climbing. Marvin's spring arms come out again and reach for Shrub. Not weighing much Marvin lifts the bulb head up like usual.

When the bulb head is stable the first thing he does is reach for the map. "Let me see what this tunnel is called."

The spring kid is the first to notice a scratched metal plate sealed to the side. There is a name on it. "Mark's Tunnel. If we get lost, make sure to meet up at Mark's Tunnel." Marvin says. The three walk forward into the poorly lit path.

CHAPTER FOUR

Many pipeways are ignored by the trio. Looking at the map and from what they have seen shows many pipes, which are expected. Been around them though makes difficult to believe what entryways Mark's Tunnel holds. As long as they get to Copper Tunnel that's all the three care about. Some pipe entries lead to what is on the map, others that are not. Palines Grove and Brick Foundation been two of them marked on the map. Shrub points these out and along with other names wondering if they have what they are called inside of them. Marvin mentions how certain areas in their exhibit after awhile look similar. Other than the Deep, names are odd like Sharp Valley. Yet the area is nothing more than another bricked room that has nothing but four pipes that lead different places. Sometimes the only differences of these rooms are the brick color, and that is mainly because of how much time and water has passed through them.

Out of curiosity they decide to look through a small pipeway that leads to the area "Iron Foam". Crawling through to reach the area "Iron Foam" the place is how they expected. It is a large room with it's brick stained by settling muck. Many pipes are present, but yet, nothing new. The friends turn around back into Mark's Tunnel.

Shrub decides to break the silence. "Alright," He brings the map down. "We been walking for three splits already, and there has been more pipeways showing up than we realized. Looking at the map is helpful but I get confused to which pipes are which and which ones don't exist on the map."

"Do you need a break or something?" Dod asks before he takes a drink of one of his shakes.

The reptile pulls out another one from the side of his bag handing it over to Shrub. "I'm tired of those things. We need...I need something real to eat."

Dod looks around at the various entry ways to the pipes. "Which one leads to an eating place?

We are using too much of my shockla anyways."

"Yeah, I'm honestly sick of it." Shrub says with his eyes wide.

Marvin would tell Shrub to calm down but seeing that Dod has not gotten irritated by Shrub so far he decides to leave it alone. Marvin looks at Shrub strangely to indicate for the bulb head to calm down though. He turns his head to look at the pipes and then down at the map. "Which one has the nearest living section." Marvin looks around squinting his eyes in confusion. "Actually, are we still in our exhibit?"

"We are, until we turn into another pipe. Otherwise this tunnel is for any exhibit really. Just none of us have ever been this far. Unless you have." Shrub looks at Dod.

"Nope." He takes another drink.

"Well, from what was at Iron Foam, nothing is that different. Meaning that the Wide Areas have a unique reputation for a reason. Reason why Lisa probably went there to complete her creation. Where else can she go?" Shrub looks around. "We just need to find some place close that has food."

All three study the map, trying to find a proper area. Dod's skinny long green finger get's placed on a pipe on the map. "There, this pipe called Mossy Drive leads to a section that has living quarters.

There should be food there."

With no reason to object they all fallow the pipe on the map. "Alright, where's it at then?" Marvin straightens up trying to find the entrance.

The bulb head looks to where the pipe should be. He sees exactly where it is indicated on the map and has the name, Mossy Drive, written on the rim. It is practically on the ground. Now all the friends need to do is step inside. Shrub folds the map, putting it into his pocket while he walks toward the pipe. The other two follow and read the name carved on the top of the rim. Like before the name should not indicate much. Marvin takes a step inside. No more than a pick later Marvin is not seen anymore. Surprised, Shrub steps closer and disappears as well. There was a quick echo that disappeared as quickly as the two went in. Dod looks at where their steps ended and takes a step forward as well.

The ground tips creating a slide. He takes a big drink from his bottle, sits at the edge of the tipping area and lets himself fall forward.

Marvin's face is hit. Not by anything solid or that can bruise, but by portions of water that fly at him. It is almost as though a hose is in front of him just spraying and never stopping. He pops up and down as water slides him and his friends down the pipe. Until finally there is the feeling of nothing cold under him anymore. No more water hits anymore. The problem with this is that he is now an object falling without any support. Falling to who knows where until the spring kid realizes that this pipeway is called Mossy Drive for an actual reason.

Marvin's back is suddenly cushioned as he smells damp moist plant life around him. Moss is felt under his hands and back but Marvin quickly moves to the side. Realizing Shrubs skinny figure falls exactly where Marvin just was. The spring kid wonders why there was no kind of warning at the entrance or even on the map. Shrub makes sure to stand away from the thick moss, irritated with the map now in hand. Just like expected, Dod falls where Shrub was.

"You know what? This is not good!" Shrub's two friends look at him wondering if they know what he is talking about. "Unless we climb that damn slide, I'm not sure of a quick way back to Mark's Tunnel. There is no other direct way, other than going through different pipeways somewhere in here."

Dod takes one long drink. There is a big gulp through his throat that seems to take a long time to down. "Well, we are screwed. This is why so many stay in one exhibit. One wrong turn, then next thing you know your lost, far beyond belief. It's ridiculous, creat."

"If this is a section that is inhabited that means the creatures here should know where to get out of, or at least the quickest way." Shrub says hearing the echo of his voice. There are three pathways in front of them. Not pipeways but they lead into shadows.

All look at the paths and each has an unsatisfied look of confusion on their face. Only lost creatures make faces like this. Far from home each know they can live in any area, if uninhabited mostly. But they are not on a mission to find a new home. They are on a mission to find Lisa.

"Look at the map Shrub." Dod says scratching the top of his head as if Shrub should have already looked at the direction they need to go.

Shrub unfolds the map making it his task to read it. Before he looks back down at the map there is something that floats in the middle pathway. Something that can be a face appears in the middle of the shadow. It has no body, so it must be a mask, one that floats. Underneath is a lamp that glows by a small lit candle wick. The woman's face is thin skin tight to the bone. The shadows at first hide most of her thin figure but she is most likely anthropomorphic. As she gets closer the eyes are seen more clearly and are the shape of diamonds. Their glare are as shiny as diamonds also. She smiles. What she has are needles close together in her mouth. Been where they are at, teeth should really be there. The pail dome of her head shows no sign of hair making her pointy ear lobes barely pass the top. Standing no more than a few feet away, Marvin and his friends realize how tall the pail woman is. She wears only a silk black dress other than her shoes that are surprisingly as small as her white hands.

"Out of all the pipes, you come down here." She says calmly.

"Yeah, we were hungry." Marvin says confused. "What pipe should we have gone through instead?" He realizes the candle. Wax might be made here. Or perhaps needed.

The tall pail woman looks behind as if she herself does not know what path to take. She looks back at them. "How about you follow me?"

Shrub is the first to break character, looking at Marvin not wanting to go. He stares at the women. "Can't you just tell us? We came down here to get something to eat. Then we need to get back on the trail. We'll pay or trade, whatever suits you."

"What trail?" She asks ignoring anything else the bulb head said.

Shrub almost roles his eyes. "Mark's Tunnel, the one that this pipe starts at."

The women looks at the pipe as if never seen it there before. "I never been there before."

Looking at the paths behind her she lifts one arm and points showing them where to enter. "You can go through any path you want. All of them lead to different areas, just like the one you came through."

Without looking back at the friends she turns and walks down the middle path. "You can follow me of course. I hardly seen anyone or anything come out of those other two."

Marvin knowing they do not have much of a choice signals to follow the lady. Dod is the first to step forward as Shrub stands and waits. Marvin starts walking while looking at the bulb head. "Let's go."

"What's a matter with you?" Shrub looks as the lady walks away and out of ear shot "This lady is creepy."

Marvin looks at the other two paths that are no different than the one the lady creature is leading them to. "So do those other two."

Clenching his fists Shrub walks toward Marvin who turns and now walks closer to the tunnel.

Not used to the ground been soft with the same moss that cushioned his fall Shrub needs to keep balanced. Moss fills certain areas of the tunnel and can be seen by what little light the lamp gives out. The three know they are getting at the end as another light starts to reveal more of the bricks and moss surrounding them. Shrub stumbles with each step as his skinny legs try to keep straight on the awkward surface. The tall women blows out the candle and turns toward the side. The only building that is present is a brick one in front of the already brick wall. Nothing special to it. Could be a house nothing more. There is a small pipe that sticks out though, but not just any pipe. This irregular pipe has a glass disk in the opening. The tall woman sees the friends looking at the metal piece.

"Now we know they have a scope." Marvin stares at the spyglass knowing what it is. The tall woman walks behind him and looks at the device.

"Exactly. Are there not any at your exhibit?" She asks looking at the three with a smile.

Her semi joyful mood makes the friends unease. None of them feel like answering her but staying silent would seem rude and make the mood even more unbearable.

"There are some, but never have I felt obligated to look through any. The only time I ever did is when we were younger and playing around." Marvin tries to remember. "The scope was mostly broken."

"I can show you in the control room what there is to see. The machines are hardly alive anymore."

"Machines, what do you mean?" Shrub says. "How can looking through a scope need a machine?"

The tall women smiles. Her needle teeth show more than ever. "You have never been out of your own exhibit before, have you? We can always tell when someone is not from around here.

Because none of them know what we are talking about." She looks at the telescope which seems so alone, so high on the wall.

For a moment the friends think they're loosing their focus on the spyglass as somehow the telescope seems to move. When it moves for the second time, the motion is seems fluid so someone has to be controlling the device.

Marvin scratches his head. "Looks like you have great security." Not knowing what else to add.

The women looks back down, her diamond eyes no longer clear but are black. There are small glares still in the black diamond eyes but somehow they changed color. "Here I can see everything the telescope can see."

The three look in shock. How can that be possible? What kind of creatures live beyond their exhibit? Some that are capable of been attached to machines? Shrub points at the lady almost not knowing what to say. "How can you do that? Your eyes are no longer the same."

The smile again. "I adjustment. You do not believe me?" The lady creature turns around. "Any of you do something."

Marvin looks at the two and shrugs his shoulders, opening his palms upside down. He is more curious on how she was able to adjust her eyes in the first place. "Like what?"

"Like that. You just shrugged with your hands open. Looked at the bulb head then the reptile." "No way. What am I doing now?" Dod bites one finger then shakes his head a little then stops.

Then he does it a second time.

"Biting your finger. You shook your head, twice." The lady creature turns around and looks back at the friends.

"So you can see us. Maybe someone is telling you somewhere but I won't worry about that." Marvin says with curiosity on his face. "Why are you showing us this? How can you even change your eyes?"

"All I do is change my focus." The lady creature blinks "A part of the machine is inside me." She smiles. "The paths you saw when we were walking in were to different areas. Never had I placed myself in any because I will admit that none of my kind want to go through. All our knowledge comes from the machines. Or new comers. In exhibited pipes that lead to only one place, the only way to learn certain things is through insight from others."

"How do you learn anything if all you get is insight from other creatures?" Marvin asks wondering what this lady does. He is starting to think she is the only one here. If she can control the spyglass, then no one needs to be behind the machine. "Are there others around? What about those two other paths that were in the room we fell in? Our map said these were living quarters with food for sale. Those paths are where the food is at. They have to be." He hopes the map is accurate. If not, what else could be here with them and the lady creature standing in front of them with eyes everywhere.

The lady creature smiles.

"We need to get out of here, and soon." Shrub says forgetting about the food. "We just need to make our way to the Wide Areas."

"And how will you get there?" The lady creature's diamond eyes close but just a little.

Shrub chuckles a bit. "We have a map."

"Not for the Wide Areas."

All three stand in silence looking upon one another. Regardless the lady creature knows enough that the Wide Areas needs a map all on its own because of the gigantic size.

"I did not think so." This time the lady's mouth stays shut as she smiles. "All I need you to do is

look for a bug. Creatures as small as you can fit where they are. Once you find him, bring the insect to me. As payment I will give you a map of the Wide Areas."

"Wait." Shrub interrupts.

"Show us the map first."

Now the lady creature's face gets a bit sour knowing she needs to show some kind of proof. She turns and looks at the spyglass. "Map for Wide Areas." She turns and smiles with her mouth closed again. The sound of sliding is somewhere. At first the trio think it's the door to the bricked house.

When they look that direction, the door is the same as before. Then there is a sound of movement that could be a flying insect. Like a buzz of some kind. When turning back at the lady creature there is a claw in front of their hostess. The three metal fingers that look like blades hold a book not a map, even though that's what it is. The Wide Areas now look bigger for some reason. The friends equally concerned with the map as they are with the metal claw. They take a step or two back and look at what this device is attached to. Wires and metal create an arm which is screwed and held together in separate pieces. They see as the claw goes back up and disappears in a square in the ceiling. The tile for it slides to close the opening.

A machine. This entire exhibit is a machine. "You can buy a map in the Wide Areas, or you can earn it." She holds out the thick book as if about to place a plate on a table. "This is all you will need to get around." She smiles, all the many needles align in her mouth. "Get the bug and it's yours."

Marvin looks at the book as if it can bite him. "What kind of bug is this?"

"I will make that decision." The lady creature holds the book with one elbow pressing on her ribs. When she straightens back up both of her hands are placed in front of her ears. She pulls forward and a bit to her left also. Her face gets removed with clicks. Now an actual mask, the white skinny face of the lady is in her own hands. Inside her head is almost hollow except for sideways gears that turns a spool between them. They are constantly moving and there are two clunks of metal pieces that align where the eyes once were. They're spigots and have nothing attached to them anymore.

Marvin is unsure to take the mask but he knows Shrub and Dod feel the same way. He reaches out as if the face wants to bite him. Turning the face around, inside is a twining mess. Maybe wires are part of the strings garbled up but he will not spend the time or effort to find out.

"Alright guys we do need a map." The spring kid swallows. He looks at them. "Or I can go by myself."

"Na, I'll go with you." Dod takes a drink of his shake. "What about you ol' Shrub?"

Shrub snaps his head at Dod. "Of course I'm going. You think I'm letting Marvin walk into some dark path he or you know nothing about?"

Taking a drink once more, Dod shrugs his shoulders.

"Let's get this over with." Marvin walks with the heavy mask but does not leave until he takes one last look at the lady's body. She stands with her hollow head now holding the map. None dare to take it, even if they knew they could.

Feeling the face move in Marvin's hand is almost like holding clay stretch on it's own. The lady told them to take the left path so that is the way they went. The path is a lot longer than the one when they followed the lady. The three wonder if she is taking them to an area that will trap them for who knows what. This entire place has been strange to the three already. Anything can seem to happen at any moment. What if the map was a fake? None want to talk, especially with the face with them.

Instead of been shocked they should have asked more about what they had to do.

"How can it hear?" Shrub was able to force out the question earlier, which has been the only thing said since they entered. The face replied that two of the wires inside still have her eardrums. That is all she had to say for them to drop back to silence.

The next thing that would make sense to ask how far this bug is. But there's no need. Up ahead is a door. The walk took awhile but has been nothing compared to when they first entered, Marks Way. As uncomfortable as it has been, the hallway is really concealed and not much air flows. The walk has been a dry one so a little relief is felt when the door is seen. The bulb head quickens a bit just to get closer. Shrub wraps his hand around the knob, ready to open the metal door. It is small. The bricks built around are solid gray indicating that there has been no water that comes by.

"I'm guessing we need to go through here?" Shrub asks.

"Yes." The face simply says.

As Shrub opens the door, the scent of old stale fruit can be smelt. Cool air rushes through to meet them and is felt relieving them of the hallway's stuffiness. "This is all you are afraid of?" The three walk in.

Webs are like blankets on what can be considered furniture. Old bolted metal seats are visible but barley. Chrome tables and aluminum vases similar to any exhibit apartment can be seen in the webbed mess. The smell of the fruit is what still baffles them. Where can any food be stored in this place? And why would it be? A slam breaks all concentration and the door is closed.

"What is this?" Marvin looks around in excitement realizing this is most likely a scam.

"All is fine until you find the vine. Then the bugs come out to dine. Pick a fruit then don't cry.

As gasoline may go in your eye. Try to find what lies inside."

"Great." Shrub brings his head up. "We are goofed. She wants to eat us!"

"I think the face plate might be going insane. That or her battery is low." Dod tells Shrub realizing that nothing is happening. "Try opening the door, I bet we can leave whenever we want."

Shrub quickly reaches for the knob. He twists it but it does not move. "I told you."

"Do you want the map? Help me find my bug and then we will grub. No one leaves until we find the insect."

"I think if we look around a bit we can find what she is talking about. I still don't know why anyone would be afraid of this place." Marvin says just to get everyone comfortable. He's not that frightened of the place, but there still could be danger.

"What is there to look for? This place is a mess. That smell must be coming from a vent." Shrub looks to the ceiling where the least webs are.

"What was it you said, find a vine or something?" Dod asks. He gets on his reptilian hands and examines corners. "There's no plants here."

"Let's just do it the hard way." Marvin places the diamond eyed face on the floor. He starts tearing through the webs. There are more objects. Pins with numbers to keep track of time. Random tin plates and cups stay at a stand still as they where when first placed. A cord is found. Not a vine but something that resembles one runs through the side. Not telling anyone because it's plastic and non- organic, Marvin still follows the cord. Tearing more webs is not easy with all the objects around. As soon as a green glow partially shines in his eye it quickly catches his attention. Shrub and Dod walk behind him. The wire is brightened by the mechanical fruit it bares. The smell of strawberries is more potent, with a strong scent of petroleum.

"I never seen a fruit harvested by machines. Who could eat this?" Shrub says with disgust on his face.

Marvin gets the face off the floor. "Is this what you are talking about?"

"Old fruit? No. We need something more natural. A bug. Only machines can eat fueled fruit.

Mostly. We need a bug! A big one." The face says.

Shrub twists his nose looking at the hanging fruit still. "Well, it looks like no bugs are around. I mean, they would've taken some of the fruit..."

"I know." Marvin does not let Shrub finish. "We bring the bug to us." He reaches for the uneven inverted triangular fruit. Pulling it from the vine takes a couple of tugs but he manages. The fruit bleeds with what can be natural juice or perhaps fuel for machines. Stinging their noses the fumes burns through their nostrils with sweetness. Marvin drops it next to it's vine. The group, except for the mask, cover their noses. Scratching sounds come from the sides of the wall. They are all startled and the first thing they think of are bugs.

"What are we going to do?" Dod says looking around as if the bugs are already seen.

Where the glowing robotic fruit once was little specks build up and cover it. Moving in closer the three realize that the specks that now cover the fruit came from all sides. They are thousands of little insects.

"Your going to miss them all. Maybe I should have a look." The faces voice is heard.

Marvin quickly brings the face where the fruit was, realizing that all the bugs are now gone. The light dims through the plastic vine that now bleeds less sweet fuel. From bright green to a dim light.

Then the light is no more.

"Too late." The mask says. "We need to find another one."

With an unpleasant look on his face, Marvin now knows what they have to do. "So we need to look around and find fruit. Why don't the bugs just find the fruits themselves?"

"They are finding more as we speak. So many webs keep the scent or them trapped. But of course, if a fruit is broken, it is easier to find." The face grins.

All three friends nod now realizing what all the webs are preventing. Another thought comes to mind. If the webs were made by the bugs, how come they would keep the fruit hidden and not easy to find? "But the webs though." Marvin asks. "Didn't the bugs make them?"

"Come on child." The mask says as if Marvin should know. "The fruit grows after the webs are finished. And there are bugs that eat bugs. The more fruit the more webs to keep them hidden. "Now

let's find our self a bug. A big one."

"Good luck with that. All those insects looked pretty small to me." Shrub says trying to figure out what webs should be removed. One of the webs waves gently like a spirit would. Again, a cool breeze filters through from somewhere. By now the group knows that its nothing but the breeze. The three begin to search.

Many attempts later, and the mask was not quick enough to spot any bugs that were big enough for her liking. The three start to begin wondering if just buying a map in the Wide Areas would be a better choice. Dod wipes his forehead drinking his shake offering some to the other two, only Shrub refuses. He did offer to the mask earlier. She looked at him as if he was joking, and in a way he was.

Pulling poles and old tin plates. The entire place is getting more of a cleaning than anything.

Maybe that's what the ladies plan is. Clean the place and she can live here instead of the brick house. Even with plates and metal hitting the floor no bugs bother until fruit is present. As so much webs are cleared the bugs show themselves plenty more.

"We're going to clear this whole room out of fruit by the time we see a right bug." Marvin looks at the mask which is now on a stool. She stays held up by the wall. "I think it's almost time to go."

"Just a little bit longer. We still got time." The face says moving up and down as it talks on the stool.

"But we don't." Shrub says irritated. "With each pick passing, our friend in the Wide Areas is most likely getting further away."

"I found another batch of this stuff." A screech comes from a small table which Dod moves. "Bring her here."

Grabbing the mask Marvin quickly rushes toward where Dod is at. All the small bugs attach to a fruit patch and then scatter. "You know what? All them little things still look, little." Dod has to say.

"I realized that." Marvin brings the mask toward his face. "Is there something you are not telling us? We are going to go if this continues. Looking for this fruit has taken too long and no progress has presented itself, other than moving furniture and having to work our way around whatever is sealed on the floor. What more is there before we leave?"

The mask smiles. Needled teeth seem to take over half the face. "I already told you. All is fine until you find…"

"Enough. Let's just leave." Shrub says heading for the door. "There were a few sledge hammers we can break down the thing."

"Agreed," Dod follows until a screech is heard from moving metal furniture again but it is not by any of them. They whisk their heads toward the sound. By default, Marvin cannot help but to face the mask the direction they all look. More screeches in portions, this time it sounds as if the piece of

furniture is trying to make its way to the side continuously by itself. As if the large giant struggling cockroach bug was caught in an act it was not supposed to be doing, the insect stops and moves its antennas toward the group. Many juices are around its mouth. By the color of the liquid, the juice cannot be the same as the fruits. Little lines, which are insect legs, dangle and twitch sticking out of the mouth as the giant insect stays in silence.

"There's the bug I need. Now hurry let's leave before he feeds his need."

Shrub has the door already opened and it slams on the wall while he runs out. Dod comes out next holding his shake. Marvin rushes with the face thinking he will throw her if the giant insect gets any closer than what it already is. There, the moss area with the sliding pipe is seen. Shrub's legs move no differently than the dead or dying bugs in the giant's mouth twitching every which way. His sharp turn causes him to almost fall. Chucking the shake over his shoulder, Dod tries his best to help Shrub while he runs but the bulb head manages to control himself. Marvin turns thinking he may have trouble also but does not. He looks and makes sure the bug is actually chasing them. Many tappings are heard getting louder from the shadowy hallway they were just in. A roach head slowly appears giving proof that the bug is definitely running behind him. Marvin runs down the second path. The brick house is already present, after all they did run this time, and the door is the only choice to go toward.

The screeching voice of Shrub echos. "That better be unlocked!" Most likely it is.

The mask stretches in Marvin's hands. He does not need to see when she smiles. The ladies

lifeless body stands where it was before. "They see what I see." Giving that none have heard what the big bug can sound like. Odd sucking and inhaling sounds come from the insect. All three stop halfway in front of the house. Instead of going inside they look behind to where they came from. The microscope from high in the wall is on top of the bug. It now has arms and legs. Copper knives take up half of the arms. The small machine pokes inside the brain of the insect. A few more yelps and the bug stops moving completely.

The three stand in silence. Surprised, also a bit saddened that they got this insect ready to be placed on a dinner plate. Yet it could have made them its meal as well. Perhaps they feel as though they should be mad at the tall lady whose body still stands with the map.

The telescope robot now stands watching. After all, it's part in this is finished.

"Place me back on my body." The mask says. Marvin does not wait a pick to do so. Spring arms stretch. It feels like putting the rims of two clay plates together. With the free hand the lady adjusts her face better and gives a small twitch of her nose and ears. She smiles looking down at Marvin. "Here you go." The map is his. They look up to where the telescope once was and sure enough it's an empty hole.

"What was this all about? Why kill a bug?"

"Bugs you mean. The bugs were bugging the wires. Now that problem is fixed. To get rid of them they have to eat each other. One will overcome the rest, thus becoming the dominant. Then that same one can even eat the ones who make the webs." The lady smiles looking at the telescope robot. "Our bladed telescope only has so many miles. And we needed to lure the big bug out. Larg bugs are only attracted to flesh. Insects never bother with machines." She smiles at the three as if no danger was involved.

"We risked our lives to clear out a bunch of bugs from a dusty room?" Shrub says irritated looking at all his friends. There is supposed to be some kind of irritation coming from them he figures, but it's not showing. "You guys think our lives were worth that map?" He points at the lady. "This creature should of told us the danger right away. The real reason we went through all this."

There is nothing but silence from the other two. Knowing that their lives were most likely at stake. Yet they have handled worse.

The lady blinks. Still diamond eyes. "The bugs kept our power low. Too many of them and they are now cleared, for awhile. One thing that keeps me going is power and productivity to keep myself and other things running." She looks at the telescope standing next to her, then she looks back at the three with a smile. "I can improve on many things for the time being. So to use power, you also need to give." She sticks out her hand and wraps her fingers around the telescope as if to pick it up from the top. But it still has it's body and knives sticking out. How to use the thing now is a mystery. Then, like the claw arm, the legs and arms fold. So do the knives which are now inside each forearm. Similar to a swiss knife.

"Here. There is a small glass inside it. I'll take out my own and break it. Then us two will lose connection. The robot is now all yours." The tall lady hands over the telescope to Marvin. She smiles and unless the machine unfolds again while he holds it, they have no choice but to trust her. "We have newer ones." From the house more smaller telescopes come to pick up the dead insect. All are shinier than the one given to the trio.

"Thanks." Marvin looks at his two friends. "We're going far. And whatever is at the Wide Areas could be dangerous."

The two just look at the robot not knowing what to say. Dod reaches and takes the piece of machinery. "I'll stuff it in my bag."

Marvin turns to face the lady. "How do we..." She or the machines are not in sight. They look to where the house is and the door closes.

Apparently the other tunnel lead to a small area of creatures. One that had a few buildings and a place to eat. The creatures walk inside the diner knowing now is the best time to get something to eat.

"What if that thing ate us. You know, we would be done for!" Dod takes a shake out thinking if he should not eat what's inside.

"Ha, that mouth was so small, my feet would hardly fit through." Shrub says as if he killed the insect himself.

Marvin thinks about the bug and how it chased them from the room all the way to that ladies house. In fact they never got her name. No need for that anymore. And they are definitely not going back. "Still, For that thing to be on you with all those legs would not be pleasant."

Standing in silence they do not know what the bug would have done to any of them. If it did get hold of someone, what would the insect be able to do? What would they themselves have done? They walk toward the diner not worrying about what happened.

The building has moss on the sides. The diner is made like most structures that are around the friends exhibit. The same steel that the pipes are made out of is the same as the building's walls. There are certain areas of their exhibit that grow moss but are usually scraped off right away. Here, the moss seems to be a permanent part of the area. The three wonder if it has a significant use. Dod decides to take a drink from his bottle.

"I wonder if this moss is different from what is around where we live? Latter I'm going to get some for my shokla."

"It looks the same, Dod. It's not much of a difference I'm sure." Marvin looks for a place to sit.

If any of the friends want to leave right away it's him.

Tables are placed all around the area. Occupants sit around eating. Some mind their business while others talk to each other. Some creatures look toward the door, but quickly turn back to eating. Stoves smoke, cooks run hysterical. One is a reptile looking creature, almost like Dod. Except this long scaled faced reptilian has a dark purple tone to his skin. In fact most of the cooks are reptiles like Dodrill. There is a black beak that seams to be moving around in the kitchen also. Marvin tries to make out what kind of creature it is, and if his eyes are not mistaken, it is some kind of skeletal body.

"Are you going to sit down?" An old aged voice from Marvin's side is heard. He looks behind and never realized that the door was closed. When he looks to his side, Marvin stares at the floor first. There are three long boned toes with pointy black nails that aim toward him. He looks up to what they are attached to and like the toes and feet, long bone connects making a leg until torn worn cloth pants covers the rest of the leg. Marvin realizes that the creature is some kind of a flying type without any skin. The skull has a beak that snaps and is pointy, just like the skull that follows it. The eye sockets are wide and hollow. "Go to the counter. They will help you if your lost kid." The old bird skeleton says, sitting on a stool. It's as if he, like the lady creature, knows a newcomer when they see one. The bone bird holds a long stick for a cane. The fingers are not fingers exactly, because they are so far apart and are long all on one bone almost.

Marvin walks forward wanting to get away from the old snapper. If the boned creature had skin or wings, there would be no where for him to use them. Nobody can really fly, not in the pipes. The three reach the bar and sit. Various small pipes run down from the top of the ceiling and lead all the way to where the cooks are. One of the reptile creatures opens a pipe vent and brings out what is a round giant slimy eyeball. Marvin never had much of a taste for eating eyes before. He just hopes it is an eye from a pipe squid. As rare as they are, the parts of squid mainly get served at stops to eat.

A creature that looks similar, but not the same as the pale lady, sits by Marvin. He has a white face but beady eyes and a small mouth. When he takes a bite, Marvin remembers how many teeth that lady had and are no different on this guy. The needles rip the eye ball, tearing a piece off as slime drips from the food and the creature's mouth. Marvin looks quickly at the waiter who stands with a notepad to write on. The reptile moves his hand slowly as if hurrying Marvin to order. The spring kid looks to his side and sees both his friends looking at him, waiting for him as well.

Marvin quickly looks at the menu, trying to spot out the most familiar thing to order. Fried grass with salt and moss. There is no name for the moss so he knows that this moss should be no different than what grows around where he lives. "I'll take the grass plate." He pushes over the menu and looks at Shrub. "What do you think of this place?"

The waiter takes the menu and stares at the map that Marvin forgot he placed on the counter. It is more like a book. Wonder if anyone knows that it's a map. Perhaps the creature, or robot, that sits next to him does.

Shrub takes a sip of partially clear water that bubbles because of added citrus. "I have not seen any pipes that are big enough to walk through. I'm going to ask someone where we can go to leave."

"Well I don't want to stay here too long." Marvin is sure none of his friends want to stay long either. "Let's ask them about Lisa. Maybe she was here earlier."

Shrub gets his food with a smile. "Go ahead." He answers Marvin not paying attention to him.

Marvin notices another boned beak creature on the other side of the counter. This is the one he saw when they first walked in. "Hello, can you help me with something?"

A solid stare on the bone creature's face shows little expression. With the boned bird looking at him, eyeless, the spring kid does not know what mood this boned body may be in. "What?" The tone is mellow, leaving Marvin still unsure.

"We've been looking for our friend. She is a water creature..." Before Marvin has time to say anything else the waiter stops him.

"Do you have something that shows her face?"

Tapping his fingertips on the counter, Marvin is unsure of anything that can help him. "No I don't."

"In that case I cannot help you. Many aquatics dine and leave and sometimes return. Come back later. Maybe she will be here then. It's a common stop for anyone going through the Marks Tunnel." The waiter turns his back, dealing with some dishes that are in front of the two.

Most likely Lisa would ignore crowded places. For all he knows she packed her meals and was done with the hassle of buying anything. Marvin picks at his food for a bit and wonders if the skull sculpture can help in anyway.

Marvin's head lifts with wide enthusiastic eyes. "I do have something. Let me show you. Dod, give me the skull." Dod hands Marvin the skull and continues eating. Marvin hands it to the waiter who only stares at the piece. He turns his head a bit. It seams like moments as the eyeless creature finishes examining. All Marvin can wonder is how anyone can see like that.

"No. There has been no murners around."

Marvin widens one eye. "No, as in the girl was never here?"

Straightening up the waiter looks at Marvin. "Not for awhile have I seen any murners. How long has your friend been missing?"

Now Marvin leans back as well, disappointed. "I have not seen her for about three courses. We just started looking for her during the one we are in now."

"Well then no, I have not seen your friend. Let me know if you need anything else." Once again the boned creature turns his back. Marvin looks at the skull as if it can actually talk just like the waiter can.

"Why would she write a note and leave it in the skull." Marvin turns the skull over hoping another note will somehow appear. Or even anything else that might have been put in.

"Now remember Marvin, she still needs to finish that creation." Shrub's voice is muffled with the food in his mouth. Marvin hates hearing any creature chew and talk at the same time, but he says nothing to Shrub. "If she wants to make a creation," He gulps in causing a ball to run down his skinny throat. "She would have to keep it in the Wide Areas. Our exhibit does not allow those. Creations can be wild or too big, remember that. Maybe she wants to stay there?"

"Ha," Marvin's smile is sour with his eyes scrunched downward. "Why would she want to do that?" Now Marvin takes a bight from his plant. His index finger becomes a single rapid tap on the counter as if he was trying to signal code with it.

"I don't know." Shrub takes another bight from the eyeball he ordered. "There are not many murners around our exhibit." The muffling continues. "You know, maybe she needs that kind of

company. Her parents won't help with that, I guarantee." There is a chuckle and right before he is about to take bite, Shrub adds on. "Everyone can guarantee you that actually."

"Would you please finish eating. We need to hurry."

"Relax Marvin. She's just a girl trying to find out where she should belong. Other than us and her family, no one talks to her. Not about her interests or anything. And we can't help her with that. So she likes to play a flute and sculpt every once in awhile. The girl never told us what she really wants. Or who. "Shrub leans back and nods at what's been sitting on the counter. "So how about that map?"

Dod hears Shrub and ignores his fried bug wings. "Ya, crack it open, Marv!"

"Well, we do have to hurry. The sooner we get to Wide Areas the better." Marvin focuses on the many folded pages in front of him. What Shrub said was to help him, yet Marvin still wonders why Lissa would not tell him what she was up to. He just like everyone else knows that there are hardly any murners in their exhibit. Lisa been as shy as she is, would create and keep a murner as her companion. Marvin forces a fake smile with his lips tight. "Yeah, she is getting older. Time for her to... do different things I guise." Marvin places two hands on top the map and tries opening it as if trying to open a lid. He looks around the map wondering why it won't budge.

Shrub takes another bight before looking at Marvin. "She probably just wants to make a creation that's all. You know she did not tell anyone about the plan because she may have been

embarrassed." Shrub looks forward, about to take another bite. "We will find out when we get there." He turns his head only to see his friend struggle. "What's a matter?"

"Marvin is having trouble with the map. We were stuped after all." Dod reaches across. "Here let me see."

As the map goes toward Dod, Shrub examines it like a specimen of unknown origin while crossing past his eyes.

The reptile tries pulling and shaking the map as if it is full of change, or buttons. "This thing won't open. Maybe a fork will do the trick." Dod reaches for the utensil.

Marvin looks around realizing they still need to leave sometime. "Waiter." He flicks his fingers at the boned creature hoping the skinless bird will notice him before anyone else. "How do we leave this place?"

The eyeless bird skull stares at Marvin. "Why you have to go through the basement. That's the route area to get back to any other pipes or the tunnel."

"The basement, now how do I get there?"

"The door is right over there." The bone creature nods to his right. The waiter starts gathering plates again.

Marvin looks around. To the left of him there is the large door that many different creatures walk in and out of. He looks back at the waiter. "One more thing. This map that someone gave us. It does not open."

The waiter places one bone hand under the map expecting Dod to hand it over. When he does the waiter examines it slowly twitching his head around the map. "Why this is a rare map of The Wide Areas." He looks at Marvin. For some reason now, Marvin can realize joy in the birds face. "You visited the Lady." With sarcasm in his voice, there is a mark of surprise.

"We all did, creat." Dod says making sure the waiter knows all three where involved.

"Whoever did, this map is sealed. Look." A bony finger points at the bottom of the spine. There is a hole wide enough for a tip of a pencil to fit through if anything. "You need a key."

"A key, she gypped us big time." Dod practically yells.

"Ha, if that be the case, name your price and I'll take it."

"No," Dod quickly says.

"Then quit complaining." The eyeless bird looks at Dod, then back at Marvin. "I'll be honest with you. This is valuable. Talk to the Lady again and see if she knows where the key is. If not, you still have a find."

Not feeling like they have much options and in need of a bigger break the three just eat. Not worrying what to do or where to go. They decide to finish what they bought and not bother with the map anymore. There's talks of seen the robotic creature again, but there is a feeling in all their gut that makes them not want to go. Finishing his food, Marvin looks at his friends. Too many things that need finding and he just needs to eat. As what little time has passed Marvin realizes that there is some creature that was talking to Dod. It's another reptile "Are you guys ready?"

"I am. Not sure if Dod here is though. The guy keeps talking about his drink as if it is the best thing in the pipes."

"Dod, are you ready?" Marvin raises his voice a little just so his friend can hear.

Shrub finally pokes the reptile rapidly. "Are you ready to go?"

"Hold on there bulb head. I'm about to make a sale."

Shrub is about to yell at the creature but Marvin holds onto his wrist. Shrub looks at him and puts his hands on the table looking around with a rushed look.

"Just give him a few more dot's." Marvin has to say.

"How long is it going to take the swamlorlakplak? That's what I am wondering." The words come out fast. The last word is no insult though. After all that is what species Dodrill is. Marvin is about to say more until Dod turns toward the two.

"Look, I made ten credit from that sale. Gave him a card also." In the reptiles webbed hand there are five buttons of random color above the light skinned palm. All are of equal sizes.

"Good, can we go now?" Shrub asks still looking around.

"Yeah, I'll leave the tip." Dod drops one of the buttons on the bar counter. Each pay for their own meal. They drop out of the stools and look to where they need to go next. Marvin puts the map in Dod's backpack along with the skull. The reptile can feel the straps sink into his shoulders just like a belt tightening around his waist.

Shrub looks at the door that leads to the pipes. "So that is the way to get out." He announces knowing that Dod did not hear the conversation with the waiter. The bulb head looks at Marvin. "Think about how we should do this. What if Lisa is not at the Wide Areas or even worse, lost?"

"That's the most likely place she will be at. And if she is lost I'm sure we can find better clues there other than wondering all around the pipes." Marvin flicks his head agitated. What else are they supposed to do. Shrub's ideas will only take them on another course. The tone of his voice actually rises a bit. "Waiting here would be too much of a risk if that's what you're thinking."

"Yeah, but what if we get lost ourselves?" Shrub looks at Marvin with a low grin. "How in all these pipes does Lisa of all creatures know how to get there? Even with the three of us we are getting confused."

"That is why we need to get out of our exhibit more often, so we cannot get lost. See, maybe it is a good thing we left." Marvin makes his way toward the large door. More reptilian creatures walk through. Marvin holds the door for his friends before it shuts.

The three look up at the sign above the door. 'The Empty' is painted in black on a flat piece of metal. As Marvin tries to look at all of them, he wonders if they should just climb the watery pipe they fell through. "I don't know. Something about going through another exit seems like we are actually moving further away from where we need to go."

"No time to worry about it now, Marvin. Our original map should have this marked." Shrub holds the map. He feels the same as Marvin but knows it is a foolish idea to try and climb the pipe they came through.

"There is always time to go back." Dod considers as he stands between the two.

Shrub looks up at Dod with a solid face. Holding in the usual temper he has toward the reptile. "Maybe you can climb it. Us two would have a hard time. We all know how far it was and slippery. We just need to read this and go the right way. No big deal."

"Okay then," Dod shrugs his shoulders. Thumbs under the straps of his back pack.

A tangy rusty smell over powers any burnt meal the deeper they go inside. Down in the basement the back wall is made of squared entrances. So many that not a single brick is seen on the wall. The entry ways are all the way up leading to the ceiling that is a dark orange to tan rust. There are so many entrances, that some creatures are showing others where to go.

"You know what I just remembered. Now that we ate we should get the key." Marvin says after seen these workers. If there is some kind of community here, than the lady should still offer her assistance just like all these employees.

"Let me go ask which path leads toward the tunnel." Dod is about to move forward.

"Wait, we have a map for that. There is no need to deal with these guys. While I figure it out, one of us should go. Actually, two would be better." Shrub unfolds the map. Where they are at is a thick piece of squared paper bulging on the map that has Empty's Entrance printed on. Shrub unfolds a layer, then another layer until the bulge spreads out to a complete sheet that is almost the size of the map itself. The bulb head looks at the naming of each opening on the bottom of the page. There are lines going toward small squares that line up above one another indicating the pathways. Above the squares, names of the entrances are labeled the order to whichever square they belong to. All Shrub needs to do is find the name, Mark's Tunnel, but it is more difficult than he thought. Especially for it been a common path. "Okay, nothing for our tunnel. Let's see." He folds the path map for The Empty looking back at the map in its original form. "Well here is the tunnel. Not sure how to get there through one of these." Shrub looks at the entrances briefly.

Dodrill starts tightening his back pack. "While you guys figure that out, I'm going to that ladies place for a key to our other map" He swallows knowing it the area might be a bit more chilling to walk through by himself.

"I can go with you." Marvin says stepping forward."

"Na, you two figure this out. It should just take one creat to go there and back. Once I come back, you two will know what to do." He walks away leaving all the thinking to the other two.

"This will take longer looking at the map. None of these lead to Mark's Tunnel. What we have to do now is find a path that goes to another pipe that leads to the tunnel." Marvin inhales a deep breadth. "The problem with that is there might be several pipes till we get to Mark's."

Shrub starts following different pipes that connect with Mark's Tunnel, seen if they lead to The Empty. "Okay, let's just see which one of these work." The two look at the map and are about to ask a few other creatures where they should go. More time has passed and the two cannot help but to focus more on the area and wonder if they should go back the way they came after all.

Dod approaches taking a drink from a new bottle. "No go guys. Her door was locked and no one would answer my knock. Not even a robot. Did you two figure out where to go?"

"We were about to just ask someone." Marvin looks for the nearest employee.

The reptile looks around. "Time to just ask one of these creats then. There here because that map takes a course or two just to plan your way around."

"I guess we have to. Let's hope the map is not that hard to read after we get out of here." Shrub says. He lets out a small laugh while looking at the map. "Some map. Can't even show us where to go."

"I agree, Shrub." Marvin spots out the closest employee.

"I am not going to ask them about Mark's Tunnel. But which one leads to Wide Areas. Or Copper Tunnel first." Marvin says before perusing the hosts.

"That is a bad idea." Shrub holds the map with a tight fist. "The Wide Areas are too far. Unless you guys want to travel through more pipes. We will have to take at least triple the amount compared to the few that lead to Mark's."

"Very true. Let's just stick with the tunnel. That's a straight way toward Copper." Dod agrees.

Marvin listens to all what his friends have to say. He walks toward one of the hosts who is a reptile, hoping he will not forget what to ask. "Hi there. Which one of these leads toward, Mark's Tunnel?"

Without moving his reptilian eyes the host points. "The third row on the eleventh entrance goes to Sludge Way. That pipe will lead you to Mark's Tunnel." The host smiles. More sharp teeth are seen like expected from a creature like him.

"What about the Wide Areas, or even Copper Tunnel?" Marvin says slightly closing his eyes, hoping there is a quicker route.

"Copper Tunnel is closer. Seventh pipe on tenth row. From there that leads to the pipe Bogs.

From Bogs you will need to go into Silk Path. Turn toward your right and from there you will go through Steel Cup. Turn left in this pipe you will find..."

Marvin smiles holding up his hand that waves rapidly. "Hold on. Sorry, how many pipes till we hit Copper from there?"

"Eight."

"Oh. The Wide Areas?" Marvin knows the answer, but he asks anyway.

"Fifty five. Not to mention some are longer than others. The empty can only go so far, sorry." There, the same smile again on the host's face. Marvin can tell that it is the same smile used so many times before.

There are ladders that go up and down on the sides of the entryways. Each one is even and are side by side. Different from the wall that the three had to enter in front of Dod's house. The friends get to one that is aligned on the third row. Marvin lowers shrinking to half the size of Shrub. Suddenly his size gets bigger than even Dod. Marvin's spring legs stretch higher until his feet pass Dod's head. On the Eleventh entrance Marvin looks down at his friends. Shrub walks forward and lifts his arms as if to catch a ball. Marvin's own arms look regular before his hands come out his sleeves stretched out creating springs. He grabs hold of shrub and brings him up.

Dod looks up at the two and shakes his head. "Na, creat. I think I'm too heavy." He takes a drink of a shake and walks toward the ladder.

CHAPTER FIVE

f the bridges were not so thin, then going through one would be no problem, even with it's rails.

Marvin's head bumps back feeling a hard press causing a white flash in his eyes. He collides with another bridge that passes above. Rubbing above his head looking at the metal bricks that make another bridge walkway above, he slouches as he goes under while holding tight on the rail. Marvin manages to look down, nothing but other bridges and nothing but shadow. For the first time ever Marvin realizes how empty of a space leads to nowhere. All the spring kid can wonder is if anyone has fallen from these stairs and bridges.

Shrub can see more of Dod's kind as they walk on another bridge beneath. He thinks the creatures are going to the same diner since there were so many of the Swamlorlakplak. Yet, the bridge and stairs bellow have to lead somewhere different. Thinking of Dod, Shrub hears him drinking from one of his usual drinks behind. "Don't you think that you will run out of those?"

Dod brings his cup down. "Not me. I always prepare for long trips. Even though I never go on any. This one has red seeds. You know, from a chiyl plant?" He takes another long drink.

Shrub looks at Dod and shakes his head very slowly, then looks forward. "Why are you stopping, Marv?"

Holding onto one of the rails Marvin looks around. "I really do hope that we are going in the right direction."

"Of course we are. We double checked the map." Shrub scratches his large head. "Not like we passed through some other bridge. We've been on the same one the entire time."

As Dod finishes his drink the swamlorlakplak holds his arm over the rail. He lets out a chuckle then he opens his palm to watch as the cup falls into shadow. "That's what I was thinking guys. But yet these things are too dang creepy to stay on." Dod looks forward at his friends biting his lower lip. "That would have been one heck of a fall."

"Come on lets go. And watch your head." Marvin continues trying to avoid any thought of falling. The Empty's walkways are secured, but one cannot help but to think of the dangers. Marvin asked a creature passing about the place. He had some information, but he himself just passes by. The creature told them. No one has ever been sure how The Empty ever came about, only that it was a separation of exhibits. Another explanation is that too much water separated an exhibit somehow, creating two. None are certain. Those who have climbed down its' rocky walls have never came back. Obvious predictions on this is that the creatures fell. If not fallen then they found a pipe to go into and never found their way back. Perhaps found another exhibit and stayed which would be common.

"There, I see water dripping." Marvin looks in the distance. The dark stained green moss to metal is a relief. As if he is back to where he needs to be. It is such a relief that the white flash from when he got bumped appears again in his eye. This time the flash is a black squirm more like something he sees when closing his eyes. That would mean it is something alive and visible. Why is it so obvious now? Perhaps it is because he has been in the dark for so long and whatever light appears from the opening to the pipe readjusts his sight. The squirm gets closer to the entrance. When it circulates around the side Marvin is sure that it cannot be his sight or else the odd squirm would go past the opening. The squirm awaits. "Guys, is it just me or is there something by the entrance?"

Shrub's large round head moves over the top of the rail, then Dod's above the bulb head. Dod is the first to speak. "Yeah, that definitely is a worm."

The word disgusts Marvin. They are no longer in their exhibit, he guesses this worm will be an annoyance or otherwise. Marvin walks forward knowing they are going to have to deal with the thing one way or another. "Wait," Shrub says. "What are you going to do?"

Marvin breaths in. "Shrub—we are going to have to deal with this guy. I suggest we do it close to the entrance. Unless you want to go back."

"We can wait until it leaves." Shrub closes one eye as if getting ready for a hit.

"You know none of us wants to stay on the bridge any longer. So does that worm. Another option is to wait for more creatures to pass by." Marvin looks at the squirm creature trying to see what the head looks like. "What do you think, Dod?"

"Yeah, sure. No more time to waste." He grabs a shake and takes a drink. It's of course any random shake from his backpack. Just something to not make him look nervous. The three already dealt with one bug, now there seems to be another.

Getting closer, Marvin can now see the eyes which are as black and moist as the worm itself. If it was not for the bumps and the thin glossy shine from around the sockets, he would never tell. The size seems to widen also. The creature is a lot bigger than he thought. Only a few feet away Marvin stops. He wants to keep walking, but the thought of this worm landing above him not knowing it's attentions would be grotesque. Even for just a moment there is silence. Not knowing why but Marvin takes a step anyways.

"Hold." At first the friends think the worm burps. Then they realize its manner is too calm to sporadically let out some disgusting gas and talk at the same time.

"What was that?" Marvin moves his head back a bit.

"Hold I said." The voice is low and still sounds as sloppy as a burp. "What are you doing?"

The high pitched voice of Shrub is then heard. "What do you mean what are we doing. We need to get through. Do you bother everyone with that ugly face, or whoever passes this entrance?" Marvin's hand gets closer to Shrubs face to make him quiet. But the worm does nothing but stare.

"Did you pay upfront? What did you think this would be a free short cut to where you need to go? It costs buttons for short cuts like these, unless you are willing to give something else. If that be so, I will not say anything and collect."

"Say anything to who?" Shrub asks not carrying about Marvin's signal. "The hosts up front?" A slur of a noise comes out, but the three are sure it's a ,yes, from the creature.

"They didn't tell us anything. Now let us pass." Shrub's face is angry. He looks behind his shoulder at Dod, wondering what he is thinking. "Would you give this guy some of your buttons?"

"No way creat." Dod laughs. "Those are mine. I'm not making shockla just to give my rewards to some worm." Although Shrub agrees with Dod, he cannot help but feel irritated that the swamlorlakplak does not hesitate to make the situation go by quicker. Yet again, Shrub doesn't make things easier at times.

"Go ahead. You still need to get through me to do that." The silk face stays staring at the three. The worm stays focused, not even moving a muscle. Only it's wide mouth has taken action. All three friends are not sure, but when the worm talks, it's mouth looks like a shadow with no teeth or tongue.

Marvin decides to finally give what the creature wants. "Fine. Let us show you what we have that you might be interested in." He turns his head looking at Dod. Dod's head moves back confused thinking that Marvin is going to ask him for the buttons also. "Let me see inside your bag."

Dod's eyes widen with his head jerking back fast this time. "Oh, okay." He passes the bag over.

Marvin fumbles around inside hoping to think of something, anything that will get them out of this. "Do you have weapons in there?" The worm asks.

"You think we came in here thinking of creeps like you?" Shrub says irritated.

There is the map and for a moment Marvin wants to give it to the worm, but it would not be worth giving the worm since it's apparently so rare. He moves the map and there's the skull and harp. Not only does he take out one piece, but both of them. Marvin looks at what he has not knowing exactly why he brought them out in the first place. In each hand he holds the clay pieces that Lisa made. Staring at the worm Marvin hopes to get some sort of reaction from the creature.

"This is all we brought with us. Other than these I don't have anything to offer. Unless you want a shake?"

The wide dark mouth of the worm widens. "What will I do with a skull and rib cage? And a nasty drink will do nothing to pay your way through me."

Marvin and Shrub hears the irritated breath out of Dod's nostrils.

"This is no rib cage. It's a harp." Marvin looks at the harp as if thinking the obvious. Come to think of it, the harp does take shape of a bone itself. This gives him another idea. "Here, I'll prove it to you. I will play you a song." He puts down the skull and holds the small harp with one hand. Marvin plucks a string than another. Not knowing exactly how to play the instrument, Marvin's grip is a bit loose on one note. Shrub and Dod lift their shoulders ducking their head a bit, trying not to cover their ears. Although the strings are still attached, the sound is more like them snapping off because of over tightening for the off tuning. Marvin keeps plucking to find a good sound, but no matter what, the instrument still makes sharp wire like noises.

"Turn it off, turn it off. Stop that. Can't you tell you are no good?" The worm says as his eyes close and open.

"Hold on, let me try one more time." Marvin plucks again. Shrub and Dod cover their ears finally. The worm does not move so easily. Instead he looks at Marvin as if adapted to the sound suddenly but yet blinks his eyes so much it's as if he has something in them. Marvin lets down his hand and stops his so called playing. "What do you want then if none of these appeal to you?"

"You go back and bring me something of value. Something that actually sounds good. Or tastes better. Either of those or do not come back." This irritates the friends greatly. Especially knowing that this worm is more than likely just a thief robbing passing creatures.

Marvin turns around toward his friends. "We are not turning back and like spittle if we are going to let this guy make us."

"I can just give him buttons if that makes everything easier?" Dod takes another drink, even been as annoyed as he is.

"No, we are not doing that." Marvin's eyes squint not wanting the worm to win in anyway. "If we make a run through him, I'm sure this guy will smash one of us in the process. I can spring to another bridge."

Looking up, the closes bridge above is too far for even Marvin's springs. Could be one of the reasons why the worm stays around this area. So creatures with abilities can't do much. The bridge he bumped his head on might be an option. He looks down at the two clay pieces hoping to find some kind of answer. Where the neck bone should be under the skull is smooth but is also hollow. The end of the harp is broken unable to connect to the skull in anyway, then he thinks of what the worm said. The two together might do something none the less. Marvin places the skull on top the harp's pillar, making it the skull's spine almost. He turns around resting the other end of the harp on his shoulder trying to balance while holding both.

"See, I told you, you stupid spring kid. That is a bone." The skull faces the worm lifeless.

Marvin places his fingers the same way he did before and plucks again. Inside Marvin's palm he can feel the skull get lighter as he holds the jaw. Marvin wonders why this would happen, when he looks up he can see the top of the skull lift.

The pierce inside each of the friends ears is much more intense causing them to press their hands on their head even tighter. Dod's drink drips from the straw onto the floor as he covers one ear with the bottom of his wrist. Marvin closes his eyes. Not even he can stand the sound. There's a curiosity to see how the worm is reacting to all this so Marvin opens his eyes. The worm who now laughs stares at Marvin, thinking his entire act is foolish. The spring kid places another finger on a different string note changing the sound to a lower tone. The worm holds his mouth half way as if confused. His eyes even squint. Marvin lets loose his fingertips a little. The tone is a low pitch whistle. It does not exactly sound like a low note, but still makes a noise of it's own.

"What is that?" The lazy slow voice of the worm questions. "What is that?" The skull says.

The sound of the harp is so loud that the friends cannot hear what the worm says. All they can see is him move his mouth up and down. Shrub looks at Marvin. "Marvin, that harp is doing something to the worm."

Marvin hears his friend as he concentrates on trying to play the instrument. Looking at how the worm reacts to all this he now flicks his head around confused. He keeps talking but once more none of the friends can understand the sloppy talk of the worm. Dod now with his hands off his ears looks closely at the worm as he rambles on still. "It looks like he is trying to tell you something, creat." The sound of the harp does not drown the voice of the worm. But all of them know the skull talked awhile ago.

The worm's head is seen from both sides. Faster and faster the worm shakes his head. When it slows the teeth can now be seen. They are the teeth of anything carnivorous, pointy and sharp. As yellow as they are, the light from the pathway is still brighter. Marvin holds tight the skull as he continues to play. "Run!" His body narrows with the path, making sure the skull and harp are no where near the sides. Shrub follows as Marvin keeps his speed toward the entrance. A cup with it's straw makes its way onto the moving face of the worm as Dod now takes off behind shrub after throwing what he was drinking. Eruption of the cup, then green liquid spreads on the face of the worm. The creature is shaking from so much confusion, he cannot tell that something just hit him. When Dod enters, the three do not stop and keep running. Marvin separates the skull from the harp for a better hold on them and looks back, hoping that the worm does not go inside. The thought of him taking up the room of the entrance while trying to catch the three frightens Marvin. With hardly any space they are easy prey. There is no telling what the worm will do then.

Far from the path, Shrub looks down the pipeway wondering the same thing. "Do you think he will come after us?"

"Not sure. We will just keep checking our backs to make sure nothing does." Trying to catch his breadth, Marvin looks down their new walkway. There is no way for them to get lost or side tracked.

Sludge Way is the path to Mark's Tunnel. "There is no excuse for us to get lost now. Especially because we escaped an ugly worm somehow."

"Yeah very true." Dod takes another bottle from his bag as his back slouches, trying to catch his breadth. "What did that instrument do? Did Lisa really make that to make noise?" He takes one huge drink.

"Well she is supposed to be at the Wide Areas. That explains a lot for this make." Marvin looks at the skull that seemed alive awhile ago. Or at least it seamed as if it had a soul at the moment. Will he look crazy if he talks to the skull? Maybe it will say something also. Looking at it does not strike any kind of threat to him. Especially now that it just got them away from danger. "Hey you. Can you hear me?" The skull stays as still as a rock.

"I think you need the harp." Shrub grabs the instrument. He plucks one string and it makes a ping sound that trembles to silence. "Maybe it needs to be tuned?" He examines all around the piece, wondering how it can do such a thing as steel someone's voice. "I want to open it somehow. I bet you whatever is inside is what freaked the worm out."

"I don't want to damage the harp." Marvin hands the skull to Dod. "We can ask Lisa about how she made such a thing, or if it was even her intention."

"Very true." Shrub now gives the harp to Dod. "If we do run into another threat, will that work the same way? I hate to say it but if something else looses their voice, I'm not sure if they will happen."

Marvin pauses for a moment. Throughout this trip he didn't think there would be any kind of danger. Yes, it is difficult to navigate the pipes. Never did he think anyone would be after them while they make their way through. "Nothing will happen. And if it does, nothing can be as bad as a large worm. Not to mention, I am not even sure if he wanted to eat us or not."

"Yeah," Dod laughs at Marvin. "What was he going to do with our bodies if we did try running through? Just throw us off with his tail and laugh as we fall down The Empty?"

The comment by Dod may not be true. The thought of how it could of really happened leaves a deep sinking feeling in all their stomachs. Marvin tries swallowing but his throat is too dry and it's not because of their run. "Can you give me a drink, Dod?"

CHAPTER SIX

The inside of Mark's Tunnel looks the same as it did before. Marvin, never been this far from his exhibit still wonders if they are going the way they are supposed to. "Shrub," He gets closer to his friend. The little bulb head turns around and stops, Dod does the same. "Are you guys sure this is the right way?"

Without question, Shrub takes out the map. "Let's see, well it does say that Sludge Way ends. The entrance is on the left." His small eyes move left to right. There is silence and without noticing Marvin and Dod are looking at the map also. "We passed two pipeways, that we knew to skip. From

there we had to go seven hundred and twenty presses." Shrub squints his eyes and looks up at the two.

"You think we walked that far?"

"Yeah, I think so." Dod quickly agrees. Marvin realizing that it was a long walk also and nods.

"It did take us awhile to get here. We should be fine."

The usual damp scent of rust fills through the area of Mark's Tunnel. More down the path they go, the dampness thickens. A wet moister sticks to the faces of the friends. A common thing to any creature in the pipes. Fluffy cotton which seems like a blanket is on the side. Not many creatures seem to rest in this tunnel, the three realize. Finally someone decided to stay here. In fact, the tunnel has not been buys at all. There ahs been no creatures that have walked through the entire time the three have been inside. They pass a few pipeways until Marvin wonders why no one hasn't been around. All are pipes so the three decide to look inside one of them. One which has no door.

They enter inside what creatures usually call a living pipe. Inside is the average bricked structure that circles making a giant tube like living quarters. The ceiling reaches high but it's all one room. The first thing seen through the circular entry are some steel steps at the far end of the wall. The pipe entryway still goes inside a bit but ends at where one end of the steps wrap around. As the friends get to the end they notice someone standing on the rail. Whoever it is has horns on a face that is long which almost resembles a bottle. This creature's eyes are round balls that stick out making it obvious wherever he looks. Now he looks at the three friends as the creature stands on the other side of the stairway.

Marvin wonders where the mouth is on the long faced creature. He's so curious that he would want the guy to talk to them. Instead the creature stays silent, looking at the three. They stay silent as well, waiting to get asked to leave. But there is no shout of rejection, so the three decide to stay, thinking this may be a resting room of some kind. All their fingers wrap around the edge of the pipe as they look down to make sure they are welcome to be inside. There was no door after all.

Not much is different that would take place in any other pipe, at first. Around the floor are white sheets that seem to just lie there. An aged wrinkled gray colored face of another long faced creature rocks back and forth on a chair. This one's eyes seem to be embedded tightly in the face, as if a needle just pressed in and out of clay leaving two small indents. The loosening of wood keeps popping back and forth as the chair the creature sits in rocks. Marvin cannot tell who or what else can be in this compartment if not for those sheets lying all over the place.

The more he looks the more the sheets seem to unwrinkle themselves. They spread out so much that the old creature is not seen anymore.

Until finally they notice that the sheets are lifting as if there is some kind of air beneath them. Then suddenly the sound of the sheets flap then thin out. The white sheets drape down like a closed umbrella floating in the air but beneath the sheets at their tip seems to be a wrapped ball. As the sheets get higher they seem to cover something but is hard to identify what the ball may be.

Marvin and his friends detach their fingers from around the rim of the pipe and crawl backward. They got nothing more than a peak of the old lady creature. All around her were beds that had sheets of their own. There are no pillows, and the floor is brown rust. But this was only a glimpse at what was at the bottom. They wanted to get away quickly before the sheets rose to their level. The three look toward the opening and see the bottle faced man make his way in front of where they leaned over.

Standing on the steel ledge that was beneath them. His hand is hidden behind the entrance and when it moves a metal door moves with it. The floating sheets are in view floating behind him before the door slides and closes all the way with a heavy slam. The three friends look at one another then at the entrance that is not for them to enter. They crawl to get out. Looking at each other, still they wonder who the creatures inside the living pipe were, or what they were doing.

Shrub is the first to talk as he wipes dirt off his knees. "Did you guys see what was around that old creature?"

"All that were there were beds." Dod wipes at his knees as well.

Marvin looks at the now closed door which is just a slab of metal and a handle bar for opening, which is probably locked now. What may be happening on the other side is a mystery. "Should we knock? Maybe they will tell us."

"Heck no, I don't want go in there. That creature that closed the door on us did not look happy with us around." Shrub looks down the small entryway. "What I really wonder is what was beneath those sheets that made them fly up."

"Helium, creat." Dod grabs a shake and starts drinking. "Pressure shoots out of some pipes letting out steam or air. The helium comes from some of those pipes. That is how these long faced creatures made the sheets come at us like that. All they have to do is fill up something light, then it will float."

"Yeah but the sheets were flat when they were on the ground." Shrub says now looking at Dod. "There was something round under those things like heads pulling them in the air."

Dod takes another drink and shrugs.

"Maybe we will find something in the Wide Areas that will explain that." Marvin says. "Yeah, very true. Let's get moving." Shrub unfolds the map again continuing down the walkway. "No need to get sidetracked." And sidetracked is what happens as the three notice light dimming from both sides of the them. At first they think the lights are going out then they realize what kind of pipes they really are in.

Shrub looks around wondering what is happening. "Who turned off the lights?

As if Shrubs words meant nothing, Marvin realizes something. "You know how we have not seen no one for a while? It's because these pipes need to be cleaned." The three look down the pathway and see as more light go out. Not because someone turned them off but because an unfolded sheet that takes up the entire path is coming their way like a giant wall. They look the other way and the same thing is happening. Marvin looks up and down and notices an opening on the ground. "You think if we jump." Marvin points to a pipe that is running downwards on the floor.

"We'll fall and die!" Shrub yells.

"Well we'll be some crushed creats if we don't. Unless those sheet are very soft." Dod looks around not knowing what other option there is.

"We jump." Marvin says as he dashes toward the opening. "Or else we will suffocate. I heard about this happening before." As he runs toward the opening the other two follow.

Inside the pipe is dark but the spring kid stretches his arms and legs able to catch both his friends. They stretch as he holds them with each hand. "What do we do now create!" The echo of Dod's voice is heard in the shadows of the pipe.

"Wer're going to hitch a ride." Marvin says. "Shrub, grab hold of my left hand. You and Dodrill hold on." Shrub listens as he is too worried to question anything now. The left spring stretches and there is still air underneath Shrub and Dod. Marvin lifts up his right hand and waits. Once the slam is heard, like two flat wooden boards slamming, Marvin stretches his right hand upwards. There is seconds until there is a dim of light again. Then the three get propelled out of the dark pipe and shoot toward the way they were walking toward. "The sheet will take is all the way to the tunnel. From there we will go to the wide areas!" Marvin has to yell so his friends can hear him. "I'm tired of all these interferences. About time we get a break."

Copper Tunnel

The three friends already knew the entrance to Copper Tunnel would not be hard to miss. The entrance looks just like any other pipe, but the brim is copper and somewhat wider than most. Placed directly where Mark's Tunnel ends. Making it the only pipe to go through. Now there are more creatures seaming to come in and out. A lazy looking green man stares at the three as he passes by, leaving from Copper. His eyes are slit, and although he looks nothing like Dod, the two share the same kind of reptilian features. From the nearest pipe, several other creatures come out and go into Copper Tunnel.

Voices echo from inside outweighing walking footsteps or anything else.

"Well we are finally here." Shrub says. "This should lead directly to the Wide Areas." They pass through the brim. More down the path a stench tickles their noses the same way the diner did, with all it's cooked food as some of it burns on a pan someplace. Here the smell is not as satisfying and is a lot more stale. Instead of fresh food been cooked on an oven it's as though something was made inside a trashcan. Not enough for the three to completely despise right away, but after awhile it gets sickening.

"So how long will this walk take?" Dod looks down at Shrub.

The bulb boy shakes his head and brings out the map. "Not as far as Mark's Tunnel was, but we still have a ways to go."

"As long as we don't run into anymore bugs, I'll be fine with that." Dod takes a drink from a shake. The ground is black. Each step leaves an oil stain in the bottom of their shoes. The stale smell gets stronger as they go deeper into the pipe. Although it's called Copper Tunnel it still is a large pipe and has built up grime over time.

Marvin walks, not paying too much attention to his friends. Never has he been to the Wide Areas, so all he can think about is how they may look like. In fact, he is not entirely sure why the place is called Wide Areas. It's still an exhibit, a very large one. How can an area be a "wide area"? Many thoughts run through his mind until he hears a voice that may be directed toward him or one of his friends.

"Aye, you kids." The sound is raspy. Almost as if whoever spoke used only their throat to speak.

There is a kind of clatter that comes after each word. "What yakes you to ya Wide Areas?"

Marvin stops and looks to see who spoke. It better not be another scum that wants to swindle them in someway. Marvin looks to his side, realizing a boned creature sitting on the side. This creature is not like the boned beaked ones inside the diner. This one's body structure is that of a five fingered creature's standards, but the ribs seem to be very wide. The face more like the flat faced reptile that walked out of the pipe, but definitely no sharp teeth. He does not seem like a reptile creature at all.

Unlike all the boned creatures before, this one has eyes with round pupils and flat molars and canines.

"You yooking for an yeasy way down ya pipe?" The bone man says. He stands up looking around as if someone watches him. "Yeye can yelp you with yat."

Marvin scratches his head wondering if there is an actual tole to pay once they exit Copper Tunnel. "Is there a price to get through once we are about to get out?"

The skull looks down at Marvin. "No. But yey can yake it easy. Yit is ya long way yown. Yon't want to climb? Yask me!" He looks at the three and puts his boned hands under his jaw. For a moment the friends wonder why he does this. The skeleton stretches his arms up bringing his skull up with them. The bumpy boned neck is now longer. It extends up as if the spine can stretch somehow. The three try to look at the bone man's back seen how his head went up without pulling the spine apart. "Yi have multiple bones."

The three look at one another thinking what the skull man said is naming an ability. The confusion on their faces tells the skull man they do not fully understand why he shows them this. His arms push up more for the neck to proceed to extend.

"I think I see what is going on." Dod takes a drink. "Our mind tricked us to what we are familiar with. As we should simply realize that there are multiple neck bones layering each other."

Shrub lets out a breadth, rolling his eyes without Dod noticing. "Most everything has small neck bones till they make out the spine."

"No," Marvin disagrees with Shrub. "Inside the spine are other small bones, like multiple spines. Making a very long neck once the bones are all the way out. Similar to straws getting thinner and thinner going inside each other."

If the skull man had skin he would smile. One hand releases from the jaw, making the long neck now more noticeable. He points at Marvin nodding in agreement. Marvin crosses his arms and looks at the skull man. "Let me guess, the way down from Copper Tunnel is pretty high. Instead of using the regular way of getting down, you will extend until we get to the bottom. Am I right?"

"Yes," The bone man pulls his skull back down, making the neck normal size. "Yay lot faster using ye."

"How do you bring us down if only your neck extends? Do your arms do the same?" Shrub says with curious squinted eyes.

The skull bites once. The teeth collide. "Yye bite ya pipe."

"Sounds kind of scary, honestly. It will cost too much buttons and time for three trips." Marvin scratches his head. "Things we do not have right now."

"How yare you going to ya Wide Areas yithout any buttons?"

"We are going to meet someone. Good luck with your, services." Shrub steps away looking at his friends so they can follow.

"Yate, yi take all three yof you yat once."

The friends realize how wide the rib cage is. Maybe they can all fit in. If they were to take the way down with the boned man, it would be more out of curiosity. "Sorry," Marvin says as he walks toward the tunnel. "We have to save as much buttons as possible." The bone man looks at the three as they walk off. This time Marvin is unsure what kind of mood he is in, but his best guess is disappointment. He stands there for a bit, eyes fixed on the three with teeth together. The bone man turns his head away and takes a few steps back. He sits back down where he was before. Marvin wonders how many creatures actually take the bone man's offer. "You think we should have just took the lift?"

"What for, to fall on our asses and land up a pile of muck? That guy gets customers every moment as someone walks into this place. Why else do you think he sits there? Probably for every course." Shrub says quickening his pace a bit. "We need to save what buttons we have for when we do need a transportation somewhere." He looks at the map knowing that the way out is near. "Come on, almost there guys."

The first thing the friends see are other entrances of pipes about one hundred feet away. Like small creatures coming in and out crawling from holes, they all move down ladders like small dots. The walls are no different than any green brick walls that the three have seen before. The difference is the many bricks create this giant round area capable of sustaining thousands of creatures. That much is evident by the many pipes that stick around and run through the top. The wall goes so far it seems to disappear somewhere in the distance. A strange fog overcomes anything past hundreds of feet, mainly from activity down bellow. When the friends reach the edge of the exit there are masses of copper to brown points sticking out from the bottom.

The rusty metal reaches all the way to the bottom revealing roofs of all shapes. The walls continue down usually homes or compartments are inside or build in the walls. These buildings attach to other roofs some with narrow tops and others without. The bottom of these buildings are only partially revealed, and that is only because they end on top of other buildings. At least, that is how it is where the friends are from. Not once did they have an idea on how the Wide Areas looked like. Only thing they knew was that many creatures live here to construct, and creations are made.

Marvin looks down at the long ladders that fade in with whatever mist or dust is down below. All this way and now he wonders if he should even go. On his side he hears his friend Shrub. "Hurry up Marv. More creatures are coming."

On the sides many creatures climb down and disappear into the dust cloud. Looking over his shoulder, Marvin knows he cannot stay in front of this ladder for too long. Climbing down a ladder is nothing uncommon for Marvin or his friends. Their exhibit has many. Difference between these ladders and the ones from their area is how far they reach. As the three climb all they can realize is that this one ladder equals more than all the ladders at their exhibit combined. It's an exaggerated thought but for how long the climb takes, it does seem possible.

Halfway down moisture sticks to Marvin's face. As hot as it is he could be sweating but it's hard to tell. At this point him and his friends realize that what they saw was a foggy mist, and not dust. Yet he also tastes a hint of dust on his tongue. Finding out that the cloud was moisture is not their heighten amusement but it's better than a lot of dust around. Down below looks like a solid game piece display that everyone likes to play at the exhibit. A board with many patterns and dots are everywhere. Little tokens of different shapes as playing pieces. In the game the player moves their token. Here all the creatures move on their own on paths that lead into the buildings that can now be seen attached to the ground. Some creatures simply just walk under the ground instead of in buildings. Others walk inside pipe entrances on whatever part of the brick wall that can be seen. That is something that the friends are familiar with at least.

Marvin is almost close to the bottom and the sounds of voices get louder. Many slams and tin smashing seem to be going on. One thing that sounds different is the same sound that many pieces of paper make that rapidly flap together while been pulled. Marvin looks over his shoulder to see where the flapping is coming from. A creature that has a stick like body with a face that has a skinny stick beak flies pass him. Something that looks like it was made out of toothpicks. There were small green feathers on the creature, and it's wings looked clear. Marvin's exhibit hardly has creatures with feathers or wings.

Standing on the bottom the city looks so much bigger as if giants built it. Marvin looks at Shrub who is trying to comprehend what to do and where to go. Dod most likely feels the same way. He takes another one of his shakes out. Marvin realizes that this time as Dod drinks out of frustration. They would try to talk to one another, but the noise is too loud. As each breath, none of them can even hear their own breadth. Not wanting to stand close to the ladder, Marvin takes a step forward. He follows the path he is on, hoping it leads to a quiet area, or even just a simple part of a building. The path winds around a corner so Marvin and his friends go around. The path continues and they keep walking as it forks off two directions. Going left wraps around another wall while the one at the right goes underground. Not wanting to go beneath, yet, the friends go around the wall. Now they realize they are in another crowd of creatures. A smaller bunch but there are still the building walls surrounding.

"We need a door." Marvin says.

Shrub can hear him and looks around not wanting to get lost. "Let's go in here." He points at a steel dark red door that has no sign above. Realizing that it's the closest one, the three agree. Turning the nob nothing happens since it's locked. A creature with dark yellow skin that almost matches a type of rust color and walks near the three. He passes them with a confused look as if wondering why they're trying to go inside. The creature looks forward continuing to walk.

"I think we should try somewhere else." Marvin says. "This spot might be for living quarters."

Shrub looks down the path. "Yup, I agree. Come on. Let's stick with the same path." Walking fast, Shrub now leads the way. He turns around the wall that the path wraps around and all it does is lead to another market like area with buildings that have no signs. The wall where the path wraps around is no longer next to them. The wall is an odd one that is shaped like a blade that expands away from it's edge. Marvin and Dod can see the frustration the bulb head has. Shrub continues another way this time he stops at what is the tip of the pathway. The other two friends stop behind him. There is a cliff where they stopped at. And under them more city and creatures down below. The three look at one another. Shrub gives a slight lift of his shoulders and walks to the side.

"What do you think we should do?" Shrub looks around knowing that they will only get confused if they walk further.

Marvin looks at Shrub. "We ask around. See if we can find out what we can about creations maybe."

"A creation?" A bitter voice comes from the side. "Why, what kind of creation?"

The three look behind themselves, knowing that it was not one of them that said anything.

Marvin smirks at what is a creature that has a large wide face as long as a cow's would be. Fur hangs to the ground and is all over the body, but the lips and pink nose can easily be seen. It's hard to tell if the creature has any clothing on, but there is a dark green cloth that wraps in top of the hump and sinks into the fur a little. "I noticed when you three came in. I knew from the looks on all your faces that you may have never been here before. At first I did not think much of it, but now that I see you again, and talking about creations, I figure we should talk."

Not having much of a choice the friends need to take the creatures' help. He's the second one to give any service. Perhaps it's common in the Wide Areas. The help is needed. Only thought to Marvin is what price this creature wants. "Alright. How will you help us exactly?"

The fur creature backs his head up a bit confused.

"I mean, do we need to pay?" Marvin looks closer at the creature. Shrub looks around thinking that Marvin should have never mentioned anything that had to do with giving away their buttons. If the fur creature wanted to help for free, he would never ask. Now that Marvin has mentioned it, the creature might change his mind taking Marvin's suggestion. Dod just drinks his shake.

"Why no, young spring kid. I walk all around these parts. I'm a simple delivery spogg. Have you ever met any spoggs before?"

The three look at one another. All shake their head when they look back at this spogg.

"I kind of figured such. Spoggs are mainly here in Wide Areas. It's too hard for us to travel through pipes. Usually if there are any that live in an exhibit, we stay mainly in one place like a compartment or large pipe. My name is Vern, not spogg just so you won't get confused. If you are looking for creations follow me. One of my deliveries is by Patties. There they specialize in parts."

Before Vern turns his large body the three introduce themselves. Walking down the path, going back to where they came from the friends can see how long Vern's back really is. Straps hold many pouches and large boxes on top of the spogg's back and even boxes on top of boxes. Marvin and his two friends walk faster to catch up to Vern's front.

Vern's head is close to the three but because of the large size of his back, the height of the spogg's head seems so much higher. Marvin is the first to speak as the four get back to the entrance area with the wet rusty pipe smell. "Does all that...stuff get heavy to carry?"

"No, why should it? My kind can carry more weight than anyone. That is why most apply and get the job I have. Maybe creatures around your size can deliver things faster, but all of them have to run back and forth to the pickup more often."

"I can see that." Shrub says to himself now noticing new buildings.

"So why are you looking for creations? You want to make one?" Vern's eyes travel down to Marvin, waiting for an answer.

"No, we are looking for a friend. She is the one who is trying to make a creation. No one has seen her for a while in our area. Have you seen any murners around here? She is young, my age. A very quiet creature." Marvin remembers Lisa wondering how things would be if she was here.

"There are murners around here, but all common. If I saw any newcomers I would notice." It's until now that Marvin sees Vern's large hand. What are a spogg's fingers look like three wide pieces of brick. Two on top one that's closer to the palm making it the thumb. Most creatures in Marvin's exhibit hardly have hooves. At least none have any as noticeable as Vern's. One large hoof of a finger points at a building. The sign says it all. "There it is, Marrow. They usually specialize in joints and such. Maybe your friend went in there. There are other places but this is the closest."

The three look at the door. "Well let's go in." Marvin takes one step forward."

"Why wait a minute." Vern says looking down at the friends. "You cannot just go in and convince them that you want to make creations without any kind of license or idea on what you are doing?"

"What are you talking about? We just go in there and say we are looking around and are interested in seeing what they have. Also we need to ask about Lisa. It should be no problem." Shrub tells Vern in his agitated voice. None of them knew about needing a license. Each know they did not come all this way to stop and worry about one now.

"Yes, but the Marrows are stubborn and have serious costumers. I can give you a delivery token to enter." Vern tells them with a smile.

For a moment Marvin thinks it will be a gift from the smogg. Then he realizes that Vern has helped them already. "Okay, the token then what?"

"You enter." He smiles. "But you will have to give me something worth an entry pass.

I mean, it can cost me my job."

"Then why do it?" Shrub says. "We can just find another place."

"Getting inside anywhere else like this won't be any different. I suggest you take my offer.

Actually, what you give me can help you out in the long run. I realize that backpack that the reptile has on has been wearing him down." The smogg smiles again.

"It has been kind of heavy." Dod takes a drink from his shake. "I can give you some." "Just drinks?" Vern says.

"We do have a skull and harp." Marvin does not know why he said that but the harp is the first thing he thought of. His friends look at him.

"That I would like to look at." With all that fur anyone can notice a smile like that.

Dod has no choice. He walks up to the smog and opens his backpack and shows both pieces. "Do you know what they are exactly?" Marvin asks looking at Vern's expression which does not change much.

"A bone and harp? Not really. I will trade for both of them, but I will not know what to do with such a thing exactly"

"Oh actually we were just wondering if you knew what they were, but they're not up for trade.

How about a shake like my friend offered and some buttons. Will that work?" Marvin half smiles hoping an exchange will be this easy.

The face on Vern already says it all. It changes not at all and he looks at the back pack still. "I have got different shakes, grass, mold, bug meat from many different exhibits. What I want to see is what's really weighing down that bag."

Without any choice, Marvin bites his lip. He feels the pressure from his friends that what he just said was a mistake. Finally the creature says something of relief. "How much buttons do you have?"

Dod has to interfere. "Enough that you need. Plus shakes from another exhibit. None that you have had before. Maybe even a recipe for one."

There is silence other than what is happening around the area. "Okay." Is what Vern says. "You guys are new so I will take it."

CHAPTER SEVEN

After putting in the token in the slot the door opens the shop. Never has any of the creatures needed something to get inside a place. When they enter the question to why the place might be called Marrows is answered. Even though Marrow can be nothing more than a common name, this building has the title intentionally. Eyes inside boned sockets are inside the boned creature that stands behind the counter. This skull is not like the skeleton that was in Copper Tunnel, offering an elevated way down.

Instead the eyes are balanced on flesh. It is easy to tell by the blood red muscle that is underneath the bone. In fact, all the flesh and muscle is held behind bone, as if the anatomy was opposite to that of any creature in living existence.

Inside is plainer than what the friends imagined. All there is are shelves of different looking skulls and other bones of various shapes. They are all almost as white as the walls. Tapping and then clicks of something hitting together multiple times is the only sound heard. Marvin looks around a corner and sees two skeleton creatures chomping their teeth up and down, looking at one another.

"Can I helt you?" The creature on the other side of the counter asks. He has a strange way of pronouncing things. The tongue holds on the top on the mouth for any pronunciation that needs soothing of the lips.

A bit plain inside, yet this is the perfect place for Marvin to find out about the skull they found. He takes it out of Dod's backpack. "Here." The skull's jaw taps on the glass counter. "Our friend made this. By the looks of it, she is trying to make a creation."

The skeleton creature moves his head in closer to the skull. There is no way in seeing how this skeleton's true expression is either. The merchant leans back up and looks toward the other two around the corner. He does some tapping of his own, then looks back down at the three. "Is there ore to this?"

Marvin looks at Shrub then to Dod. The two friends exchange looks as well, making it obvious that they are confused somewhat. "Yeah," Marvin says slowly.

"Let eey see it, ease?"

The bony palm of the merchant opens up in front of Marvin. The red flesh is what sticks out most between joints as the bones blend in much with the room. Marvin is about to grab the harp from the backpack, but as he does the two skeletons at the corner are looking right at him. Straightening up Marvin does not get the harp from the backpack. He clears his throat and looks at the merchant again. "Tell me what this skull of a murner can be used for first. Aren't you supposed to know?"

"Eey are." The merchant straightens himself. "It is nothing ore than a regalar skull. Just need to know it there eey ore."

"Just tell us what the skull is for?" Shrub interferes not knowing what the skeleton said. "It is ore creations. Illing to i it." The merchant sticks out his hand again.

Shrub looks at Marvin. "He wants to buy it from us I think."

Marvin stays staring at the merchant. "We cannot do that. This is our friends and we need to find her first." Two pairs of footsteps get placed behind them, and they are not from costumers.

"It is too dangerous, to carry around. Let us handle the skull." The merchant's eyes do not leave from staring at Marvin's. He wonders why they want the skull so much. It looks as if it can be placed with any other of the skulls in the shop. Somehow it is as though the merchant can realize that it has a special power.

"No," Marvin says not knowing how to get out of the shop with the two standing behind him and his friends. There is an instant pull that Shrub and Dod feel. Marvin hears it but is distracted as the skeleton falls forward reaching out toward him. Those eyes so wide come forward causing Marvin to flinch. His reflexes from his legs are not by instinct as he springs up to the ceiling, trying to get away. The top of his head feels like as if something heavy fell on it as he collides with the top of the ceiling.

The springs of his legs compact immediately for the second he stops in the air. On his way down Marvin springs them back out. The bottom of his shoes come forward straight to the merchant's face. The impact causes the skeleton man to fall backwards hitting the wall behind the counter. As Marvin falls he lands on top of his friends and their attackers. All five lay on the floor ruffled to get back up.

Dod's red tongue comes out of his mouth and hits one of the skeleton's eye. The hit is so hard that the skeleton presses both hands on his sockets. Immediately Dod grabs one of his drinks from the bag and pours it on the face of the skeleton who has his arms wrapped around Shrubs big round bulb head. The drink does nothing much, but the skeleton shakes his head rapidly to get the liquid off.

Marvin then gets up and shoots his hands toward the door knob. He twists it but it doesn't turn. He notices that there had to be some kind of control scheme behind the counter somewhere for the merchant to activate. Marvin still holds the knob and lets his body shoot forward as his arms compact.

Quickly Dod get's up and tries to pry the arms off of Shrubs head. He is about to shoot his tongue at the attacker but he forgets about the merchant behind the counter. The straps of his backpack press into the front his shoulders causing him to fall back. He yelps by the brief pinch of pain as he falls back. Unzipping the backpack the merchant is desperate to see what's inside. With the merchant behind Dod, it is hard to tell what he's doing. Marvin notices the skull on the floor so he extends his spring arm for the grab. Once he brings the skull in close he stares at the piece wondering, can the skull do some kind of trick? Similar to what happened with the worm. He faces it toward the skeleton creatures.

Nothing happens.

No time to waste, Marvin runs toward the skeleton on the floor, wearing out Shrub. The spring kid kicks the skeleton on the face but the skull is too tough for the hit. Marvin's ankle gets a tightening feel wrapped around. As he looks to the floor the third skeleton grabs hold of him, his left eye's veins are blood shot red.

Slipping his arms out of the straps, Dod lets the backpack slip off. He punches the skeleton on the face but nothing but pain spreads throughout his fist. "Oh!" Dod shakes off the pain. He shoots his tongue, but the skeleton moves his head. The merchant looks at Dod. The backpack swings toward the reptile only moving Dod a little to the side. He grabs hold of what is his, hoping that none of the shakes open. Some liquid drips on the floor, then a burst of green slush shoots in the air.

The harp is displayed in front of the merchant. His eye lids are permanently wide to show the look of surprise that is on his face.

He grabs the harp, letting go of the rest of the backpack. Dod falls backwards with most of his shockla spurting everywhere in the room along with other objects.

The harp is in his grasp. With amusement, the skeleton looks at the instrument. "That's something I'm looking for."

Marvin kicks the one with a red eye now as Shrub tries to break the other's grasp. Lisa's clay skull lies on the floor barley a foot away from Marvin to reach. One arm extends grabbing the skull and bringing it back close to him. The clay skull collides with the head of the skeleton on the ground. It is enough to knock the skeleton's grip away and put him to rest. Marvin sees Shrub been carried away.

Bringing his arm back, Marvin gets ready for another punch with the skull. The spring extracts holding the skull and is able to knock the skeleton on the floor, dropping shrub as well.

Dod and the merchant see this. Knowing that his comrades are slowed down, the skeleton behind the counter holds tighter onto the harp. He stares at the back door where the two were talking at first. The friends know that the skeleton wants to leave, so they walk closer.

"Give us back the harp. Why do you want these pieces so much?" Marvin asks.

Shrub with an angry look on his face looks at Marvin. "I think we should just knock him out." "I want to know why they attacked us. These guys did not even want to bargain first." Marvin looks at the merchant waiting for him to say something.

Shrub looks at Marvin a bit confused then at the merchant. "Would you have?" "No," The merchant says.

Dod mixes a few of the partially empty drinks in one cup. He puts his focus on Marvin. "Maybe they did not want the chance of us leaving with those things. Either way, we need the harp."

Marvin looks at the skull in his hand, then back at the skeleton. He realizes now that the creation Lisa is trying to make is more important than he thought. "Why not tell us what is so great about these two pieces?" A simple question that Marvin expects that he will not get an answer to.

The skeleton merchant shakes his head slowly. The teeth do not separate this time as he speaks.

"No."

Marvin stays staring at the skeleton. He shrugs his shoulders and tosses the skull again letting his arm extend all the way. The merchant hits the wall for the second time. Quickly Marvin's other hand grabs hold of the harp. He looks at Dod checking if the backpack is still intact. "Can these go in still?"

Finishing mixing all the shakes that Dod can, the reptilian gets up and attaches pins on the pocket that was opened. "Yeah, I just need to put them both in the same pocket now." Dod leans up looking at his two friends. "By the looks of it, that skull will not get damaged easily. So I don't think the harp will either. Do you need your sleeping bag? It's kinda torn up."

Shrub walks toward the wall where there are towels and clothed bags. He takes one of the towels handing it to Dod. "Forget the sleeping back. Wrap this around the harp so the strings won't get caught on anything."

The harp gets wrapped and put away. All three look around the room wondering how to leave. Attempting to open the entrance again is pointless. Marvin tries the back door, as dangerous as it may be, but that is locked also. "There has to be a switch over here." Shrub walks over the bone legs of the merchant. He cannot tell if the bony hands will reach out for him or not, seeing that the eyes are looking right at him. A lot of tearing drips as the skeleton lies motionless. Shrub ignores the body and looks under the desk. Marvin was right about there been a switch because there are several. "Ugh, guys."

Before he is able to say anymore, Marvin and Dod are beside him. "Which one do you think unlocks the door?" Dod asks rubbing his chin.

For a while they examine the bottom of the desk that actually has more to it then the top. "I say we try for the one that has the longest pin. If they need to lock the door as desperate as they were, that should be the easiest one to reach."

Realizing that the skeleton's know the control scheme by memory, it should not be difficult to know where all the controls may be. There is no other option since all the switches look almost the same. "Well, this one is longer." Shrub puts his small finger tip below the switch. His finger is almost as thin as the switch itself.

"Do it." Dod says without any hesitation.

Not thinking about it anymore, Shrub clicks the switch. Another click that sounds heavier inside the room is heard near the door.

"That had to be it." Marvin rushes toward the door. His hand wraps around the knob. Before he opens it, he looks at his friends. "Let's also report these maniacs."

Dod and Shrub who now stand close to Marvin nod their heads in agreement. The door opens but the streets that were The Wide Areas look different to the point where they are not streets anymore. They are not even the same color. The rust that once was walls is now a red brick pathway leading toward a red flashing light brighter than the bricks. Marvin thinks they are at the back door. He turns around looking at the same view from when they walked inside. The red eyed skeleton's bony hands moves slightly. It is a minor movement still indicating him awaking. Clicking of the other doorknob sounds rapidly. All three already know that the back door is trying to be opened. With one more stare Marvin looks down this new hallway. The three stare at one another and all run inside at the same time. Dod closes the door to the new hallway, as none of them know where they are going.

CHAPTER EIGHT

"This leads to somewhere not good for any of us. I know it." Shrub slowly walks looking over his shoulder every so often. The brick pathway leads only one way toward red lights further down. Shrub always so anxious keeps staring at the backpack, wondering if their lives are worth the clay pieces.

"Those skeleton's really wanted those bones. Are you sure all this is worth giving to Lisa? I mean we can just look for her without them."

Marvin looks down at Shrub not wanting to answer him. The walk has been nothing but time consuming. Right now the spring kid just wants to keep his mind off of everything they are dealing with and get out of the mysterious place. "I think these are proof against those marrows. We have already been seen with them and still here in the skeletons turf, I do not think ditching them would really matter. Once we reach the surface you can go back if you want. I had no idea that we were going to run into this much trouble."

Shrub's voice raises. "It's not that I want to leave. This is all too risky for returning those bones.

The danger made me forget why we are really here."

"And you Dod?" Marvin turns looking at the reptilian creature.

"No man, I don't care. I had nothing better to do." Dod says only half listening to Marvin and Shrub's conversation. He examines the walls trying to figure out how they were made so deep into the ground. "Whatever we do, we should not stop. Those skeleton's up there might be after us. Should be after us."

"Of course. Keep in mind, the merchant changed the rooms somehow so we will not leave. This is still their territory. I think that room must have been an elevator of some kind. I have no idea. If the buildings can move, anything can happen." Marvin looks as if he hears something in the distance. "Hold on." He says to his friends in whisper. He walks with a hunch knowing the end is near. More red shines into his eyes causing him to shade them as he walks closer.

Looking down the stairway, it is like stepping into a giant warehouse that is used for storing materials and containers of gargantuan size. Although there are many squared containments all lined up, chains hang and dangle from the top. The red lights filter through creating a grid shadow cast upon the three. Marvin's first thought is why chains hang through a fenced ceiling? The red-light shines above revealing particles of dust falling, still there is no indication what exactly is causing the light.

"Now where are we?" Shrub's high pitched voice asks. "Some kind of storage!" He looks up at his friend with those wide eyes squinting like usual. "After we go passed all those storage's, there might be more of those bone heads."

Now it is time for Dod to squint his eyes. He looks down at Shrub confused. "What are you talking about?"

Although what Shrub was trying to suggest did not come out clear. Marvin still knows what his friend was talking about. "The stairway in front of us will only take us more closer to the creatures.

Normal for them but dangerous for us."

"Yeah, well..." Dod looks to the sides at the bottom of where they stand. Nothing is on their right, Dod is more satisfied on what he sees to the left. "Look, there are openings on the side." He looks at Shrub and Marvin with wide eyes. "If they know we are in their exhibit, at least they will not know where exactly. Quick, let's go." The reptilian creature brings his bare webbed feet down beginning to climb as his tail dangles past his ankles.

"I can lower you." Marvin suggests.

"Lower, Shrub. You know I weigh more." Climbing down is Dod's main concern. He looks down, making sure each step does not miss a crack or bump on the stone stairway.

Grabbing Shrub under his shoulders, Marvin's arms extend showing their spring form. He lowers Shrub. When Marvin's spring arms loosen and dangle, he knows Shrub has touched the ground. As if the hands disappear the springs close into arms making a small clap. There is an echo that follows, and Marvin knows it is not him. He looks to his left inside the brick tunnel. A new light creeps through each gap that connects the bricks together, shining on each one. The spring kid knows that whoever it is does not care if they are heard. At first he thinks the clan has cubes rolling inside cups, because that is what is heard. Then as shadows of skinny shapes of skulls and ribcages are quickly distinguished on the wall, Marvin knows who it is. There is nothing but flaky movements of bones as they get closer. But the teeth of each skull chops at different paces.

Below, Dod has already reached the ground. He thinks of climbing back up to help Marvin as he stands stunned. Shrub waves his skinny arms in whispers. Both can see the glow getting closer.

Marvin blinks his eyes as if he were out of a trance. He looks down and sees his friends trying to get his attention. Gripping his fingers on the edge is easy, the stairway may be a bit narrow on the sides but is also cracked in some areas. His head dips forward and very slowly it almost reaches where his hands hold. He sees the fenced ceiling then the other side of the walls as he now turns around. His back touches the side of the stairway and his arms and legs come apart. Once his feet touch the ground he lets go of his grip. Marvin's body comes together making a clap sound again. All three press their backs against the wall and look up to see the marrow creatures.

A blinking light flickers. On the edge of the stairway small flames reach out and quickly disappear. Even though the three friends cannot see what is creating the small flames, they are sure one of the skeletons is holding a torch. To their surprise, none of them look down. The rattling is heard in the distance and fades as the flaming light fades as well.

"They are gone." Whispering from Shrub is heard. "I say we stay hidden, as if someone is still up there."

Nodding in agreement Marvin and Dod look at the entryways that they all agreed on going through. There are five and each are shadow pathways. Not like the pathways by Diner but these are digged through holes. Without anyone saying a word already each stand in confusion and a repetitive fear runs through all their minds knowing that pathways always have something unpleasant in them. Dod who is on the right looks at Marvin and Shrub with a smile. "Now what do we do?"

Shrub opens his mouth yet no words come out. He scratches his chin as he is about to say something but still does not. Silence once again in the giant hollow compartment, cave of skeletons. The three do not even know what kind of building they are in.

"Let's go inside one of these holes." Dod says.

"Are you crazy? We do not know where those lead to." Shrub sniffles, he looks at the holes and shakes his head.

Dod looks also realizing there is not much of a choice. "Well, where else do you suggest we go?

Where those skeletons went perhaps?"

"We can wait until they leave." Shrub's sarcastic tone comes out. "I am sure there are other paths going down that way."

"Alright guys, enough." Marvin breaks in. "These tunnels need to lead somewhere and I'm sure the skeleton people are going to search this entire place from bottom to top. I am surprised they passed us, unless they themselves do not want to be near these holes. There are other places that they know of also. So we need to figure out how to get out of this place which is their home..." Marvin pauses. "Did you hear that?"

Shrub lifts his head trying to hear what Marvin heard. "Hear what?" "I thought I heard someone speaking."

Suddenly a sound. A voice maybe? Inside the tunnels the sound of gravel been pushed gets closer. Something must be dragging. But then there is a cough. The gravel sounds seem to smooth out. Suddenly they realize that it is someone's voice clearing.

"I'm sorry to crawly"

"But we came stomach growling"

"No one need to worry"

"Just need to tell ye, for we see you camping"

"So let us eat all you that are small, ye."

What can be one of the most ugliest green faces, uglier than the worm from the Hollow, appears from one of the holes. The eyes on the thing are like white balls with pupils as wide as the inside of pipes themselves. It is not a worm. Worms do not have many pointless legs that stick out from the sides like wings. The long face has a mouth that is a hyenas smile. The molars on the thing are so big that there can be bucked teeth on it, but the crooked assortment all matches.

"Who are you?" Shrub asks. A confused look on his face.

"No need for me to say, I just come for a stay."

"What kind of stay?" Marvin asks stepping back remembering this green creature mentioning something about eating them, and not to worry about it.

"Oh, new? What brings you?" The teeth of the green creature clack together with the last word.

Shrub looks up at Marvin and whispers. "Should we tell him that we are lost?"

"No, creat." Dod tells Shrub. "He can go back into that hole and report us!"

"I don't report to anyone, fellow. So mellow." The creature blinks. Upfront the hideous creature, no one can see the eye lids, but it blinks.

All three continue to step back, not feeling comfortable in front of the thing. "We need to go. Sorry to bother you." Marvin tells the creature."

"You guys are leaving already?" The large ball eyes look from side to side. "I thought you came here to see me?"

"What are you talking about?" Shrub asks.

His rhymes continue. "The small critters come down here. And I greet to eat."

"What kind of creature would do that just to feed you?" Shrub looks at the creature more confused. The three back up even further.

"If you guys stay, you can see for yourselves if you may."

"First," Shrub says. "We do not even know where we are. Can you tell us how to get out of here and then maybe we will throw you a shake or something."

Dod looks down at Shrub, upset that he is offering him one of his drinks.

The creature blinks his eyes again. The pupils turn to each of the friends. "The only way out is through the top of those stairs. Or come through me if you dare."

As if already knowing the answer Marvin looks at the ground. The spring kid thinks to himself that there has to be another way. With his spring abilities, he can spring them out. He looks to the ceiling. "Come on guys. Let's get out of here."

"No wait!" The creature says. "Don't you want to meet who I eat?"

Shrub shrugs his shoulders not caring to show that he is uninterested. "Why?"

This time the creature is able to move his entire long head. "Because you guys might decide to get eaten also."

"No, creat." Dod says. "We would rather jump inside a clogged sewer pipe with crap. But I will offer you this." He takes one of the bottles from his bag. "I got some shockla here, maybe it will shock ya."

"Be careful Dod." Marvin warns.

"What is that?" The creature's head moves with curiosity.

"A shake look. But remember, only the first one is free. Now open wide." Dod removes the lid, knowing not to get so close. The large mouth expands revealing the mandible teeth that are so big that their alignment takes up most of the mouth. As if standing in front of a heater which smells like rotten food, Dod cannot help but to pull back his head as he smells the breadth of the creature. Behind the teeth there is red that fades into a green. Dod for a second thinks he is looking into a garbage bin. What can be a green slimy worm moves between the teeth. Then Dod realizes that this is the tongue. A bright green of a glow pours on the tongue. Quickly Dod backs up after the shockla is out.

The cheeks of the creature swoosh as he tries to see how the shake tastes most of all. "That is really good. Can I have more."

"Sorry creat, remember only the first one is free."

The eyes are half covered this time as the slimy creature looks at the three. They quickly move away and a smile forms on the face. There is a tapping coming from behind. Along with it, a type of rattle. The three look and right away move to the side. Another skeleton. Do they feed themselves to this creature? Marvin takes a closer look until he realizes that the skeleton is not like the ones in the shop. "It is the bone man from Copper Tunnel." Marvin says.

"What, do you think he works with these freaks?" Shrub eyes the bone man with a smirk. "I mean, what is there to eat if he is going to eat this guy?"

The bone man sees the three but ignores them. He looks with the only flesh he has, which are his eyes, at the creature in the hole. "Yeye yam here to be yeaten."

"Aww, I have had skeletons before. This one will digest slowly. The large mouth of the slime creature opens. Dod recognizes the breadth once again.

"Wait," Marvin says. He looks at the boned man. "What are you doing?"

Interrupted, the bone man looks at Marvin. "Yeye shall feed myself yo yis creature. It will be for ya good cause."

"Why would you give up your life just to be eaten?"

"No one yiks my lifts. Nor does yany one need them. For yat, I will end my yife, giving it a purpose."

"Have you tried giving lifts somewhere else? Or even tried doing anything else." Marvin looks at the boned man wondering how he found out about the creature in the hole. "Just because you can expand your spine, does not mean you have to use that as an only job." Marvin's hands fall on the ground with the loosened spring arms. "Look, I can expand too. Does not mean I need to use my arms and legs for only one thing."

The bone man's head moves slightly left and right. "Yeye yever thought of that before. Not often do yeye go into ya Wide Areas."

A wave of disappointment fills the creature in the hole. He knows what Marvin is doing and does not like what's happening. "Hey wait a minute. I still need to eat. Come here and then you guys can talk after."

Shrub is sure the creature eats another way. Especially because this "skeleton man" is a volunteer. "Go eat somewhere else. I know you do not rely on creatures who just suddenly show up to be eaten."

"I don't, they make appointments, most of the time." The creature smiles.

Marvin looks at the skeleton man, he not only sees someone who should not let themselves get eaten, but someone with great potential to the group. "Well, just come with us. We might need your help. And if not by your neck extending but by you knowing about The Wide Areas."

"Wait," The face on the creature in the hole is now that of anger. His veins stick out like worms pushing their way through. His eyes, blood shot red. "You cannot just take my food and not offer a trade. One of you has to commit." "Here have some more shockla."

"I don't want that crap. I need meet, I need marrow. One of you come here and see no tomorrow."

The creature pushes himself out more which frightens Shrub. He thinks the creature is actually going to get out and try to eat one of them. "Guys, maybe we should just give him the skeleton."

"What?" Marvin says. Dod can also be heard saying your crazy man, while then taking a drink of his shake.

"Ha, just kidding...sort of." Shrub smirks with worry. "But this guy is about to explode."

"Explode!" The creature moves closer. His eyes pulsating with rage. The heat from his mouth comes out as a mist that could kill any kind of stink it once had. Yes, it is a mist and the three would not disbelieve if fire shot out. "I am going to eat ALL OF YOU!" If any fire would come out, the creature stops it from happening. The four back up and almost run as the angry hole creature pushes itself forward. All that is on his mind is to get at least one. Why only one when he can get all! Just as a magnet would on opposite ends get closer to other opposite magnets. This worm does the same toward the crowd as they keep going further back.

Not sure if the worm is almost to his full extent, but a lot of it's body can be seen. It chops a few times not necessarily near any of the friends and does it rapidly trying to get whatever it can. Not able to avoid the chomping the friends spread out. None pay attention to go as far as the stairway ends but all are at a far distance. The four friends re-group seeing the entire body of the slug. It's round body makes it uncomfortable for turning. The chopping starts to slow down. The pupils in the eyes turn looking all directions. The slug notices the four standing in front of the stairway. Slowly it wiggles its body. With all of it's arms, none serve a purpose.

With a sniff, Dod tries looking at the three. "Um, let's move."

There is no reaction from Shrub, but he cannot help but to answer. "This guy is way slow."

Heavy breaths can be heard. The veins pop out more and the blackish green leather like skin expands like a balloon where the stomach is at. With how slow the slug is he finally manages to face the tunnels in the walls. Heavy breadths continue and he tries squirming toward the middle tunnel. The small arms on the body rapidly move but like before are not even close to touching the ground.

The three friends stay looking at the slug, feeling like there is something they should do. The skeleton man just stands there.

Confused, Dod does not even take a drink from his shake. "Should we push him in?"

Marvin does not answer quickly. He bytes down at the question, which would be the same reaction as if one of his parents asked why he never likes to clean his room. "He might byte us."

The slug ignores them. He keeps squirming. Finally moments later, his head ducks. The expanding stomach and moving arms slow down. The heavy breathing sounds are no more.

Shrub, like a rodent, walks up to the body unafraid. The teeth are closed and the round eyes are as visible as they were before. "This guy is dead." Shrub looks at the skeleton man. "You live here.

What kind of creature is this? Do they die easily?"

"Yime not sure, actually. No one yows what kind of creature this is. Yey just say yey know he needs to eat."

"I know what kind of creature this is." Shrub says staring back at the dead slug. "One that is so fat that it's true features have been hidden. Ha, he is so fat that he could never get out of those holes. Look how bloated he just got from squeezing out of the tunnel!"

"That's nice Shrub, but can you get away from that thing now." Marvin says getting nervous. "He could be faking."

"Sure," Shrub steps away. "But he ain't faking. The veins are gone and he is bloating by the..." A second of pressure is all Shrub feels hit his head. All he sees for that second is black. Then he realizes that he is slipping on the ground. His bulb head is wet, but it is not sweat. He looks around and sees that all his friends and the skeleton man, who are now suddenly sitting down, are a different color. They are all painted a slime green, almost the same color that the moss is sticking to the walls but just a bit brighter. He looks in front of him and sees no face, but what is a rib cage covered in the muck.

"Damn," Dod says amused. "That guy just exploded!"

"Great, now we are covered in this crap. What do we do now?" Shrub looks at the other three still sitting down wiping away the blood.

"We go into one of those tunnels." Marvin says.

"You are crazy. That slug can have more friends that we will walk right into. And there will be no way to move around in there." Shrub flicks his arms trying to get any heavy weight of the slime off.

"Yot exactly." The skeleton man says. "You know, we never knew ya bout any more of yees slugs. Yother than this one. He would yome out of yother holes around ye area."

"He might be right. If this one got fat on his own and had no choice but to live in there because of that. This condition could be avoided by others of it's kind." Marvin looks at the tunnels. "Those tunnels lead to other areas around The Wide Areas. Besides, if we go the other way. Those other

skeletons can get us."

Shrub shakes his head realizing that it is too much of a risk. "I still don't like it, Marvin. Who knows what else can be in there. I say we take our chances going toward where those skeletons went. Maybe we can find a vent or something."

"We should of asked that slug if those other tunnels lead somewhere else." Dod takes a drink of a shake. He looks at the slime, suggesting to himself that maybe it can be part of a recipe. He smells his arm and shakes his head. "Now that would be a mistake."

Marvin unsure what to do looks at the skeleton man. "Do you know where we would go if we go toward the end of this large room? Those Marrows kept going that direction. As a matter of fact, how did you get here?"

"Ya path. Yit is almost ya-round the area where ya Marrows went through."

"Well let's just go through there." Shrub says looking at both Marvin and Dod. "Why take our chances in those tunnels that can get us in more danger?"

"Yee cause, more Marrows are who let other creatures come in."

They all stay silent, knowing whichever way they go danger is going to find them regardless.

Shrub is the first to speak. "If you say that was the only slug around, I think we go through the tunnels." He points at the skeleton. "But you better be right."

Everyone looks at Marvin. "Well, I guess, but we better find our way out of there quick." He looks at the skeleton wondering what he is going to do. Shrub is not usually the one for worrying about extra weight. But he sees this skeleton as a good navigator, or even someone that can bring the group up or down in certain areas that Marvin cannot get to. "And you, are you coming with us? what is your name anyways?"

"Zeet."

"Okay, well, now which tunnel do we go through, Zeet?" Shrub looks at the tunnels knowing the middle one is out of the question.

"Let's go through the last one on the right." Marvin says as he examines the opening. "Something tells me that one leads away from the Marrow area and into the Wide Areas. Does everyone agree." All shake their heads. Picking any tunnel is as mysterious as the next. The group waits a moment in case any of them needs to say anything and nothing is said. The four go into the tunnel.

CHAPTER NINE

As the group walks on each think the area would have the same stench of what the slug smelt like. Instead all they can smell is the dirt that surrounds them. None have said much of anything. Mainly just to make sure no one or nothing is around. For the most part the tunnel has not broke off in too many other paths. Whenever they come to a fork, the group would always choose the path to the right.

"This might have been a more dangerous idea than we thought guys. What if we are going in circles or what if this does lead to the Wide Areas but is still too far for us to last?"

"Don't worry, we still got a lot of shockla." Dod says while he drinks a shake. "I myself have walked in pipes that have been just as long. I am sure you have also."

"Yeah, but at least I know I'm in or around my exhibit. I don't know how some creatures just travel along any pipe and that is their home. If I knew we were going to be doing the same thing, I would of brought bags and a blanket." Shrub realizes that they are surrounded by an area of dirt that has been more compressed. Most areas have had the dirt not disturbed. "Look. We are around a more compact spot. Looks like that nasty slug was around here before."

Marvin feels like telling Dod to not have such a light opinion about the walk. Then again why worry too much? If they see another slug, then maybe the humor will dampen the fear. "We been walking for a while and have not seen anything." Marvin faces Zeet. "You have been in the Wide Areas. What does it have to offer?"

"Yeah Wide Areas. Yot of creations. Many compete with each others and try to yovercome how ever yey could."

"Then how come we did not see any of these creations when we were there?" Shrub interferes. "Everyone has heard of them. So why were none on the streets?"

"I know. We just fallowed a huge, what was that creat called again? Ah, spogg or whatever."

"Yay usually are inside yay place they are made in." Zeet says only moving his eyes as he walks as if something is wrong. "Ya floor here is yerly cold."

"Meaning, that there should be no slugs around. Right?" Shrub asks with an unsure voice. He touches the dirt wall which is as cold as it should be been underneath the ground. "Or maybe we have finally reached an end." As he feels the cold dirt a glimmer of light not only reveals itself but also more details of the bumpy dirt wall.

As relieved as they are by seen a bright circle that makes an exit, the site beyond still leaves them worried. Worried because they are not quite sure whether the circle is a pathway to someplace they prefer or another stop that will lead them to danger. Once in front of the opening on the other side of them there are many pipes that create a wall of their own. Standing on the edge almost does not seem to be a way down as endless pipes around them run down and all around the area endlessly. They create two walls that fade away into shadow on both sides as well as the top and bottom of the area.

There is a dirty green square plate of metal on the other side a few feet below. Pipes continue to run around the floor and up the wall. Even though it is hard to notice no one can see the bottom. The random sheet seams to float in this pipe infestation.

"Pipes that are not tunnels." Shrub says in amazement.

Marvin looks at him. "Or at least that is what it looks like. I mean, I doubt anyone can go through any. Each look too small."

"Don't be surprised." Shrub says. "We know plenty of small creatures that can crawl their way through. There are pipes in our exhibit that are small and big that are unsuitable for anything living."

Shrub thinks for a moment as if looking at these pipes can answer any questions that have always made the creatures curious. "I am guessing that this is where some of those pipes come from."

"Every pipe?" Marvin asks. "Nonsense, not every pipe that makes up an exhibit can come from this one place. Look, we cannot even see the end in some of them." All realize that, even with all the

pipes that make the two walls. Then again, looking to both sides the pipes continue on fading away into the shadow. "Let's get down."

"Yeye, don't see why not." Zeet's neck stretches two clicks above the friends as they look. "Yeye can definitely reach yat floor."

"Honestly, there is nowhere else to go." Marvin says as he stands up from sitting. "Zeet, can you take the two of them? I can manage on my own." The spring kid loosens his arms a bit trying to see what pipe he should grab.

"Yes. Yeye can also yhold ya three of you yat once. One just needs to hold on to my back." "No need to worry about that. Like I said, I can manage on my own." The hands of Marvin are already gone. His arms become the stretched springs that they are and already he can feel the tube shapes on each hand. One feels as cool as gripping ice, while the other is no different than room temperature. His body is gone instantly. His two brown leather shoes turn into a flash of streams in the air. Holding on all the way on the other side, Marvin holds and looks up. Looking at the others they stand where they were before. Then Zeet looks at Dod and Shrub indicating them to come closer to him.

The rib-cage seems a lot bigger from the inside, like an actual cage. Shrub and Dod holds on to one side. Shrubs large round head touches the front and back of the rib-cage causing him to hold lower than Dod pushing the reptilians body close to the ribs. It is an uncomfortable fit but they are able to manage. Nothing seems to happen until they hear a clacking as if cogs of gears are at work. Then the lower jaw of Zeet floats above them. His passing is not as fast as Marvin's, but is still yet a convenient way of getting around. Zeet's head is face to face with a pipe with his teeth then grip on a flange. As if some sort of skinny bridge is above them the two start to get closer to the other side as well. When their feet become afloat they grip tighter. Shrub would say something but is too frightened this time for one of his sly remarks.

With each clank of Zeet's spine moving forward the more Shrub is relieved. Dod on the other hand seems to not be bothered by the lift. Instead his mind drifts on wondering more of what kind of place they are in. His curiosity outweighing the anxiety of the high depth. When Zeet gets to where Marvin is, the skeleton does a kind of flip with his feet landing on ground. As Zeet stands the two in the ribcage are released. All four look at each other as if making sure they are complete.

One thing the group notices is one large pipe that instead of connecting to the metal ground, it runs between the nearest pipe-wall and the sheet they stand on. The dim silver pipe stands out not only because it is so close and large, but the color seems to be foreign to all pipes around the area. Could just be because it is the largest pipe sticking out of the clutter from the pipe-wall. Regardless, the pipe hangs alone. "Yat a large pipe. Yaybe a way out?"

"Probably. I do not think creatures climb to this spot very often." Marvin says as he looks around the floor in wonderment.

"Whatever this spot is." Dod says taking out a new bottle. He looks at it and puts it back away realizing that he might run out.

All cannot help but look around. As quiet as it is the area has a kind of humming to it. Small machines at work somewhere either around or beneath their feet. The four wonder what other works can be going on around or beneath them, if any.

As the friends stand a kind of tapping is heard from the side from where the large pipe is. The four walk and notice two rail handles which curve going downward over the edge. Underneath their feet a low vibration of power at work gets felt. Only walking closer did they realize that the hook rails were not pipes. They look over the edge not only realizing that the two curved rails make a ladder but there is another compartment floor tucked between where they stand and the pipe wall. Following the tapping sounds a small creature's back is seen sitting. His busy state is working at some controls and types rapidly. Most creatures have three to five fingers per hand, but this one has an assortment of what looks like spiders crawling all over the computer desk.

"Maybe we should ask him where we are at?" Shrub looks down upon the creature as he types.

"No," Marvin answers quickly. "It looks like someone else is there."

The creature pulls something from the side that can hardly be seen. Clay is the first thing the group notices in astonishment. With each shape that was crafted, the many fingered creature seems to place them on other parts of machinery. He pulls out wire from the floor which is already assorted by a spool it comes out of. From where the four stand they see as the creature puts the wire through a needle. The needle starts to go through the clay, twining the wire attaching both the machinery and the clay. At this point the four already can assume that the combination of the two things can create something all on its own.

Marvin slowly moves his head toward Zeet, not moving his eyes away from the site. "Is this how creations are made?"

"Yay make yem all different ways." Neither does Zeet take his eyes off of the creature down below. "Usually ya skeletal structure is formed. From yere, they add on different parts."

"What kind of parts?" Shrub asks. His voice had a type of wisp in it.

The working creature looks up. Four different faces are what he sees. The creature stops what he is doing and stands up.

"Get down from there. Who are you?"

The four back up right away. Making themselves no longer in sight. "Oh, no. What do we do?" Shrub says in a panic.

Marvin looks around realizing the only visible way out is through the opened pipe next to them. "We do what he says. Get down." Before anyone can say anything else, Marvin shows himself with one hand up. "We are lost. There is no harm that we are trying to do. We are going down?"

"No!" The many odd fingers straighten out like twine twisting together. "Stay where you are." "Didn't you just want us to get down?"

"Just stay up there. I do not need you to see what is down here."

"Can you tell us how we can get out of this place? Been here in the first place has been one big accident." Marvin says while looking down. There is a bit of an echo.

"You go through that pipe, kid." The creature walks toward the ladder shaking his head. "Of course you do not belong here so you do not know how to use such an object." As the creature climbs the ladder Marvin steps aside. He looks around the area below trying to make out what the creature is using for the creation. If it is a creation, Marvin wonders, but what else could it be?

Before Marvin completely moves out of the way, there is a murmuring grunt from where the figure sits.

"What brings you four down here?" The creature looks as though a hanger is under his shirt with pointy shoulders on each end. Facial hair runs through his sideburns almost all the way through to the creature's pointy chin of his light leather like skin. He has big eyes that seem to almost take up all his head. His mouth sticks out creating a muzzle type of area on his face. The nostrils are also big. Not as big as his eyes but flare out as if always angry. "Come on, speak up. You kids are already in a tight spot and there is no way out."

"We just need to get into The Wide Areas." Marvin looks at the creature not knowing what else to say. "If it is off limits than how come there is a worm hole on the wall."

"Because it is a damn worm hole. You should not worry about that anyways. There are plenty of worm holes around that are not worth my time to worry about. As a matter of fact you guys were supposed to get caught by a slug in them. You are lucky he never saw you."

Marvin looks to his side knowing that the other three keep that they killed the thing. Marvin looks back at the creature. "Well we are here and we need to get out."

"There is no way out other than this pipe. And I have the number sequence for the suction to take me out. You guys go back through exactly where you came from or else things will get a lot worse."

"What if I climb us through yat pipe with my spine." Zeet says.

The creature knows that Zeet got the crew here. Neither does it interest him or does he care who these creatures are. "You're not climbing no pipe, skeleton. Just get out of here before I get hold of Breakers.

The three friends do not know what Breakers are, but they have a feeling that they are not friendly. In their exhibit there are patrol creatures that mainly serve their use if children miss behave or go missing. Hardly do the older creatures cause trouble. When they do the situation gets settled easily with one another. Here around these areas and these tunnels, creatures are so much more different.

Marvin feels as though he should explain, but then the moan again. "What are you making down there?"

The creature bites down on his teeth that the four now know are sharp. His brows point down, slowly revealing the frustration. "That is it. You are disturbing my progress since you are not delivering anything you have to go."

Before the creature has anything else to say, Marvin remembers the skull. "We have a skull we want to show you."

The creature opens his eyes again. "What?" Not sure if he should be interested.

"You want to know." Feeling like there is no other option, Marvin reaches behind Dod and takes out the skull. The harp points out, so he takes that out as well. "We have been trying to figure out what these things do." Marvin holds both out in front of the creature but not too close. If this crazy creator or whatever he is tries to attack in anyway, something the friends are already familiar with. He may try and trick them in someway to steal. "Have you any idea what can be done with these things?"

The eyes widen from the creature. "These are not things." He copies Marvin's words. The mad creature wants to ask where the spring kid got the skull and instrument. But he knows he wants them for himself. The face becomes normal. Even with the partial moans coming from down below the mad creature keeps a stern look. "I can show you what they are. Scanning just needs to be made."

"What kind of scanning?"

"None that will damage the skull or harp. Oh no, but I do need to see what they are made out of." The creature looks around the sides as if someone is watching. "Go down the ladder where I was."

All the fingers start tangling with each other.

"You first." Marvin says not wanting to take an eye off the crazed creature.

A long smile appears on the face of the creature. His eyes nearly close and there is a kind of sinister grin as if he wants to hold a laugh back. "What is this. You think I can do something to the four of you? I'll go first if that makes you happy. Although it makes no difference."

"Then it should not be a problem." Marvin says feeling that he should be as stern as possible. "Yesss," The creature looks to the side quickly. "No problem at all." His head does not move at all as he turns until it is time for the mad creature to align himself toward the ladder. The multi-fingers look as if they are crawling when he climbs down. Marvin is the first to follow with the skull in hand. He gives Dod the harp as he goes after Marvin. Then shrub and Zeet are the last to come down.

The section that was hard to see is a workshop filled with spools and working panels. Electric wires are not only wrapped with the spools but run throughout the area. Many are next to electrical machines that have the many switches and levers that must be used for the creations. Out of all the machines, wires and controls, a body sits like a ragged doll ready for shot injections. With so much clutter a scribbled mess of wiring and even springs hang above the body. The body looks as if it is part of the room with some wires from the spools running inside of the arms and left leg to keep it together. But if the mad creature was stitching parts together, he is far from finished. The body is missing the right hand and both feet still. The head is another part that should be missing also because it is not seen. Then wires, springs and threads slightly move at the same time that the moan is heard again. Revealing themselves above the shoulders on a round surface just as hair would appear, which slouches indicating that the head is bowed and just as nonfunctional as the body.

"We can put the skull here on my dash. I think that would be best." The mad creature says breaking any focus the group had. Even Zeet who has seen and has some knowledge on how the creations are made seems amazed by the sitting body.

"Gnnaa," The mummer of a grunt is heard again.

"Quiet." The mad creature says and looks at the body beginning to type as he does so. He looks back at his dashboard. "Place it there on top of that round glass. I can readout what that skull is made out of."

Marvin looks at the dash and it's glass top. It is an egglike shape almost and once again there are wires and such beneath it. The mad creature stops his typing and slowly turns his head to look at Marvin. He does not say anything for a few seconds. "Well come on. Put the skull there."

Not seeing any objection from his friends Marvin puts the skull on the uneven circular glass top.

Dod still holds the harp. From all the times he was holding one of his shakes, he now grips the instrument. Holding it he feels as though he should take a try and play it. Maybe not. Something must be done about holding the piece. He wiggles his fingers a little to warm them up, licking his lips. Then he thinks to play it would be a bad idea now. Hand tightens to a fist and squeezes tight. He can wait.

Like marble on glass the skull gets placed on the counter. The mad creature smiles with that sinister grin. Marvin thinking that he should not have done that. Knowing how persuasive the creature was to get rid of the crew, maybe showing the skull to this mad creature is a bad idea.

He only asked for the skull. If both were important, in time he will ask for the harp. As of now, Marvin is not sure.

A light shines beneath the skull. Two rods that carry the lights turn slowly, examining the skull.

One screen gets many characters. They seem to spell out almost an entire page. The group does not know what any of it says because the writing is foreign to them, but the mad creature nods his head. Some of the dials light up. The creation that sits footless moves it's head slightly letting out the short grunt sound. The mad creature looks at it for only a second and continues reading the screen.

"What is it?" Marvin asks.

The mad creature says nothing. When he finally decides to speak it is because he himself needs answers. "It is a skull. Where did you say you found this again?"

Marvin looks at his friends. "A friend made it. Why?"

The mad creature's question was not answered completely, but it does help indicate the origins of the skull none the less. "So a creature factory?" He turns and faces the four.

"No. Pottery shop." Marvin says as if the answer will give him more answers. "From a different sector. What is so amusing about the skull?"

The many fingers wrap as the mad creature smiles. They look like an assortment of tangles strings. When undone the fingers look like they go through a rewind process that only the creature can do himself. "This skull is made out of clay? Impossible. What you have here is a real skull. Once you showed it to me I can tell what it was immediately. Could you not tell that it's not pottery. Of course young creatures like yourselves could not tell the difference between a real skull and an artificial one. But this here is a skull of a murner. Murner's can live in pipes that are filled with water, giving them an advantage to go almost anywhere. To have an actual skull of one would be an advantage for a creature that is capable of breathing in water. And you have two bones of one." With a press of a button the rods light and start to turn underneath the skull. A grunt from the side is heard again but the mad creature just ignores the creature sitting completely.

There is a bit uncertainty that hovers over the friends after what the creator just said. "How is that possible? We found these in a shop. With a note in the skull."

The creator looks at them with a face that he himself is unsure how a note could have been in the skull. "Let me see the note."

Marvin checks his pockets and the pockets of the backpack. He looks at Shrub and Dod who shake their heads that they do not have the note. "I must of lost it."

The creator bites. "It is not important. These are bones that you have though. Now for the other part." The mad creature tells the friends without looking at any of them changing the subject.

Marvin taps his fingers on his leg. "What are you going to do with them?"

Turning back around the creature looks at the group. For the first time he smiles. "I am going to place it on the scanner next. A few runs and everything will be finished with the skull. Is there a problem with that? Do want me to find out where these are from?"

"Yes. I'll wait until you are done with the skull." Marvin stares at the creation that sits and groans. "Who is that?"

The mad creature smiles again this time the smile is more dull and his lashes do not move. "That is my creation. Why would you ask me young creature?"

Looking around astonished. Even trying to keep his distance from the mad creature, Marvin gets a tinge of excitement in his stomach. "Well, what is it going to be used for? The creation."

Pressing his lips the mad creature does not want to tell Marvin, so he does not. "That my young friend you will have to find out in Wide Areas. Sorry. You do not need to know right now anyway." He breaths in and looks at Marvin. "Now that you give me the ribcage, I can analyze and see how the strings were put on. Although I know it should not be a ribcage completely. But to do that I would have to keep both pieces here for a few courses."

Shrub takes a step forward. "Wait a dot. We showed you what we have, and you cannot even tell us what you are doing here?" He looks around the area making it obvious that he wants to know more about the place. "There is a lot going on but we need to know how you can figure out what this skull is exactly. Before we give you anything else, I need to be certain you will not press something to give us the boot."

"Yit is a far yay down." Zeet's teeth tap one another as he says this behind Shrub.

"Yeah, and not so long ago this creature wanted us to get out. I want something for collateral.

Or at least show us how we can get out of here. Who are you and what is your name?" Shrub says getting a little upset.

The fingers of the mad creature tangle once again. "Well, you have every reason to think that young bulb head. There is no need to get angry though. Would you not get mad at even your mother if she barged in your room while you were busy? Would you want her out immediately? My name is doctor Shrogow and this is my lab space. Around the Marrow area I use to have a bigger one but they

chop and are on my case too much. I decided to not pay rent and find an area where no one will find me. And it has worked so far until now." Shrogow says with a mad face that loosens up the more he talks. "It is all fine now. I see you guys may be lost and you somehow made your way into the pipe hallway so I am not upset. Especially with the prize you have brought. There is no need to be upset."

He smiles with his more expressionless smile again. He thinks of how he can bargain with the creatures for the bone pieces. "Maybe other than showing you how to get out, I can trade you for, one or both these pieces?"

Looking at the doctor, Shrub still does not trust him. None of the friends do. With Marvin and Zeet's abilities, they can leave at anytime. They also know that this could be their opportunity to find out where Lisa may be with so much equipment around. As long as they know Lisa is all right, none of the bones will matter as much. A hidden creature alone should not attack like how the marrows did.

"Show us how to get out and if you can help us find our friend."

"I can search around, but how do I know you are not robbers. I will give you the code out when all is done. It will take many resources to find a specific creature if one of you is missing." The creator says looking down at Marvin. "With more scanning, I can use my free time to search around whatever cameras I can and perhaps ask others in Wide Areas."

Marvin remembers the marrows. "Try not to ask any skeletons. I just don't like them. You can examine the skull while we keep the harp. Since you have something of ours and we have nothing of yours."

Pressing his lips tight, the doctor has never been one to bargain. Hardly has he had to negotiate with anyway also. "Alright, I will search for whatever friend you're looking for. In the meantime it will take a while to scan and get results for the skull." The doctor walks away. "Sit tight."

"She is a murner, by the way." Marvin says as the doctor walks toward his workstation. Slowly Shrowgow turns his head to look at the young creature. "What?"

"Our friend, the one that we're looking for. She is a murner."

Dr. Shrogow smiles. "I'll find her."

***

Splits go by and time with the skull has taken longer than expected. Almost enough for an entire course to go through. The friends decided to stay on the upper floor where they first entered. Away from the doctor. Each of the friends take turns with naps as none trust Shrowgow. The entire time he has been typing and writing, looking at the skull. Hardly attending to the creation that is most likely asleep. Dr. Shrogow has stitched the feet and taken out any cords running through. The creation seems to be complete but still misses the right hand. Marvin looks down the area to keep an eye on the doctor as best he can. Dod is still awake as their other two friends nap for the moment. With the doctor down below, Marvin finds this the perfect time to explain a plan. "We need to think of something in case this guy goes haywire. He might not keep to his promise."

Shrub is not liking anything that is happening like usual. "Call me evil, but I want to send that creation loose." The bulb head makes sure his voice is at a low tone. Very little voltage can be heard partially drowning out their voice. For all they know this doctor has something installed that can catch what they are saying no matter how far. Yet he does hardly get any visitors and the area is a privet spot. Shrub looks at Marvin with the thought. "What do you think?"

Marvin's nose quickly moves side to side as he thinks. "That's none of out concern." He looks at Shrub and Dod. We should not jump to scenarios thinking this doctor is all that bad.?"

"What if he didn't?" Dod brings his arm down to rest on his knee. "What if he does exactly what we think he is going to do. While he is working on that skull there are other ideas going through his head to get rid of us somehow. He is communicating with others in order to help us after all."

Marvin nods in agreement. "True. I am going to ask him if he is working with the Marrows still.

Just because he is doing his work elsewhere does not mean he does not provide for them still." "Go ahead. I want the guy to be telling the truth." Dod says.

Marvin climbs down the ladder toward Dr. Shrogow. "Excuse me doctor."

Shrogow turns around with an expression on his face as if he did not know anyone was there.

"Yes, what is it?"

As Marvin walks closer, he becomes uncertain what to say. The angry look on the doctor's face reminds Marvin that he already told them what he was going to be doing, so why would any of them need to ask anything else. Then Marvin remembers the Marrows. "I just had a quick question about the marrows..."

Before he says anything else, Shrogow interrupts "Yess?"

The spring kid clears his throat. "Do you still work with them?"

"Did I not tell you that I do? But do not worry, I will not bring you up to them. All I do is provide whatever they order. That much is obvious, yes. I'm not the only doctor creator in all the Wide Areas." Then a mad grin turns into a side smirk. "But none are as good as me."

Not sure if the doctor is basing himself on facts or on his ego. Marvin does realize it's difficult for anyone to bother him in this space. For the doctor to have what he wants, maybe the Marrows do hold him at high value.

"I see. Well can you show us how to get out of here? One of us wants to leave while the rest stay."

"I need all of you here. If I find your friend, I do not want to spend time looking for someone else. You have no place to go up there in Wide Areas anyway. Someone will rob you and take anything you have. A group of young creatures such as yourselves are the easiest victims to be mugged. Trust me, I actually live here, unlike you." He tuns around and types some more. "If you want to see more screens like earlier let me know. Otherwise let me finish."

Marvin climbs up the ladder. Shrub and Dod who stepped closer to listen to what Shrogow said waits for Marvin. "Not much of a mellow guy is he? You actually want to stay in here?" Shrub asks as Marvin reaches the top. The three turn and walk toward the center of the floor. "We can find our own way out, other than that pipe. You and Zeet can get us out just by reaching across this pipe hallway."

"I know, but we do need to find Lisa and what that skull is also, if we can. If we do just leave than how will we find our ways around The Wide Areas?"

"My thoughts exactly creat." Dod looks at Zeet who is the only one sleeping. "One of us should still get out of here. Better it be two."

"Of course. Even though the doctor wants us all here. But that is not up to him." Marvin stays quiet and thinks knowing none other than Zeet have been at these Wide Areas. Even though he talked to Shrogow earlier, splitting up can be dangerous. "You think that is a good idea? We do not know this area and there is no way in keeping in touch with one another." He breathes in then out.

"I know, and there is no where we can meet up. But there are two things wrong with us being here. First reason, I'm bored. The other we are wasting time waiting. Two can keep an eye on the skull and this doctor. The other two will leave and figure out where we are going to stay after we get out."

"The skull might give us a clue to where Lisa went." Marvin looks toward the ladder as if expecting the doctor to be listening in their conversation. "But I still do not trust this doctor and staying here is hardly helping." He looks back at Dod who is now scratching under his chin. "If we do split up, whichever two leave should somehow stay close around here if possible. Not saying that is easy, but it should be in consideration."

The entire time the group has been here, nothing has happened other than the work the doctor has been at. The three know climbing or whatever means it takes to get out should not be too difficult. The common question is where would they go? The slug hole they came out of is a maze and still remains deadly. With the help of time they managed to get out of there alright. Climbing any of the pipes around might lead to dangerous areas as well.

"We need to ask the doctor on the way out." Marvin says. "Climbing through all this is too much of a hassle and none of us know where we will land up."

"You are right. But I am not going to ask the doctor anything. Even if he decided to send us through that large pipe that he uses. He will send us some place dangerous I be. Better to find another

path, even if it means climbing to the bottom of this place." Shrub brings up as if there is no danger.

The bottom, Marvin thinks. To take that chance is worse than the slug hole. "Well, I suggest you climb up not down. So you are saying you want to go?"

"We both know that is best, creat. Plus I still want to get the word out for my shockla. We drank too many." Dod squeezes the words out, now ashamed that he drank as much as he did. "You got the harp and that is your friends skull. I have not talked to Lisa much, yet neither has many other creatures, but we both know each others faces. It will not be hard to notice her."

"I think you should take Zeet." Marvin knows Shrub gets irritated with Dod. It is not a problem for the reptile, when Marvin is around.

"That's what I was thinking. It will be more difficult for him to climb these pipes. Our new friend should know some areas better than we do and his neck stretches."

"There is no arguing in that." Shrub says nothing liking the plan. Marvin looks at the ladder again then back at Dod. "When are you going?"

"Now. Umm, or maybe I will let the skeleton sleep? Na, lets wake him." Dod walks up to Zeet whose eyes are covered by eye lids that are hidden under the skull when awake. He taps his foot. The body of the skeleton stays in place, only the foot moves. "Hey Zeet. You need to wake up lazy bones." Dod gives him another tap. "Come on creat. It's not like you've been sleeping for like six splits." The more he taps the foot, the harder they get. Seeing that there is no progress in waking him this way, Dod taps the ribs instead. But he taps the ribs a little bit harder than he expected to. "Zeet creat..." Dod would not back up if it was not for the eyeballs going up in the air. For a moment Dod and Marvin think they are two different creatures from who knows where. Then the red and purple strings below them are attached from inside the sockets of Zeet's skull. The two balls are back inside. There is a single slap sound after they get sucked into the sockets. As if coming back from the dead, Zeet leans his upper body up, blinking profusely. He rubs his eyes with cuffed fists.

"What ye want?" Zeet tells the two expecting a good answer since they have to wake him up so suddenly.

"Sorry, Zeet." Dod hunches a bit as if trying to spot any differences on the skeletons face. "I am leaving. You want to come?"

"Yint we have to yate here?" Zeet blinks a few more times and looks at Dod.

"Ya, if you want to bore your eyes out of your sockets like you just did. I mean like, would you want to stay?"

Zeet stares at him for a moment, running the situation through his still waking mind. "Yit don't matter to ye. Lets go."

As the two get ready, Marvin walks over to where the doctor is. All the clicking and clacking is still going on. Still not able to see Shrogow, Marvin feels like it is all completely normal. I'll just stay here, Marvin thinks to himself. When he approaches Dod and Zeet he cannot help but feel worry for

them and even Shrub and himself. "Alright, I will just tell the doctor you left. If he asks." "Tell him whatever creat."

"If too much time has passed, we will meet at the end of Copper Tunnel. How long would you say?"

Dod looks up, eyes partially closed thinking that a short time would be unnecessary. "When I find Lisa, we will go there right away. If not, by the end of this course."

Shrub brings out his time-keeper pin and looks at Marvin. Nineteen. The same time of the course when they left. "We been gone for an entire course. Will another course give you enough time to look for Lisa before meeting up?"

Dod thinks. "Okay, at nineteen tomorrow. That should be enough. And if you finish here, I suggest you go straight to Copper Tunnel. Don't try to look for us or Lisa."

"Agree. That will only make things more difficult." Looking at the Pipe Hallway, Marvin knows it will not be easy to find a way out. Then again, there are so many pipes that it could take less time than any of them think. "You guys better go. Keep to the schedule and be careful."

"Got it. I got Zeet and shockla on my side." Dod flicks his head up and laughs as he walks away. Zeet fallows and the lizard this time does not drink any of his shakes.

***

Dr. Shrogow climbs up the ladder. When he sees only the spring kid and bulb boy sitting down, the doctor is more than sure that the other two left. Marvin and Shrub look at the doctor unsurprised. "Where are your two friends." Shrogow asks in his shriveled voice.

"They left." Marvin answers.

"What for?" Shrogow says as if worried.

All Marvin does is shrug his shoulders. "They wanted to."

Staying put like a statue, Shrogow looks at the two as if he really needed all four waiting around. He shrugs his shoulders as if it is not important.

"What did you find out about the skull? Any news on our friend Lisa?" Marvin asks. He stays looking at the doctor in a normal way. All Marvin is concerned about is what is going on with the skull and Lisa. If Shrogow brings up the other two again, Marvin will accuse the doctor of a plan to rid of them all for the skull and harp. Instead Shrogow follows up on Marvin's question.

"The skull is not delicate but a special piece none the less." "What makes it so... special then?" Shrub says.

"Has it done anything unusual, something very obvious?"

The two look at one another. Their eyes show the same uncertainty. When they look back at the doctor, Marvin tries not to tell him too much. "We made it talk once."

"Really?" The doctors left brow pushes up. "How did that happen, with the harp?" "Yeah, with the harp."

"What really baffles me is where it was found. Whoever created the skull must have did it in secret. Like I said before this is an actual skull. Some really good creators do know how to mash bone to their liking, shaping the kind of skull they want for whatever creation they need. I think that method takes too long and there is no need. For your friend to make one is highly unlikely. Especially a child in a random exhibit. This is more bone than anything. If like you say, it was made somehow, there have been no traces of other substances at all. For me to continue I will need the harp."

"Yeah, sure." Marvin tightens his grip on the harp not ready to hand it over yet. "Are you done with the skull?"

"Come on child. We both need to work with each other to get everything figured out. That much is obvious." Shrogow holds out his hand.

Marvin presses his lips and hands it over. The doctor smiles and goes back down the ladder. "We should go down there and watch him." Shrub gets up.

That was something Marvin wanted to do before Shrub said anything. "Let's go. Of course the guy is not telling us everything. He knows something else. He has to. We should have been watching him more from the start." As they walk toward the ladder, Marvin does not distinguish how easy it would have been for Dr. Shrogow to hide the skull. Even call in someone he knows to get rid of the bunch. "You remember what Dod and I suggested about that creature?"

"Yes, and it's not a good idea. That thing can attack us instead."

"My thoughts exactly. So watch out. Just because the creature looked like it was not having a good time, it may still follow orders from the master." Marvin puts one foot down.

"I know. None of us have experience with this place or it's creations. "Shrub smiles sarcastically knowing nothing about creations. "So expect the worse. Why do these damn steps have to be gaped so far apart?" Shrub says as he struggles to climb down.

Marvin ignores him. When he reaches the bottom the doctor right away sees them. "You decided to see what I am doing?" Shrogow tells the two as Shrub drops on his feet lightly, clearing the last step.

"Yeah, I don't see why not. We have nothing to do up there." Marvin says seeing as the harp is now on top the glass scanner.

There is a slight pause before Shrogow answers. "Fine deed, fine deed." He turns around and starts his typing. "I would like to keep an eye out if any of my valuables were been tested. Where did you say your two friends went to?"

Marvin cannot think of anything that would throw the doctor off track in case the doctor tried looking for Dod and Zeet in anyway. There is still nothing that has proven the doctor friend of foe. So he tells him what he can. "I don't know. They just left and we stayed."

"Alright. That's just fine." Shrogow continues typing.

Marvin looks around the room. Behind the creation the compartment of machinery is at high velocity. As if creating a hum of some sort the electrical current stays within unison of the voice of the creation. Why does it suddenly make a noise now? Marvin and Shrub wonder.

They look at the doctor making certain his expression at the sound that is not normal but he doesn't. "What did you find out about the harp?" Marvin asks.

"The ribcage needs to stay here. They both do. You children cannot be caring around such valuable materials. These need to be taken care of in the hands of a creator. Now that your part in this is finished, you should follow your other friends.

"Of course we are not going to do that. What, do you think we are stupid. Those are ours." Shrub looks at the doctor, angry even as if ready to put up a fight with him.

"You do not even know son." Dr. Shogow clicks a switch on the counter of many controls. Straps that were on the creation snap and come undone. As much as it resembles a doll, the creation moves exactly like one that is a puppet pulled by it's strings. Even though it does not have any. Springs and wire strands fall back behind the creation as it lolls back like that of a lifeless body. Shrogow twists his hand around a nob as he smiles with a sinister face that has bewilderment. The creation's head falls forward. The mouth is even, with a face that has no expression. The eyelids stay shut. It is the lashes that point out that this creation is female. The hum continues making the surrounding pipes rattle.

The doctor continues to smile. "She was not ready before. Maybe I was not able to get all of you but the marrows will assure your friends do not get out of here." The many teeth to the doctor look as if they were one solid white piece in the mouth of Shrogow. "They will not make it out alive."

Marvin and Shrub look as worried as two lost pups. Shrogow turns the notch even more so the creation will become more alive as more voltage runs through. She still misses the right hand but to Shrogow, she is more than enough for the two. One bare foot steps off the step that guides anything to the high operation chair. The creation does not necessarily have a decent balance as the next foot takes place but she still stands.

"Hhhmmm," The hum of the creation is more audible as the nob turns down the volume of the machines. Although the mouth is not stitched with the wiring in any way, the mouth remains shut as if complicated to open. Shrogow hardly has use for the mouth. All he wants is the created life to destroy.

"You should know my voice my dear. I created you." Shrogow smiles and says looking at the creature amused. The creation keeps walking and turning her head as if looking to the ceiling trying to figure out where she is with closed eyes.

"You should know my dear. We are in tune with one another. In unison. Like all my other creations. Now open those eyes and kill, kill, KILL!" The doctor says with a smile still remaining.

"Hhhmmmm," The voice almost sounds too sweet for destruction Marvin and Shrub think. But if she gets any closer with those eyes closed, one simple step can lead her off the edge into nothingness. All Marvin has to do is grab hold of Shrub and stretch his arms elsewhere and bring his light friend with him.

"Come on. Open those eyes. You need to do what you are made for." Shrogow keeps the same bit of excitement in his attitude only because the two creatures are there. Inside there is a miss count of some kind, the doctor thinks. That something might be wrong with this creation. The ears are on, she should be able to hear him. Why does she not open her lids? Maybe scanning the skull and harp

disrupted the process somehow. That is it. Shrogow thinks. There is too much of a natural occurrence from the skull and harp that somehow disrupted the entire process.

The creature stays walking as if trying to figure out where she is at, other than trying to find out what to do. Marvin sees the harp on the table and steps closer as the doctor talks to his creation. "Distract him if you have to." Both hands leave the arms. The wire is stretched but is still compact than usual since Marvin does not need to stretch out too far.

Shrogow with wide eyes looks as the harp and skull leave his desk. "What are you... how did you do that?" Only now the doctor realizes Marvin's physical advantage.

"Not as smart as I thought you were, Shrogow." He places the skull on top of the harp, preparing to play a tune like before.

Shrogow laughs. "Stupid boy. You cannot use a tune to manipulate someone or thing that is already influenced."

Marvin looks at the harp and skull. Not really worrying about what the doctor said. "I told you I used them before, so I will do it again." Marvin places the skull. His fingers touch strings at random and plucks. The tone is low on the longer stings. Marvin moves his hand closer to the smaller ones, knowing that they are higher hoping that they will match that of the hum of the creation. Even Shrogow looks at the creation curious, but nothing happens. The doctor smiles.

"I don't know why I am so worried about you kids. I did not signal the marrows before because I wanted those pieces for myself after I got rid of you, but I guess that won't happen. So I have to hear them bombard me with questions. I rather deal with that than waste anymore time."

Shrogow is about to press a button on the control board. As he brings that hand with those many fingers on the switch, Shrub runs from the side and pushes him. The doctor crashes against the wall of many other controls, but holds onto the chair where the creation once sat. He looks at the bulb head boy angry.

"Damn it Creation! Do what you are supposed to do. Can't you hear my voice?"

Finally, the creation flicks her head toward the doctor. This worries the friends and Shrogow smiles. Shrub's stomach impacts with the air coming out he realizes that the doctor just kicked him. "I hate using my energy for insignificant things like you. But yes this has became more complicated than I thought." He looks at the creation. "Creation. Kill."

She walks with closed eyes and a lifeless body. Both arms rise but with only one hand for any kind of strangling.

"Come on let's get out of here." Shrub says to Marvin. "What are you waiting for?" Griping the harp tighter, Marvin begins plucking more, this time letting the tone ring out.

"Hhhhmmmm." The same tone and hum comes from the creation as her wired stitched lips stay shut. As the sound of the harp gets in unison with the hum, the skull opens.

Shrogow rushes to the computer and twists the dial, making that of the machines hum a lot louder. Marvin stays focused on the plucking, keeping the tune going. Shrub covers his ears hardly baring the sound. When some dials reach their peak, glass pops and shatters. It's not a lot, but Shrogow flicks and knows that his machinery will not last if he continues the match up. When he sees the creation stop and bring her arms down, that is when he turns down the dial. Unlike before the creation ends with such animated movements now bringing up her arms more fluidly with lively gestures. She only rubs her throat with one hand. Moving her head in a confused way the creation tries figuring out what went wrong with her suddenly. With the humming not heard, more than likely she just lost her voice.

"What did you do to her you children! After all my work I have to deal with a bunch of kids." Shrogow walks toward his board and opens a drawer.

"Use that instrument on the doctor." Shrub tells Marvin.

Marvin listens but then sees a wire in the doctor's hand. A small glisten of a spark is at the end.

Playing the harp again, Marvin points the skull at the creation. "Let's see if you can open your eyes."

Like blinds instantly pulled up, the lids of the creature flick open. Both eyes are the same and are wide enough to take up most of the face. The irises are a blue abyss that are lifeless. Small pupils that are smaller than the smallest marble in any collection look toward the direction of the sound of the harp. Examining again, this time with her eyes open, the creation sees the doctor who now stands still.

"Come over here." Shrogow says in a commanding voice. "Are you not listening to me still?

Come over here and we are going to kill these children."

She stands looking at Shrogow examining him with squinted eyes. Then another voice, the same one she heard before.

"Listen to me." Marvin says, this time not playing the harp. "Don't listen to your creator." Marvin swallows not sure what to do. "I will give you your voice back."

The creation looks and blinks at Marvin in wonderment.

"Don't you dare fail me. I created you. Some bunch of kids are not capable in any way of overturning my process. So you better get over here for your own good!" Shrogow looks and points at Marvin. "He stole your voice. A voice that I will have to put back. He does not know how to do that."

There is a pause as everyone in the room looks at one another, other than the creation. Only small pulses of electricity zip and zap. Marvin places his fingers back on the same strings that he used to match the hum. The skull opens, the same hum is heard.

"Hhhhmmmmm." Marvin lets the string play out as the creation looks at him.

"Shut up you child." With a flick of his hand, Shrogow lifts an electric cord and swings it toward Marvin. It not only hits his shoulder but knocks the skull off, putting an end to the hum. Shrogow lifts his hand again. His breathing stops at the throat as it tightens, and the skin gets pressed in. The left hand of the creation is held around the doctor's neck. "*What, are you doing?*" The choked voice says as Shrogow looks at the creation with wide eyes.

There is no response, obviously, as the wide dead blue eyes of the creation look at Shrogow with an expressionless face. Marvin and Shrub wonder if there is something they should try and tell the creation. As she squeezes harder, the doctor grips the hand trying to take it off.

"Stop." Marvin says. The grip loosens as both the creation and doctor look at Marvin. "Stop?" Shrub looks at his friend as if he made the most pointless decision of his life. "He could have died. No need for that to happen."

Shrub looks as the doctor who's face is almost blue and bewildered. "Yes. He tried to kill us!" "Well do you think she should do it? Kill, is one of the first words she heard since she woke. Do

we need a death on our hands. Well again? Killing is something she would not do if she had a more attainable mind. Even if this is what we want, in the future it might be something she only knows since she committed it."

"Or maybe she is aware as much as we are. This doctor needs to be rid of. He will follow and do what he said he would, which was to kill us in case you forgot." Shrub feels like making a command himself. But he feels like the creation will only listen to Marvin who already managed to do so. "Come on Marvin. We need to do something and get out of here."

Marvin looks at the doctor's face. Does he need to die? That same confused face stays stamped on Shrogow. "You can hear me. So can you understand if I tell you to let him go?"

The creation with that pale face looks at Marvin then looks at the doctor as she loosens her grip. She does not leave him alone. Shrogow ducks his head and closes his eyes as she begins to tap the top of his head like some kind of house pet. This confuses everyone, but also makes them realize the creation's influence on things must have been by seen and hearing things. Wondering if he should tell her to stop, Marvin steps forward and looks for a rope or twine of some kind.

"Come on Shrub. Let's see if we can tie him with something."

Shrub scratches his head while shaking it slowly in disappointment but yet still helps search. "I think we really should get rid of this guy for good. He will be after us and send the Marrows." Yet even Shrub does not know how exactly to get rid of the doctor. Before, he would of tried tricking him off the ledge. That would be out of spite from the situation. Now to purposely grab hold of the doctor and toss him over would be difficult. Not even Shrub can purposely commit murder in such a way. Unless

Marvin commands the creation to do so. Even with that, making someone else to take care of dirty work would still be as cruel. Or even more so. "She will have to watch him. But I am not sure how long that can happen. We will have to learn how to keep in contact with the creation."

A dangle of wires get discombobulated pulled by Marvin. They are all still attached to the wall bringing power to whatever machine they are attached to. Shrub grabs hold of a hand full of wires also. They both walk up to Shrogow as if they have a net of some kind.

"What are you kids doing?" Shrogow says as he flicks the hand of the creation away. He tries to move but even the creation grabs hold of him. With the tight grip she pets his some more. "Ugh, stop doing that. You are going to get me...get away kids!" Marvin walks in front as Shrub goes around.

Shrogow has no choice but to kick as he attempts to move the creation's hands away from his face. Soon enough his arms stop moving as he stands stiff.

"Well what are we going to do, just leave him here?" Shrub asks. "He can starve and will die anyway." He eyes the doctor as he stands wired and tied up.

Marvin looks at the controls. If there is a device that shows a way to signal for someone to pick him up then that would be best. There are patrol creatures in their exhibit, so there must be a kind of patrol in Wide Areas. "We can call someone to get him. Tell them what he tried doing to us."

"And what was that?" Shrogow says sarcastically. "Making my creation?"

"No. Stealing and trying to kill us with that creation. We can make this simple by you telling me what code it is to get out of here. Either way, Shrub and I will figure it out just like our other two friends did." A lie.

The creation with her light dead blue eyes looks at Marvin. It is frightening for the spring kid to look at the blue irises surrounding small pupils. With her one hand she points at the controls. Marvin and Shrub look and wonder what she is trying to tell them. The doctor bows his head and shakes it in regret.

"The way out?" Marvin asks. While Shrogow shakes his head no, the creation shakes her head yes. "I know, but do you know what the code is?" Marvin walks closer to the controls trying to figure them out the best he can. There are over a hundred buttons and switches. Hardley a way to figure out which will help him with the way out. The creation points toward the pipe on top of the next level with her skinny stub of an arm. "You still cannot talk. That's right." Marvin decides to ask. The creation just stares at him with those dead blues. He looks back at the controls, fingers wide mapping out the dashboard. "Doctor, can you help me out?" Marvin asks but with a smile. The humor is heard through his voice and the doctor responds with the same irritation he has been feeling.

"Screw off you child."

"Let's take the wires from out of her mouth." Shrub looks at Shrogow. The doctor just looks at him with an angry face.

Shrub grabs some scissors and brings them toward the creation. "Hold still."

She stays quiet for a moment and even looks around the room. Not knowing what to do she leans forward. Shrub snips away the wires while he hears a laugh.

"Ha-ha. I hope she bytes your fingers off. Wait until you need to take them out. It might hurt you know." Shrogow says with a smile.

"Shut up." Shrub says, not entirely knowing what he is doing. If anything he will leave the wires on and figure out what to do when they leave. He clips some more and leans back. "I think I got them."

The creation widens her mouth. Touching her lips she pulls the stitch wires out herself. "See," Shrub smiles and looks at Shrogow. "No problem."

The doctor twists his lips and shrugs his shoulders not pretending not to care.

Marvin looks at Shrogow after seen his reaction. There is a tap on Marvin's shoulder. He looks back at the dead blues as the creation points at the green button. Marvin points at it with a signifying look on his face. The creation nods. When pressed nothing happens other than the button staying pushed in. Nothing happens other than power running through the machines around them. The creation flicks a switch and a sound that is of air instead of surgical electric power is heard above. The switch automatically turns down and the button pushes out of place.

Shrub looks at the pipe above. "That pipe sucks things through when those controls are pressed.

There is no damn code, the doctor was lying the whole time. It seems someone would need to stay down here and flick the switch though. Maybe the creation can do it?" She looks at the two, then at the pipe above. "So she wants to go with us. I guess we owe her. We also did take her voice." Shrub looks at Shrogow. "Hey doctor, mind if you do us a favor?"

"Screw off, child." He insults shrub the same way he did Marvin. "Never mind then." Shrub looks around for another solution. "Shrub. Go up there. I can take care of it." Marvin says.

Looking at his arms which are now together, Shrub knows Marvin will definitely be able to reach. Without a word, the bulb head climbs the ladder toward the pipe. He stands under it waiting. The same controls are pressed. One moment Shrub is seen, then he disappears as the wind sound is heard and the pipe sucks him away. The creation is next, the same thing happens. The first thing to see move up are the wires and strings that are considered hair. Then the creation is gone. Marvin makes his way under the pipe. Marvin takes one last look at Shrogow before flicking the switch. When his arm slinks out and flicks the switch, it is his hand that is the last thing that leaves the area.

CHAPTER TEN

Dod and Zeet tap their way crawling through a pipeway that was one of many before leaving the Pipe Hallway. They chose a random pipe to go through. After so many slits have passed, the two manage to find an opening. "Look creat." Dod points with eyes that are tired he could find a reason to rest now. "It's light."

Zeet on the other hand is hardly as tired as Dod. If they needed to go further, than maybe the skeleton man, Zeet, would start to feel his bones rattle. "Yit yis yonderful to see the light. Shall ye go?" "Of course Zeet creat." Dod says as if about to fall asleep, still looking up to the light. He takes a drink from one of his shakes. Not only because he is thirsty, but because he needs to prepare for any surprises. Since trouble has seem to find them most of the way.

Brightness hits outside the rim of the pipe. Dod shades his eyes with one hand as he temporarily gets blinded. Zeet does the same holding on beside him. "Yot is yis place?" Zeet asks as if asking both Dod and himself.

"Not sure. I need my eyes to adjust." Dod notices the floor and simply drops out and falls to the ground. Grains of gold are beneath him. It is like salt but is thicker and probably not good to taste. Zeet does the same by throwing his legs over the rim and falling in a sitting position. The impact on the ground was not a hard one. "

"Yit yis, sand." Grains of yellow sand fall through Zeet's skeletal fist as he looks at where they are at.

"What is that?" Dod stares as the sand falls through Zeet's fingers.

"My sand clumps, chump." An old rasp voice is heard. Still Dod's sight needs adjusting but he does see three legs. All three are as skinny as sticks. One stands partially in front of the other two. With a few blinks there are only two webbed feet. A stick pierces the sand. Apparently the creature that speaks does not have three legs after all, but holds a cane. Dod looks up to see who holds the cane.

"Looks like you climbed up the wrong pipe." A face that has eyes bigger than his face but a face that has fur all around that the mouth is not seen. A bare pointy nose seems to force its way out of the fur. The nose looks like a normal nose until it opens and speaks. "What kind of creature are you?" The creature asks?

Dod realizes that the nose is a beak similar to feathered creatures. The nostrils are so small he could barley tell that they are on the beak. "Swamlorlakplak. Now what the heck are you man?"

"A swamlak what?" The odd creature remembers the insult. "Get up you fool. Who do you think you are?"

Both dust themselves getting up off of the sand. "ye found yis place. Who yar you?" "Tarvo. I've seen many skeleton's before. Hardly do I keep in touch with any though."

Zeet looks around the area. He sees piles of this sand everywhere wondering what their purpose may be. Then he realizes that not this much sand could just be anywhere. "Zyou create this?"

"Yes. But it looks like you are not here to buy." Tarvo looks at Dodrill. "Especially this one.

What's your name kid?"

"Hey creat, I'm no kid. And..." There is a tap on his arm by Zeet.

"Yee can yelp us out. There is no reason to be so yimpatient." Zeet says then looking at Tarvo. "I'm, Zeet."

Trusting the skeleton, Dod wipes more sand off his legs and answers Tarvo. "Dodrill. You can call me Dod. It does not matter to me. What do you have going on here?"

"Sand of course. You never heard of sand? The rich pay by the buttons to get their own pile." Tarvo looks at the pipe behind them. "That is one high climb of a pipe you went through. I got to give you two credit for that. Now I got to close it off on both ends. Making sure no other creatures get through. I usually use it for garbage and waste. But if creatures are going to find their way, I would rather have it blocked." He turns his back on the two and looks at the sand piles. He tries to see if he has any to spare. "Maybe I'll just clog it up with wasted glop. You never know what you can find in those pipes that can ruin a batch."

Dod sniffles and looks around now more interested. The top is the odd ceiling with fencing like a warehouse but no chains are hanging. "Well I am somewhat of a maker of sorts myself." Dod tells Tarvo more than confident.

The furred creature turns and looks at Dod. He has straps on his chest and many pouches that hang from his unusual travailing tan leg trench coat. "A maker of what?" Tarvo asks as if Dod is lying.

"Shockla, creat. You never heard of it?" Dod smiles as if to have a one up on the creature.

Not saying anything, Tarvo finally answers. "No."

"Well, it is time you try some." Dod takes a bottle from the backpack. He hands it over to Tarvo who grabs it suspiciously. "With so dry of a place, you will need more than anyone."

Tarvo takes a sip. "Taste like worm piss."

Dod almost insulted looks at Tarvo with a sour stare. "Only you would know what worm piss tastes like. During your search for this... sand."

"Ha, a funny creature here. Take your shake. I'll even show you the way out. And I don's search for the sand, I make it." Tarvo turns his back and starts to walk.

Zeet walks close to the creature keeping the same pace. "Yait a second. Ye need to find a friend.

How do ye get to ya Wide Areas?"

"Wide Areas? It is far from here. But I will take you to the nearest pipe that leads you. So you guys can get out of my fur quicker." Dragging the cane, Tarvo looks and pokes at each hill of sand as if checking a thermometer of some kind. Sand pours from small pipes above creating hills that are not finished yet. How many buttons would it cost just to have a sand hill, Dod wonders. Zeet walks as normal as could be.

"So how long does it take you to make all this sand? Are you a rich creat?"

"By rich that would mean I am left alone, so no. I am always in business and buttons do not mean much when all you do is collect them. Although the piles are great to look at." The end of the cane goes into one of the piles. Dod and Zeet wonder why Tarvo poked the sand so aggressively.

"The sooner we get to the Wide Areas the better." Dod says as he looks at each pile they pass by. "Do you go there often to sell sand?"

"No I have enough clientele. For me to find more would be too much that I would not want to handle." Tarvo pokes another pile. "Looking for clunkers. I never like leaving them when all the minerals and pieces combine together and make a clunk. They are as hard as rocks, thus never breaking down." Tarvo keeps walking. Dod and Zeet follow wanting to find the pipeway that leads closest to the Wide Areas. From there they can meet up with Marvin and Shrub and find Lisa. While the two wait at Copper Tunnel, there are still ways of Dod and Zeet to ask questions to where she may be. The time has passed enough for almost half the course to go. By the time the two get back to the Wide Areas, most likely the entire course would be over.

"Yeah it is going to take us some time in The Wide Areas. We actually need to find and meet up with some friends at Copper Tunnels entrance. Do you have any suggestions on how to find someone around that place?"

Tarvo listens to Dod as he walks. He stops and before he leads them out he looks toward his small hut. A little area where no sand falls but is still surrounded by many piles. With a dim light inside and so much sand it is as if gold lightens the area, that without the sand it would be nothing but darkness. "Follow me you two. You guys are probably hungry. Those shakes of yours are not going give you the strength you need to travel around. Come inside for a while."

Dod feeling insulted once again ignores the comment about his drinks. He cannot ignore to appreciate that Tarvo wants to help in some way. "Alright, whatever you say. You doing okay, Zeet."

"Yof course." Zeet says as he follows Tarvo with no hesitation.

***

The lighting from the exposed bulb is more noticeable now that Dod and Zeet sit inside the small hut. After a few fried leaf stems, fruit juice and wine, which Tarvo said not to tell their parents about, the two feel like they are good to go.

"Thanks, creat. That climb made me hungry." He looks at Zeet. "The meal was so good, I did not even see you eat, Zeet. How do skeletons swallow that stuff.

"So what are you guys looking for, a friend and that is it?" Tarvo asks.

"Like we said before, she is a silent creature. Murner. If you left from here more often I wonder if you would have seen her."

Tarvo shakes his head. "Not me. Just hopefully she finds her way around the city. It is filled with more desperate creatures than that of which is in your exhibit."

"Ha, I can tell." Dod says and picks at his food some more. "From what I told you about the worms we met up with, and a couple of marrows as you call them, I think I would rather pick any exhibit over this place."

Looking at the two, the old long furred creature taps his fingers on the table. "You know what, I have something for you. In case you have any trouble in the future." The first thing Tarvo does is grab his cane and takes himself toward some cupboards that are above the sink. After opening one he takes out a plate that has something that may be the likes of a potato. "I want you two to have this." Before he puts it on the table, Dod and Zeet already know that it is a clump of sand. "This is when clunkers first start to form in the piles. Since I maintain them never do they get any bigger than this."

Dod looks at the clump. Question is why Tarvo would want him and Zeet to have the wasted sand. "Alright, thanks. Maybe I can throw it at someone who tries messing with us."

Tarvo claps his hand on his own forehead. "No, child. If you find the right creator, the clump can form into a figure with life. The sand relies on sand to live. But a clunker with the right paper and gloss can keep it intact. Even grow to great hight"

"Really?" Dod takes a closer look at it wanting to see the clunk actually move. "How come you have not done this to help with your sand piles?"

"I have!" Tarvo says walking closer to him. "It takes courses to advance. So I have very few. A lot of dedication creating something out of a clunk. Depending on how you raise it. Since you make

that drink, I see you're dedicated enough. Believe me. This can turn into a living thing. So it will take a lot more patients and care than some nasty swoosh."

"Younds like a lot of work." Zeet says. "Yet, worth the yeffort."

"What are you talking about. Of course it is. I found it just on time. Too soon it would crumble.

Too late its, well like I said, a rock basically." Tarvo sniffles.

***

Straight ahead is a gate that has silver bars running down. Tarvo simply pushes it open and already they are in a circular bricked area where only a few pipe openings are surrounding.

"Do one of these lead to Copper, Tarv?"

Tarvo looks at Dod with his brows frowning down. "Not exactly. You will land up in the Wide Areas though. If you want to get close to the tunnel, I suggest you take the second one." He looks and points with his cane.

The pipe is one out of five. Dod wonders why there are so few if this merchant has a vast business. Then again, Tarvo is a secluded and busy creature. "Okay. So number two. Where will it take us in the Wide Areas exactly?"

"The merchants district. Buy a map and find your way around the place. That way you do not fall in anymore compartments that you are not invited into. Do not forget to get that paper gloss also." Tarvo steps away allowing the two to enter the pipe.

"Oh well, we do not plan to. Tell creat's about my shockla will you? You got my card. I know you know many that would like the drink." Dod says entering the pipe. He looks at Tarvo. "Thanks for everything, Tarv. We owe you. I will feed and water that clunker. Will also get what you told me to.

Wrote all down on paper in case we forget."

Roling his large plate like size eyes Tarvo looks down at Dod. "Don't treat the sand like a plant.

Quit fooling around."

"Right." Dod walks into the pipe and is not seen. Zeet waves to Tarvo and then follows after.

***

Falling out of the pipe is like any other after the air stops pushing Marvin and his two friends. He is the last one out but realizes that Shrub and the creation are already sliding down a gold hill of some sort. There is no longer the cold smooth slide as Marvin's stomach feels like it rises to his chest during free fall. The pipe that they came through is now far above Marvin. There is a kick under his butt as he lands and begins sliding behind the other two. They all wonder what the rough yellow grains are that bring them down. Dod with Zeet, already found out that this golden grain material is sand. Sand is something that Marvin and Shrub do not know about either. What does look familiar is the floor which looks like stained green on metal sheets. Surrounding the hill is a shadow for the ceiling cannot be seen.

The pipe was a straight direction. That would mean that this path should be the only way Dr.

Shrogow goes though. When all three land on the metal floor, Shrub is the first to speak about the hill. "What is that?" He looks up to the opening of the pipe, now so far above. "In case we have to, do you think we can climb this again? It is like shards of metal after being grinded."

Marvin grabs a hand full of the yellow sand and watches as streams fall through his fingers. "I know but it's way too soft. All that I can think of is that it is the dried muck that stays so deep in the water. Even when that dries it is not as hard and fine as this. Must be a certain kind." He looks at the creation who cares nothing of the sand. Instead she turns her head in all directions trying to figure out where they are and what they are doing. "Everything okay?" Not knowing how to properly communicate with the creation. She ignores any voice that is around and takes a step forward.

"I don't think she heard you." Shrub goes up to her making himself visible. "How are you? Um, you still recognize us from the doctor's place, right?"

She looks down at Shrub with her large blue eyes that have pupils that can hardly be seen. She touches her chest with the tips of her fingers. The creation is still unable to speak, Shrub remembers. The creation without moving her head much taps her throat as if to tell him what she cannot do anymore.

"Oh yeah. We need to get your voice back. Marvin, can we reverse the skull into talking to her in some way?"

Looking at the creation both know communicating with her will be easier then they thought. Although confused a bit, she is still aware of what happened before and how to communicate in some way. Marvin wonders if the creation wanted to get away from the doctor. What kind of pain do the creations have to go through in order to come alive. "Let me see." Marvin places the skull on the harp once more. With a simple stroke on the strings there is nothing but a tune. He strokes the strings again and the same sweet tune comes out. "Hold on." Marvin says wondering if there is a certain note he needs in order for this to work. "I am sure this thing cannot only take voices."

"Yeah well, that's all we've been doing. For all we know he probably can sneak on other creatures more quietly now. This skull and harp may be too much of a risk using." Shrub looks at the instrument as the skull sits on top the harp. There is a slight look of fear. If the instrument took something from others before, then it can take something from anyone. "Do you think this can do worse from what you are trying to attempt now, Marv?"

Pressing his lips, Marvin looks concerned. He looks at the creation and really wants to give her voice back. "She got us out of there. I would feel like a slug-chump to just not give her what is hers."

"Well, what do you think?" Shrub looks at the creation hoping she will indicate some kind of answer. "Do you think we can wait on your voice? Maybe we can find someone in the Wide Areas that can give us more information on what to do. Thinking about that, looking around the Wide Areas with a creation might not be a good idea. Has looking for anything there been?" The Wide Areas have been nothing but trouble. Now would be a good time for them to decide whether not to go back in or not.

"While everyone tries to kill us over the very things we know nothing about." Marvin says.

Both stare at the creation.

The look on her face is like a stone bust which cannot change expression.

"We can't just stay here. Not like we have been in the Areas for a long time. There has to be more than just a bunch of creatures wanting what's ours." Marvin looks at the creation.

"Alright, let's go. We just got to be careful." Shrub says frustrated. "Try the harp again. We need her to talk. By chance the creation will help us through The Wide Areas."

Marvin looks at Shrub as if he can help. Both know that he knows nothing of the instrument- mechanism. Marvin plays the harp some more with simple strokes. Nothing happens.

"Alright. That thing isn't working. What kind of device did Lisa make here? Didn't she think about who it might affect?" Shrub says once again frustrated.

"If that was her intention." Marvin answers. "There has to be some way to..." Below where the neck is at on the harp, there are pins that have flat heads. He turns them, tightening the strings a bit. "I will tune it differently. Not that I know much about tuning an instrument, but this might help. He begins to play it again plucking and stroking the strings. It does not make the harp melody that it did before, instead there is a hum of some sort. The tone goes up then drops over and over. Marvin's eyes turn to look at the ribcage instrument. "Is that her voice?" Marvin keeps playing surprised.

"I don't know. She only groaned when she was on that chair." Shrub looks and listens. Like an odd wind in the air there seems to be a voice. "Did you hear something Marvin?"

Before Marvin can answer the creation cuffs her one hand and coughs. Hearing the cough the two are convinced. "She got her voice back." Marvin looks at the harp as if he made the thing himself. "All you have to do is tune it. I wonder if I play it now, what will happen."

"Don't do it Marv." Shrub says quickly. "We just got her voice back. If we try anything else, maybe ours will go next. Or perhaps hers again." The creation coughs still while the two are astonished. Shrub thinks blinking his eyes. He looks at the creation. "That is, you can talk now?" Looking at her waiting for an answer, the creation moves her hand.

"Y-y-yes." The tone is high but not too high. The smoothness makes it sound sweet and calm. "I- I can speak now."

"Ha, we did it." Shrub claps once and looks at Marvin and the creation with a smile. "Sorry for taking your voice. But we don't know how to work this instrument quite yet. How are you feeling."

The creation blinks and looks around like a camera adjusting to a setting but not taking any pictures. "I – feel – normal. Never have I been out of the doctor's chair."

"Him, he's not a friend." Shrub says examining the creations wondering what to ask.

Marvin looks at Shrub but quickly shifts to the creation. "What did you do before you got there?"

"I do not know. Ask the doctor."

"Maybe we should ask someone that knows more about creations. I would not doubt if the doctor has to get rid of the old memories before he begins a new creation. If memories have anything to do with the process. That is since she does not remember anything also. I wonder if the memories can even be stored and sold." Shrub says staring at the creation. "What is your name, do you even have one?"

"No. The doctor called me, creation. He said that my owners will name me when I get to the arena."

Now more amused by what the arena is Shrub does not worry about the creations name. "Arena.

What goes on there?"

The creation blinks her eyes once. "Even I don't know what the arena is. Why, don't you?"

Shrub looks up at the creation who is about twice his size. "We are not from around here. Our exhibit is far away. Not sure if you know anything about going inside the pipeways but they lead to entirely different living areas. How do you even know about the Wide Areas when you were just woken up not too long ago?"

"The doctor would tell me, what he said I needed to know. But he never told me about any exhibits."

"I guess if you are in The Wide Areas there is no need to, depending on who you are." Scratching his large round head, Shrub questions.

Marvin interrupts looking at the two. "We got to figure out where we are. This shadow is like a mist. The more you walk into it, the more you can see what is around. Do not split up or else it will be difficult to find our way around." He looks up at the creation. "You have no name. Do you have any idea what might be close to one?" Marvin asks if that should help.

She blinks her eyes rapidly. "I do not know. I was put together."

Marvin looks at Shrub trying to already think of a name but not getting anywhere. "What do you want to be called?"

"Things like that do not really occur to me at the moment." The creation talks in a robotic manner. She is too new to the situation and to the world she just walked into.

Confused, Marvin looks at Shrub who is thinking. "I don't know. What do they name creations around here?" He scratches his head again not even sure what the girl is really made of. It looks like whatever she has can be skin. Then it looks like a solid frame of what can be clay. "I do not want to just keep calling you creation. Since you are from this area that we know nothing about." He taps his fingers. Then Shub's eyes widen. "How about Clara. You like that?"

"Sure." Replies a simple answer from the creation.

"Good," Shrub says and looks around. "Now let's get out of here."

***

There are many hills surrounding the area. Still none of the three can figure out what they are made out of. Wondering in the shadow filled area has been a stretch of a walk. There is a fog that keeps rising like a moisture of some kind. None know what to say other than to look around and try and find a way out. With the piles of sand around there is a kind of dampness to the air which brings out the rich wet smell out of the piles. They may be surrounded by walls but it's hard to tell.

"Well great. I am starting to think we should climb the biggest hill there is. Maybe then it will lead us somewhere." Shrub says irritated.

"You know that might not be a bad idea. And you never seen this before, Clara?" Marvin asks.

"Never. Perhaps before I was created, maybe I did know what the hills are made out of, or maybe I did not."

"Then what do you remember exactly?" Marvin says. Even he tries to keep up with the creation as they walk.

She looks forward not stopping. "Honestly. Not much. I do remember Shrogow saying he would tell me more when the process was finished. But I, we left before that."

Marvin wonders if she needed that last piece to properly cope. A bit of worry strikes him.

"Well that's good." Shrub interrupts Marvin's line of thinking. "That makes you a more thought productive creation. Now you can create any memories you want. Not many other creations can think for themselves I am sure. Yet, what do we know about them. Hey Marvin. You think Clara would like to come to our exhibit sometime." He looks at her with concern. "It's different than here. Not so many wide spaces.

And no matter if you get lost, more than likely you always find your way back home."

"What if you do get lost?" She asks.

"Only once did Marvin and I land up in another exhibit. It seemed to have a much smaller rate of creatures, but we found a pipe that lead back to ours. So if you get lost, you can just live somewhere else I guess." Shrub looks up at the creation's eyes that are wide yet with such a small dilation rate. The blueness of them stick out most. Even when she just concentrates on walking.

"We been in here too long already. Time to clime one of these piles." Marvin places one foot on the sand and it hardly sinks in. He crawls the rest of the way up until the tip of the hill is near. The fenced roof shows no clue of anything different. There are other hills where pipes drop sand while others just lead to the top fencing. He climbs the rest of the way up and holds on the fence. Grabbing on to the ceiling he wonders if he should climb. "Nothing different up here..." The spring kid does not feel the ground anymore, yet his legs feel like they are getting covered. Marvin starts sinking. The tightness around his ankle feels as though something is pulling him in. Never would he have guessed that the sand would cause anyone to sink since he just walked up it. "Don't come up here! The hill is not stable! I'M SINKING!"

Shrub and Clara look at one another in shock. Shrub places one foot on the hill just to get a better look. Something takes hold of his shoulders. The sand itself tries to pull him in. When he looks at what is in front of him there is a sloppy face as if melted, but it is not melted. The face is made out of sand and makes up an entire being of itself. Shrub's eyes widen. A tighter grip on the back of his neck yanks him backwards. He knows it's Clara with her one hand trying to get him away from this creature. The grip on his neck is relieved. He feels sand drizzle down his shirt. With eight missing fingers, the creature looks at his hands and realizes the strength of the creation that just pulled Shrub breaking the sand creatures fingers off. The sand creature goes back into the hill. Shrub looks up the hill where two springs are been expanded and trying to reach anything he can.

"Marvin, keep holding on!" Shrub yells hoping his friend's head is still above the hill.

Trying not to let go Marvin is ready to hold his breadth. He knows when he gets buried it will be hard for his springs to bring him up.

"What should we do?" Shrub asks Clara as if she has a type of experience with any kind of danger.

Clara looks at Shrub then the hill. "Not sure. Maybe give these things what they want." "Which is one of us? I do not think so." Shrub steps back. The springs are now almost nothing but straight wires. Clara walks closer to the sand ready to go get what is pulling Marvin.

"What choice do we have? Maybe the best chance he has is if I go inside and tear them apart myself."

Another sloppy face comes out. The entire body jumps out the hill. "If it was not for those springs, we would already have your friend."

"What are you going to do with him?"

"He disturbed us. We do not like been disturbed." More of the creatures come out. Grains of gold fall on Shrub and Clara. Shrub has to spit before his teeth press down on more sand. The one who lost his fingers approaches. "We are going to turn him into sand... by eating him. And you two will make fine sand yourselves."

If Shrub was not so small and head so big and round, the sand creature might be able to wrap his entire mouth around the forehead. The monster does not see the bulb boy's legs. One foot hits between the legs of the sand creature and gets stuck as if he just stepped in mud. The face gets more sloppy instantly with an awkward expression. He has no choice but to let the jaws go. Shrub's foot comes out. Sand falls through the creature's fingers, the same way blood would. The other three creatures come toward the two. Right away Clara's one hand comes down in a chopping motion. The head of one of the sand creatures goes in two. Then she yanks her fist to the side and one half of the face shatters into streams of more sand. The creature is not dead but walks around with half a head.

The finger-less one goes toward Shrub. With his bulb head he runs toward him and rams into the creature. The impact does nothing. Sanded hands with only thumbs get placed on the side of Shrub. The sand creature lost his fingers not so long ago, already he tries grabbing if they were still there. So when he tries grabbing the large round head of Shrub, only the thumbs rub. Quickly Shrub backs up realizing he cannot do much. The sand creature comes toward him very slowly with arms up but finger- less. As shrub moves back the creature slows down. He might know their weakness now. He steps further away from the hill. "Clara, get away from the hill. They need their...sand."

She looks at the remaining sand creature and swings as hard as she can. The strength of the creation causes the entire head to explode with grains of sand bursting in the air. "What if we dig up that hill." Accrues to Clara.

Shrub could not agree more. He attempts to run under the legs of the headless sand creature, causing the monster to fall instead. The finger-less one gets closer to shrub. With his small legs Shrub attempts another kick. Moving to the side the sand creature avoids him. Behind him is the hill. The other sand creatures are gone. Shrub sees a pile of sand not too far from the hills but assumes he got too

weak and went away. Clara walks up to Shrub, ready to attack the sand creature. Finger-less, the sand body turns around and goes into the sand as well.

"Quick, lets dig." They start at one end clawing at the hill. Sand goes under their legs rapidly, getting spread out behind them. Grains start to drizzle down the hill trying to fill in where the missing sand once was. Shrub feels something solid. It is still sand but a lot harder than what the hill is. "Oh great." He realizes it is a foot.

Clara looks at the foot and simply grips it. She throws the sand body over her shoulder. There is a yelp then somewhat of a burst like a water balloon. The sand creature's legs have a few gashes from the fall. His fingers are twisted as he crawls toward any sand hill. Too far away, he crumbles like a week sand castle creating it's own pile of sand.

"Make sure they do not stick their hands out." Shrub says.

"If they do I will break them off. I did not realize I had this much strength, even with one hand." "Neither did I." Shrub says as he digs. Then he looks at the pile. The sand creatures are living

beings, like them. Clara herself is parts of living and artificial creatures. "You think one of those hands can stay on you for awhile?"

Clara thinks. If she had two hands, then this process would be a lot faster. "I do not know. Let's find out."

Suddenly there is an attempted attack from two more sand creatures. With less sand on the hill, Shrub and Clara back off, making the creatures having to catch them. When the two step forward, especially Clara, one sand creature escapes jumping back in the hill. The other one is not so lucky as he gets closer to the creation, not realizing his fellow comrade just left him. Clara holds his head still as Shrub holds the legs together. "I got him, but damn thing moves so much."

Clara tightens her hand around the left arm and squeezes. Sand falls from her fist and the sand hand falls. The creature tries biting her since that is all he can do. Like a carpet that is rolled, the two swing the body back and forth. They toss it away from the sand pile. There is a burst from the creature but is easily ignored. Clara gets the hand and attaches it to her arm as fast as she can. Nothing happens as she tries to move the fingers. They twitch partially, perhaps because of whatever nerves the sand monsters have, but the hand does not stick.

"Here," Shrub seeing that she wears a sash walks up to Clara. He tears a piece off and begins wrapping it around tight. "Better?"

The fingers move a little bit more. "Kind of stiff. It feels as though I'm made of tight wires."

Shrub is amazed. "So you do have some kind of control though?"

"Should do for now. We focus on your friend." They rush to the hill and continue digging.

Shrub looks up while he takes out more sand. "You okay, Marv!"

Spitting sand out of his mouth, Marvin lifts his chin as best he can. "Doing great." Now feeling less pressure on his chest he can breath better. Sand lowers and he pulls himself up as much as possible.

He can see the two down the hill. Marvin feels like he is about to get sick. He thinks he starts to see things, noticing that Clara has a sand hand. Breathing heavily, he tries talking again. "Guys can you hurry? I've only been hanging here for a while to get pulled apart."

None of his friends down below can make out what he just said. But by the tone of Marvin's voice he sounds tired. They dig as fast as they can, keeping an eye on him.

Not talking too much the spring kid has been pulling himself up and down catching air whenever he can. Less sand the easier he's managed.

The two stare up at Marvin as he holds on, arms stretched out. "I can almost get out." He says as his feet kick forward pushing sand on Shrub and Clara. Whatever was holding him before must of let go. His springs compact. Helping Marvin to hold on to the ceiling better. Letting go of the ceiling his feet kick forward and the spring kid allows himself to fall. Marvin lands in completion. "I never want to deal with this stuff again." He says as he looks at his feet, hoping everything is still intact.

"They were going to eat you. This stuff is called sand apparently." Shrub says hoping his friend is alright.

"Good thing they did not. Maybe the creatures got too scared once you started digging. I was bobbing up and down on top of that hill as best I can. If you were not here I would have been swallowed!" Marvin looks at Lara's new hand, now feeling a lot better than he did while he was hanging. "Looks like it helped you out. How does that hand feel?"

Tightening a fist made out of sand, Clara looks examining the new ligament. She and her new two friends try and see if any crumbs fall, or if the hand itself will somehow crack and fall apart. "It seems to be just fine." Is all she can say as if getting the hand was too easy. Shrub would also agree.

"Well, we better keep moving. These sand creatures seem to not know when someone is around unless their piles get touched. Let's make sure we don't do that." Marvin continues to walk not knowing exactly where to go. With the guidance of the skull and harp, maybe it can talk them in a certain direction or hopefully somehow use it's power in another way the group did not know about. If any more sand creatures come out, Marvin figures he can use the instrument the same way against the worm at The Hollow. He takes the skull out from his outstretched pocket. He reaches for the harp in the other. It's gone.

When Shrub looks at the wide-eyed look on Marvin's face, he already knows what happened. Marvin stares at the creation in hopes that somehow she has the two pieces Lisa made. An answer he already knows.

"We need to break down that entire hill." Marvin says and rushes toward the sand. Shrub follows as both dig away decreasing the pile some more. Clara not as radical does the same but goes as fast as she can.

So much time passes. The three would stop frequently to spread the sand in all directions.

Sometimes even adding additional sand to another pile. When each of them scratches the hard ground, all they see are blots of the rustic green floor with partial scrapes of whatever sand is left.

"Where did any of them go? Not a single sand monster was in there along with the harp?" Shrub says worried.

Marvin looks around not noticing much of anything other than the new small piles and scattered sand they made. "I don't know where the harp went. But if they tossed it to another pile, then we will be doing this forever."

"We got to go. I hope the creation Lisa has in mind will be able to use any kind of other ribcage.

It was a very good one yes, but let's just hope that we did not need it for anything that will help with finding Lisa." Shrub says. Marvin can tell he is getting as tired as him.

"About her. We have not even been around any Wide Areas enough to actually find any clues to where she may have went. Infact maybe she does not need these. As long as we are safe and find her

the same way." Marvin's voice rises. With the loss of the harp, anger is now flashing over his face like a wave of hot water. He still wish they had the instrument for it's benefits though. "Are we going to have to get out of here without finding her?"

"Calm down. Let's leave this damn place." Shrub wants to suggest that Lisa may be back at their exhibit but decides not to in case it infuriates Marvin more.

"If I did not climb that hill we would still have the harp."

Clara looks down at Marvin. "Worrying about the harp is going to hold us back just as much as the pile of sand was able to hold you. We have to keep looking for a way out."

CHAPTER ELEVEN

etting back to The Wide Areas did not take long. If the two knew of the troubles that their friends had, then they would feel a bit guilty that they got out so easy and with a souvenir. "Hey creat. You know this place? How can we find the entrance from where you would stand around and talk to other creatures?"

"Yat should be yover there." He points toward where most of the bigger buildings are. "Ye would have to yo through the main central yarea. Yets keep yoing straight."

Looking at the area at a different perspective, Dod wonders what the place might have to offer.

He knows not to get distracted, but they still need to look for Lisa. "Well let's go." The two start to walk." So what does this place have to offer, Zeet? I mean all I ever hear about is how creations stick around here. Somehow they make the place the way it is." He says wondering if he should pick some up gloss for the clunker.

"Yes. Yey build. Just look yat all the high places." Zeet says as he points up. The buildings are tall. Dod remembers his view from the entrance and how the bottoms of most faded into the dust clouds lower into the city.

"I know but I would figure that is because of all the room they have here. In exhibits, there is no way such structures can be built.

172

Unless they broke all the pipes." He looks at Zeet with a sarcastic smile. "Which is what some creat tried to do at one point. Dirt filled up that pipe, which is what everyone knew would happen. What we were told that if a pipe happened to be opened up, there would be nothing but empty space. Which is what The Hollow is. An endless area that leads to most likely, well I would say ummm, anywhere or nowhere. There is a rumor that water may fill other areas. That's uncertain though."

"Sounds yike a lot of things are yon certain about your place."

"Things are. You can dig for answers, but that might create another opening for a pipe. Or like I said, flood you with sand. Even water maybe." Dod looks around. "Say I should sell some Shockla.

What's our time?"

"Yat I don't know. I gave everything away before I yent to the slug."

"Well great." Dod sees a store that is embedded into one of the tall buildings. There are sheets of paper that hang from the ceiling. "Let's go in here and see the picks." He reads the sign that says,

Cloggers Den. "Seems innocent. Now we don't want to go anywhere dangerous. Right creat? Also need to find something that both of us can keep in touch with one another."

Zeet has nothing to say. He knows Dod picked the place because of the paper. As both walk in, the scent of plant with an aroma of mint lingers. Must be what the papers are made out of. There is a hallway that has many buttons that are basically the hallway itself. Above them are small pipes. There is a zip like sound as if something has been ripped. Dod looks up and sees a paper above his head.

Another zip sound, sure enough a paper comes through and hangs from the ceiling along with many others. "Oh look..." Before Dod has anything to say a voice interrupts him.

"What is it you need? Sending something?" A skinny creature with a pencil thin face looks down at Dod and Zeet. It has an odd gray that matches his one piece jacket. His legs are as thin as his head.

"I just wanted to see what the picks are my friend." Dod tells him. There is a time keep that has a large pointer aimed at the number 26. "Wow. We have been out of that doctor's place for seven splits." Time has been a hard thing to keep up with. For all Dod knows, Marvin and Shrub should be back at Copper Tunnel's entrance. Which he expects they did leave Shrogow's place unharmed. "We are kinda in a hurry and we are looking for someone." Dod looks around a bit, trying to find the paper gloss Tarvo told him about. Then he remembers his shake. "Would you like to try out a shake of mine?"

The long face moves and points to the roof the same way a time hand would. "What. You came here to sell?"

"Not really sell." Dod's green scaled face almost changes to a darker green as if to blush. He realizes that he is not as good of a salesmen that he thought he would be. Clearing his throat the reptile tries his best to notice where the eyes are on the merchant. "The reason is because I have various kinds of drinks for different kinds of situations. Kinda like, you know, for a job and stuff." He smiles trying to hold in his embarrassment and sloppy tongue that always weakens when Dod gets confused.

The skinny creature smiles as well. Dod can tell because of a horizontal black line appearing high where the creatures face should be. He scratches the side of his head as if trying to think of something to say. "We do not buy. We sell. If you need a delivery we will do just that."

Dod looks up. "You mean, those papers are from all around these Wide Areas?"

"They are from everywhere." The skinny creature looks at the time-keep, then back down at

Dod. "Now if I can accommodate you with anything let me know. Other than delivery, I am not sure what else you need to be here for."

Delivery can be a good way to get hold of his friends, or even Lisa. "Is there way you can send a message to someone that we don't know where they are at. Or to a doctor?" Dod looks at Zeet. "What was his name?"

"Shrogow."

"There you go." Dod says with a smile.

"Ha," The laugh is dull. "You would need to climb the Spyglass Tower for that. We can send messages around from ten to a hundred buttons. I doubt you have that." The long face gets closer to Dod in an uncomfortable way. "If you need a missing creature report, go to the observation finders. You find we send. It's not our job to look for others or locations. You need to know that yourself."

Both friends stay still with unease. Zeet looks at Dod knowing a solution. "I know where a Spyglass Yower is."

"Well, let's go." Dod says throwing his arms in the air not wanting to waste anymore time. "I'm sure we don't want to take anymore of this creat's time. Right?"

"Of course. If you ever need something delivered, this is the place to go to. I own it." He says with a smile that is more enthusiastic this time. The owner can already tell Dod and Zeet are not from the area. So any unusual hold backs are forgiven.

"Can you tell me how you make your paper? I can use the formula. Perhaps even for my shockla."

The merchant scratches behind his ear with the smile now fading a bit. "It's moss. Like a lot of paper. You should know that. That smell comes from a certain flower that keeps the paper from ripping so easily. I also add a gloss to keep it more intact."

"How much for the gloss!" Dod gets excited. "Will you sell some?"

"Small bottle is only three buttons." The owner of the store scratches behind his ear again, this time with an average thinking look upon his face.

"How about two bottles of shockla for half the price?"

The grin on the shop owner's mouth twists. "How about you give me two...shocklas. As a bonus I will keep them out and tell whoever gets them about you." Although the owner's response is unsure. Dod figures this a good opportunity to get more of his drinks out. He does not say but most anything can be a meal for this skinny creatures apatite. He should just drink the shocklas himself.

"Sure my friend. Here are some of my cards to give. If anyone is interested, I mean, when they want more they can contact me by letters."

"Yes, yes, of course. Now come now step by the register and we will be through here."

Zeet wonders why Dod would buy such inconvenient things in their matter of trying to find someone. When will the reptilian creature need or use such a substance at a time like this? He looks at Dod. "Yon't forget to get something to communicate with."

***

The Spyglass tower is somewhere deep in the middle of the city. Main reason why is because it has to be. Little did Dod know that just because the tower has a giant microscope on top, he did not think of the tower looking any different from any of the other buildings. And in more ways than one, it is completely different. When Zeet and him approach the tower, many creatures are seen walking inside because the actual building itself is not seen. The creatures are seen as if stepping in the air. Walking up invisible stairs leads them toward the ceiling. It is as if there is another city with inhabitants unaware or caring about what is going on beyond them. Zeet walks up to a glare. With a closer look at Zeet, a small hint of his reflection appears. Dod can now tell the entire place is made out of glass. He does not know why. Maybe the means of looking upon everyone else equals the lookers to be completely exposed themselves.

"Yere. We need to pay." Zeet tells Dod at a stop.

The reptilian boy looks at a vertical copper knob to pull open the door. There is a copper box that looks as if it floats right by this handle. "You don't have any buttons do you?"

Zeet shakes his head. Dod does not know if he should be annoyed that Zeet is completely empty handed. Then again, he was never supposed to be part of this trip. Besides, the skeleton has helped out in many ways. "Just that I'm running low create." Dod says as he takes out a hand full of buttons. The slot in the box is like any other. Ten small buttons for entry. Two medium for entry. One large for entry. Dod puts one of his largest buttons in. Not sure if the entry is only for one creature or will cover both Dod waits to see what happens. There is a click, and they both walk in.

Never has Dod seen so much glass before, as hard as it is to see. Yet it is not difficult to navigate to the top. Rails guide all the stairways. Dod does not know why he could not see them before. Perhaps he was distracted by the creatures walking beside them. With a slight turn of his head, Dod realizes they are all painted on the one side facing away from the stairs. Painted the same patterns the buildings that they are in front of. How did they get such details in? Dod wonders. What if someone was to not see the rails and fall off? Dod thinks. Not sure if it has happened so far, but there are not many creatures inside, or at least for today.

There are six telescopes that of course can be seen as Dod and Zeet almost reach the top. Each hang over the glass ledge ready to be used. Before the two are able to go through the door. There is a desk, and it is not glass. "How many the merchant asks."

Dod looks at the birdlike thing that has small eyes. "Two." "That will be fifteen buttons each."

"What, I spent a large one just for entry already?"

The bird creature looks at Dod use to newcomers. "If you want to find out where anything is at, it will not be cheap. Now are you both going in?"

"I yid not know you had to pay. You go ahead. I yill wait here."

Dod would like Zeet to come with him. Especially to tell him what certain areas maybe. He is sure there is a map or a directory of some kind to tell him what everything is. "Ya Zeet stay here. If one of us should look it should be me so I can spot out our other friend." Dod drops five small buttons then another two mediums on the counter. Counting the buttons the cashier presses a different type of button of her own which is attached to the desk. The door opens and Dod goes outside.

The price Dod payed was more than worth it. He can see everything with the telescope. But not Lisa or any of his friends. None have arrived at Copper Tunnel's entrance. He realizes that just because he now has the eyes to see everything does not mean he can find all the answers. In fact, the Marrows might be after them still. The only reason why they have not found Dod and his friends is because they got lost themselves. The Marrow's building is where it was before. He looks after zooming in and seeing much of everything. It is the same from the outside except it turns and dips in the ground like an elevator. Those bastards. That's how the group stepped out a different door. Mainly he is concerned about his friends. What if that creation came alive and did the doctors bidding. What if she attacked Marvin and Shrub? Perhaps splitting up just made things worse. No need to change course now. The only solution he has is to wait at Copper Tunnel. First Dod wants to see if he sees any marrows around the city. There is that huge furry creature, what was his name, Vern?

Nothing is of importance. Too bad none of the friends are at the tunnel's entrance, but that is where Dod and Zeet will still go next. Since he payed, Dod figures to spend a little bit more time with the telescope. There is a line of Marrows on a certain street. He is not sure what they are doing in a group like that but Dod does not want them to see him when they go back down into the city's streets. A little bit more up the road he sees a giant box. It is not like any other building, but does seem to stand out on purpose. And it does stand out, because the building is meant to. Why does the sign light? Why is the creature standing in front of it have a frog like face but a long rough reptilian body. Both eyes are even different colors. One is red and the other has a metallic like object inside. The fingers reach to the ground and are metal with blades. That has to be a creation. That building must be where the creations are. Other than been used to build the place, they live inside that box that's for all to see.

Dod spends the rest of his time on the telescope mainly looking for his friends. Every few moments he looks toward Copper Tunnel's entrance. He figures this would be a better way of finding them instead of waiting at the tunnel. He hears someone walk up to him, so Dod looks to see that it is another bird creature.

"Your time is up. Unless you want to pay again. But you would have to wait in the line this time."

Even though Dod is not going to pay again, he decides to look at the line of only two other creatures. "No I'm leaving." He stares at the city without the help of the telescope and sees many little dots on buildings. Buildings that now all seem attached to one another again. The box though. That seems to be different.

CHAPTER TWELVE

As if there was no way out, Marvin, Shrub and Clara find a wall which is made exactly like the metal green ground. The upward green rustic sheets with bolts to hold them together are a relief to the group. Following along the wall there is a rustic red sheet of a door no bigger than Clara. When they go through their mood is not as in high spirits. Without the harp, it feels as though a piece of what they have been fighting for is now missing. In addition to that the skull might not work. A light blinds them. Each has to shade their eyes.

"Where are we, back at The Wide Areas?" Shrub gets confused as to where else light would be coming from. What he hears his friend say is so far the most disappointing thing throughout the entire quest.

"I do not like this." Apparently, Marvin's eyes are the first to adjust. All he sees are streams of lights like straws coming toward him that glare out of fences. The fences from the ceiling are now the walls. But what crawls on the fencing are that of the marrows. They climb like spiders. Some even have multiple legs like them. They have been in the marrows territory the entire time. The door shuts, but this time it will not open.

"What are they caring?" Shrub asks. The answer is obvious. Limbs, bags and tools of various designs. Designs for creations. "Let's go back." He turns around quickly only to push a door that does not open causing the bulb boy to ram his shoulder hard. Despite the brief hit, Shrub presses his back against the door. Before he can say anything a skull with it's embedded eyes comes down from the ceiling. How did he come down from so high, is he on a web of some kind just like a spider would be? The teeth like pistons on a motor tap rapidly. Already an entire squadron of skeletons surround the group.

They all start to clatter their teeth. It is more like a thousand rattles going off at ounce. Marvin, Shrub and Clara cover their ears, mainly because the sound is so violent and is also the sound of them getting caught. When the rattling stops all Marvin waits for is for each of the skeletons to grab hold of the three of them and start pulling them apart to add to their creations. That or he does not want to hear the odd speech as they talk. But a path clears in front of them and a familiar face appears. That odd narrow face with the snout pointing toward them. The wide eyes of Dr. Shrogow looks satisfied. He stops in front of them and smiles.

"I knew you would never leave from here." He stares at Clara's new hand and smiles even wider. "I like what you did with my creation. Now I will have her back along with the ribcage and skull."

Already on check, there is no point in Marvin holding anything back. "We do not have the ribcage." His back flicks to the side. A marrow pulls Marvin, yanking the skull away from his arms. Shrub gets held quickly. Clara sees as the two get hassled. Without thought her hand lifts knocking a marrow to the ground. About twenty hands come upon her. A large needle attached to a syringe goes into her neck. The plunger presses in and down goes Clara. The marrows drag her body away.

"You better not do anything to her!" Shrub yells.

"Of course I am. Need to erase her memory you see. Contaminated her mind is. Now it is time to get her a new one and the reason is because of you two." One of the marrows gives the skull to Shrogow. Then the marrow looks down upon the two friends. Anger is in his face. "So it looks like you did loose the harp. Tell me where the location. Then we can find it. You are already caught, there is no point in not telling me."

Marvin stares at the doctor defeated. There is no answer.

"Oh come on. We can beat it out of you. If you die before you say anything we can just search the entire factory. Or I can just tell you this. Your friend Lisa's life depends on it."

The look turns into confusion more than anything on Marvin's face. Then he realizes something.

His friend Lisa has been in the marrow's territory the entire time. Shrogow was lying. If that be the case, then she might have already been turned into a creation in some terrible way. "She has been here the entire time?"

Shrogow laughs and looks at the floor. He stares back at Marvin. "No fool. She has been with you the entire time."

Marvin looks up at the creation beside him, that his friend Shrub is already looking upon. "Clara?"

"No." The doctor's eyes turn into satisfied anger. "Even before you took the creation." Marvin and Shrub then realize the answer but say nothing letting Shrogow continue.

"The skull is hers. This," He brings the skull closer to Marvin as if to give it to him. "is her." "Makes no sense. There was a note written by her inside."

"A note which was written prior. Which was then put in after. You said you found it in a pottery shop. She must of fell in the kiln and the skull was then put on the shelf when found. Then the note was also found somewhere in the room perhaps, put in by someone thinking she made the skull. The girl made another pottery piece which the note belonged to. You never seen her parents much have you.

Water creatures like these are rare. Bones from them carry the soul once dead. Water holds in the spirit unless empty. That is why it's heavier than a regular skull. This is not pottery. Water is trapped inside the hollow areas in her bones. Meaning the rib cage, or harp, is also hers. Have you never seen the clear bones of certain fish on your dinner plate? Those ribs make fine strings my boy. Now if you tell me where the harp is, I can put her together. We will let you go as a reward for these fine bones."

The same marrow that handed the skull to Shrogow chops his teeth at him.

"I know, I know. The next event is soon and we need to see how our latest works hold up." Shrogow looks at Clara's dangled body in disappointment. "Too bad we could not sell her. But at least we got her back and the skull."

Marvin wonders if he still had the harp, would they been able to escape all these Marrows. The skull, Lisa, has got them out of many situations, yet has got them in so much also. Maybe if the two get back together somehow, then there might be a possibility for escape. The skull seemed to have a mind of it's own before.

"Let's take them. They need to get caged for now so we can make it to the arena on time. When the event is over we will get more answers. Do you agree?"

The marrow shakes his head rapidly. The grips on Marvin and Shrub tighten as they are pulled away. There is nothing either of them can do now but to see where they are going to be taken.

Other than cold brick walls the bars are the only things that separate Marvin and Shrub from leaving the cell they now sit in. One marrow stands down the hallway making sure no one or nothing tries leaving.

Both wait and wonder what the marrows and Shrogow were talking about when they mentioned an event. "So wherever they are going, that is where the creations are been used." Shrub says sitting on the floor.

"That is what I'm guessing. Marvin taps the back of his head on the wall sitting on the only mattress. "We got to get out of here and fast. I know Shrogow said he was going to delete Clara's memory. Depending on how long this event lasts, we still got time."

"Yes I know but how? Your arms are the only thing we have. Shrogow said the marrows will clip them if you strain one hand outside the cell."

"That guard is standing by the door. We need to think of another way." Marvin gets up and walks toward the bars. He smells mold and water build up. The green bricks look worse here more than they did anywhere else. Water drips in the distance somewhere sounding its lifeless echo's. This gives Marvin the idea that the ceiling might not be secure. He goes back up to Shrub. "I wonder how big the pipes are above us."

Shrub looks up and sees nothing but concrete. "You think there is someway in getting up there?

It would have to be in the hallway. Something tells me that hardly anyone is held prisoner in this place."

"Maybe I can loosen something in the hall. If only that guard was not there." Marvin looks over his shoulder to make sure no one is listening in their conversation. The guard knows they are conspiring in on something. Of course they would, but none of it matters.

The marrow guard will see anything they do. "I don't know what we got exactly. What do you think?"

Shrub leans back, his hands go behind his head. "I don't know anymore. All we have been doing is thinking. And all this time we were looking for Lisa, she was with us the entire time. I think now's the time to rest and wait."

Resting would be the best thing to do. With rest comes refresh. Marvin's mother always tells him. But they cannot rest. Clara is going to get her mind erased. Whether she wants that or not she still helped them in two situations that were impossible to get out of. "I know Shrub. But Clara is still in the hands of the doctor."

The very name of the doctor makes it feel like the inside of Shrub's stomach twists. He feels too tired to do anything but time is always running short. Different from when they were home. "I remember." The bulb boy leans up. His hands lift and fall as if they woke and quickly went back to sleep. "What do we got?"

There's nothing that they got, which is read on the expressionless face of Marvin. "Nothing so far."

Shrub lays back down. Resting would probably be the best thing for him until Marvin can think of something. He can wake him when that happens.

CHAPTER THIRTEEN

Clara does not know how she came to live. Only that the snout face of Shrogow appeared in her sight once she opened her eyes. Never did he insult her how she was made, why would she need a new memory if that be the case. In fact he always would say she was perfect. Maybe it was the doctor's ego that made it as though he does not make any mistakes. Yet later he still needs to correct her. Suddenly, she is a mistake? Once again she is strapped in another chair. One that is much more uncomfortable with a line of pressure on the forehead. Fact is her forehead has a leather strap sinking into her partially made artificial skin, keeping the head from moving at all. She does not like this, who would? If every time she made a mistake, would that mean another readjustment? At least with Shrub and Marvin, her two new friends, they would not care if she made a mistake. So far they had not.

Two skeletons sit across looking at monitors that indicate so many places within the facility. The tools that look similar to Shrogow's lay all around, something the doctor would never do. All his stuff was organized and put in specific places. A door slides from one side and disappears into the wall. Whoever comes in is not Shrogow, but definitely someone that looks the part. He is a creature with a twisted face and nose that seems to stretch out more than it should. If the marrows had skin this is what they would look like with details of their bones showing. There is hair that is placed on top of this creature's head. And that is what it looks exactly like. A patch of black hair that was glued on top just so he can have any. Behind him is what you can call his assistant. She is also what you can call a marrow with skin, but she has no eyes. At least her nose looks more attuned with the skin. The hair is silk and combed almost too perfect. Although she does not say it, Clara wished she had hair like that. Better than the wires and whatever Shrogow stitched on top of her head.

This guy's big nose is what examines Clara more than his eyes, it seems like. He looks down at the sand hand and shows that he is impressed by completely not doing a thing. The doctor turns his attention back to examining Clara and looks at the table next to him.

"This is a Shrogow piece." The doctor says but there is no answer. His voice has a crackle like sound in his throat. "I hate it when I get his leftovers." He says very low but the crackling sound makes it louder than he actually anticipates it to be. "All she needs is a memory swipe?" He says louder and looks over at the marrows who's backs are still turned as they sit and type.

These marrows seem to always be doing something. One turns his head not all the way but answers the doctor by slowly nodding his head up and down a few times.

"Good, because I have work to do. That hand though. Not a bad idea. This is what they mentioned in the report." He looks up aiming that long nose at Clara's face once again. "Hi, I am Sharp, and I will be your doctor for this swipe. You and your little friends came from that area where they dump the no good sand at. I have not seen the video-clip but I am looking forward to how you got that hand." The long nose finally turns, to Clara's relief. "Sweetie, scoop."

The very word is one that Clara has not heard but is sure Shrogow had whatever a scoop is.

Maybe he used it when she was unconscious. Regardless she does not like the word. The eyeless assistant hands a spoon like instrument to the doctor, which has a point at the end of it.

"Now this will not hurt I am guessing. If they want me to take care of that doctor's mistakes, I want a little something more out of it. Especially if I am already busy."

How will it not hurt if Clara can feel the cold point of the scoop's tip on the top of her hand. Just because it is sand, does not mean it is not part of her. The point digs in. The head of the spoon slowly disappears as it digs into the sandy skin. If her mouth was not strapped she would scream. Her eyes widen the more the instrument goes into her hand. All the doctor does is look as if the sand is some kind of a new creature to be examined. He presses the instrument further in. He stops, now noticing that bone could be struck, or something like bone. He twists the object. There is now liquid that comes from her eyes because of the pain. Do all creations have water come down their eyes, Clara wonders for a moment. When the blurriness clears, she sees sand in the cup of the spoon which slowly crumbles and breaks. This does not surprise the doctor, for any sand creature that dies crumbles up the same way.

The doctor looks inside the newly formed wound. Now his eyes widen letting out amusement. He realizes that the sand was forming bones after all. Not normal bones but now broken sticks of sand that support the hand with the new body it hosts. Sand creatures do not have bones so this was all constructed with another living organism. "I will need to take the entire hand." The doctor looks left to right. "If I can get away with it. Maybe just a finger. If it falls apart just like the skin the risk is not worth anything. I guess I should go and visit the Sand Dumps on my own sometime."

"Ut oing on oer there?" One of the marrows asks with tongue slaps and lipless talk.

"Nothing." Dr. Sharp says in a mellow voice, leaning back a bit. Cleaning the scoop on his leg. "I'm just examining the hand since it looks damaged. The swipe will not take long. Let me look at the thing for a bit, since you pulled me away from my progress."

The marrow does not say anything for a while. He shrugs his shoulders and looks back at the monitors.

The doctor rolls his eyes and starts to adjust the strap around her forehead as if it was not tight enough. If Clara was not tied up, she would grab hold of his neck the same way she did Shrogow when her and her two friends escaped. Although she cannot do what she wants, her hand makes the false movements anyway. She looks at Dr. Sharp with angry eyes. Nothing she can do only picture the hand, he took a scoop out of, choking this creature to death. His small eyes now widen as much as Clara's do. Thick red liquid splashes on the screens behind him. The marrows flicker in surprise as if the computers suddenly exploded. How could they have exploded because they are still on with slight red splashes on them. The marrows feel wet with no sign of the smell of smoke or damage.

Sweetie's eyeless face is now dripping red liquid as if it was red wax melting, and that pretty blonde hair of hers is now drenched like a paint brush dipped in red paint. It makes it hard to see the surprise in her face. It is not hard to see the surprise on Clara's face though. Although she did not get the blood shower treatment like the rest. The sand hand feels wet like it just got poured in a bucket of water. The doctor got a treatment of his own inside his stomach, more like through it. The blood came from him, that is why he is not soaked or moving. Maybe Clara's hand did not go around his neck like she wanted, but the fist through his guts will do just fine.

The marrows see the hand which looks like a creature all on its own soaked in blood, looking around to escape out of Sharp's body. Where the fingers are is a mouth letting the blood just drip out. It twists and turns behind the doctor's back as if trying to find its way back inside. They are too surprised to do anything at the moment. At first because Sharp is most likely dead or going to be. Then because of the hand. They should of known something new on a creation might have its own ability.

The sand hand gets sucked in and there is a plop sound indicating something fell on the ground.

Dr. Sharp falls to the floor also. His hands shake too much to hold his belly, or to put his guts back inside. Maybe he can try doing it later with the scoop. Clara herself is amused by her hand. The wrist looks different because it is stretched as if it was rubber. The wrist shrinks in just like Marvin's spring arms do, but fits perfectly back into place forming the hand that it once was.

Sweetie kneels and covers her eye sockets. She does not even step closer to Sharp. She just kneels and inhales in making it seem as if she is crying, but no one can tell. One marrow grabs a bar while the other presses buttons on the dashboard. He makes sure not to turn his back in case the hand stretches out for him next. Slowly the marrow gets close to Clara. Her brows frown like a wild animal about to be caught by a catcher. Instead of reaching out, the sand hand squeezes causing the fingers to touch together and point out. The wrist squeezes its way through the strap that bounds it. The marrow

quickens before the hand is all the way through but is too late. Clara's hand is now released. She reaches bringing it toward her other wrist.

The marrow stops now seeing that the hand is out.

The hand goes to the other bound wrist and rips off the strap. The marrow runs and gets closer not realizing his speed or the blood on the floor. He kicks his feet up in the air, trips and falls hitting the back of his thick head on the ground.

Clara pulls apart the two straps that bound her forehead and mouth, then the ones around her ankles.

CHAPTER FOURTEEN

Waiting at the end of Copper Tunnel can be boring. Staring at the city makes Dod an even more anxious creature as he sits. Zeet on the other hand can stay standing for a long time and does not worry about much. How can he do it? Dod wonders. After all, he did try finding work by standing here for an entire course each day. The city never seems to die down. And of course, many creatures come in and out of the entrance. The noise on top is not as loud as it is in the bottom. Hoping their friends do show up makes the volume not matter much.

"Time to go Zeet. If I stay here another split I am going to, to..." Dod pauses trying to think of the words. "I don't know what I would do. But I feel like our friends are not going to show up anytime soon. I don't know a lot about this place but I think those marrows might have seen them. If we stand here longer, who knows. Maybe the marrows will see us and try taking us in."

Zeet looks around considering what Dod told him. The city is usually not a bad place. Living can be difficult, but that is the price if you want to check around Wide Areas. Reason why Zeet has not went around as much as he would like. "Yeye don't know. Yabe ye should stay a little bit yonger. Yhen again, you could be right. Yain concern is to know if Marvin and Shrub are alright. Been in ya room with a creation and it's creator can lead to death. Two dots have passed. Yothing has happened. Yot even your other friend has been seen. Yaybe one of us stays and ya other goes?"

"You think? This is too big of a place creat to be doing what we are doing. Who knows if two dots are too little or too much." Dod looks toward the direction where the big arena box was at.

Although now difficult to see, a large sum of speckles of creatures, in air and ground, go that way. "I am going toward the arena." In the reptile's hand is a device that is no bigger than his palm but has many buttons on it. He presses one of them. Two antennas come out from the top. Both have BB sized copper balls on the tip of them. "Alright creat, keep in touch." He aims it at Zeet who now takes one out and does the same. The antennas tap one another. There is no kind of current or sound heard, but a green light slowly dims to life on the both of them. "We may have each other's codes for these things. But this way with one touch of the first lower button, we will get in contact right away."

"Yeye knew it was ya good idea to get tellercomunicators. Why did you buy that paper gloss though?"

Bringing one hand up slowly, Dod moves his head to the side. "Don't worry about it creat. We both know after this there is a clunker to maintain. Around my exhibit there is not a lot of paper gloss sold. Now if you see a small creature that is a murner like the picture I showed you, ask her her name. Of course contact me right away. Even contact me if you get in trouble."

Zeet blinks his embedded eyes. He looks toward the city not completely sure if where Dod is going is safe. He is more concerned about him getting in trouble. "You do ya same. What is it ya say, yeate?"

"Ha, ha. creat, man." Going down the ladder like always is simple for Dod. Zeet not only hopes Dod comes back but Marvin and Shrub also. In fact he really wants to meet the murner creature, Lisa. If she is with this group of friends that Zeet wants to be part of, then that should mean she is a good creature. One worth this entire trip.

194

CHAPTER FIFTEEN

"This cell, the punishment, the boredom." Shrub sits for what seems like the hundredth time. In fact it may be.

"Would you just stay still?" Marvin looks outside the bars. The marrow guard stands in the same spot and has not moved. "I need to find something." He looks at Shrub. "That roof. If I can just reach…"

"You've been saying that the entire time. Once your arm breaks the ceiling what then? I distract the guard while you take the key? If he has the key and if he does not call any more of those marrows. I think we sit here and wait. Plus he is always watching in case you use your arms. They know about the springs, remember?"

"To get pulled apart and be part of a new creation? What about Clara? We still need to do something about her before they take her memory. And what about…"

Now Shrub cuts Marvin off. His voice rises the same way he does. "I know! All our damn friends are out there still. I mean come on, I don't think they want to kill us. It is not like we murdered anyone. All we did is steel their creation and they, they wanted to steel from us at first." The bulb boy points at the wall toward the gourd who cannot see him. As if it is only his fault. "Now we played a game and lost. It's time to take in the swampy waste storm of defeat. At least we tried." He looks toward where he was pointing and brings his hand back wondering why he even pointed. The bulb boy sits back down, the back of his large head scrapping the brick wall.

Marvin looks at him with disappointment. He knows Shrub is right and as of now with each split passing everything gets more difficult to figure out.

***

Time passes. A door opens. Marvin and Shrub both sit not saying a single word to one another. The rapid tapping teeth clatter. Already Marvin knows that another marrow came in to talk to the guard. He gets up to see what is exactly going on, even though he does not know what they are saying. The new marrow that just entered looks toward Marvin as he clatters his teeth. The marrow points at him and keeps his skeletal hand up while he looks back at the guard talking. The guard starts clacking his teeth also, at the same time. The only time any other creature would talk like this is during an argument. Yet in this situation it does not look like they are arguing. There is even a nod from the guard a few times. Something happened. Most likely something with Clara. If it is bad for them then it should be good for Marvin and his friends. The sliding door opens, but only halfway. The marrow that just entered quickly presses something on the switch board to close again. The clacking stops for a moment. Then begins again as the two struggle.

Blackness was on the other side of the door, so Marvin did not see who or what was there. The door slowly starts to open and the button on the console is working but partially for some reason. The door itself seems to be fighting with the marrows trying to open and close. The guard marrow tries closing it himself with force as the one at the console keeps pressing the button.

The black line of shadow gets wider. Like a void of suction the marrow at the controls gets vacuumed into it. The guard forgets about the door and backs up. He gets his defense bar staying on the side and walks toward the cells backwards. His teeth are chatting at a rapid speed. The door opens revealing more on what was on the other side. The shadow shows the sand hand of Clara. Her body is revealed, brown rust all over it. Then Marvin realizes that it is dried blood. She stands on top of a pile of bones looking around the hallway. She sees the guard and walks toward him.

When she gets no more than a foot away, the guard raises the bar. With the sand hand she grabs him by the wrist. Her other hand lifts in a fist ready to hammer down. When it strikes the marrow's forehead, he drops right away. There is nothing but relief on Marvin and Shrub's face.

"How did you know we were in here?" Is all Shrub can ask. "No time." She looks down at the guard, there is no key.

"The control." Marvin says quickly. There is a horn like sound that rumbles in their ears. It is not loud but by it's repetitive pulse the three know it's an emergency alarm.

Clara rushes to the controls. "I will lock the entry door."

Shrub looks up trying to see if there is another way out other than the entrance. "I don't think the way in is the best way out." The cell door opens and quickly the two leave. "Where else can we go? Do you think the ceiling is a good escape still?" He looks at his friend.

Marvin sees a security camera's lens aiming down right at them. "They will know where we went." Turning his attention toward the roof, Marvin's spring arms stretch. The metal sheet where the drops came from does not break. The hit pinches his knuckles after hitting the top. Clara shows up, grabs a bar, and starts to hit the ceiling. Marvin helps more, ignoring the pain as drops of water and crumbs of the ceilings rust and dust fall on them. The sheet removes completely. "Grab on to me." Marvin quickly says.

"Go. They are no match for me." Clara tells him with abandonment in her voice. "Take only Shrub."

"You're not staying." The springs stretch again and Marvin goes up. Stranding inside the ceiling Marvin looks down at the two. "Shrub lift her." He says not knowing how much Clara will weigh.

Shrub wraps his arms around Clara's legs not carrying if she is too heavy. He lifts as Marvin pulls. It's difficult to get her halfway inside but she does the rest. Her figure is slim, but she is a creation after all. Clara manages to pull herself up.

Marvin brings up Shrub. He stays quiet, all three do. They hear a pound as if a trash bin was been kicked. Just like a trash bin, the sound is like dents are being created. Then another slam. All three look at one another. Eyes wide open, their mouths open. All know a marrow cannot make that sound on a door that thick. They run.

CHAPTER SIXTEEN

Whatever the talk has been about, even though Dod has not been in the city to know what that talk is, it is going to happen here, in the arena. The boxed building that everything seemed to be magnetized toward is called simply Box 48. Where the other forty seven are, Dod does not know. If there are any more than forty eight, he does not know either. What he does know is that there are creations in the arena past split twenty.

The wide faced creation guarding the door that was three times Dod's size may not be fighting. Up close the skin looks like green dyed dried clay. So many details in the creation, looking at him far away played the guy no justice. It is after all the first live creation Dod has ever seen. He stood and stared at the reptilian as he paid the ticket booth five medium buttons to get in. With blades twice the size of Dod, he would think that the wide faced reptile would be one hell of an opponent in whatever the arena has to present.

Paying to attend the show is not why Dod came here though. He is certain that it is a good idea since everything seems to be catering to this one place. There has to be answers to Lisa. And wherever his other two friends are they might have landed up in here as well, for better or for worse. The back row actually works best for his investigation. In fact, he is not even going to sit down. What Dod is going to do is lean against the wall like some of the other attendees and watch from there. More like examine and see if he can spot anyone he knows. If there are any marrows around, he will definitely keep an eye on them.

The arena sure is big, for Dod's standards. How often has he been in one to begin with? Chains hang from the top of the ceiling and the inside is round with patches of the steel to create a barrier. It's big enough to fit forty of these creations. The place must be big for all the weapons also. But why, Dod wonders. Do all these creature's get enjoyment by watching creations beat one another up until death possibly? He walks around the back area to only where his ticket allows him.

One more split until the creations are going to enter the arena. Although nothing has happened on the fighting floor, the place is loud. Creatures talk to one another. Sound of buttons been placed on trays. Trays falling. Creatures falling. Dod unfamiliar with anything that has to do with creations wonders what will be shown.

Finally something happens inside the fighting floor. A copper ring comes down from the ceiling and hangs. Not sure what it will be used for but it does not look anything of the sort for creations to use for fighting. Dod is about to ask someone standing by him what the hanging rings are exactly. After each other exchanges looks and Dod sees the large eyes on a fat head that looks no different than the sloppy body that's attached, he decides not to ask the angry looking slob. Instead he looks back at the fighting grounds and the rings now hanging above.

More rings come down and still the show has not started. When a small creature, could be creation, grabs hold and steadies himself inside one of the large hoops placed in the ring, Dod realizes that this might be a pre-show. He is a small one that has ears that hang down to his shoulders. Although he has no hair or fur, the ears can be mistaken for either. His eyes are big and has a small mouth. The creature or creation waits in the ring he rocks it back and forth. Dod cannot believe that the little guy will do nothing else other than rock. The next ring is too far.

Sure enough as if attached, spokes of a carriage wheel were to take off on their own, the little guy takes flight. He makes it to the next ring.

Although not inside, his hands grab on to the bottom rim. He pulls himself up and positions himself the same way when he first started. The creature or creation, makes it all the way through. Few creatures cheer him on while most don't even pay attention. There is still rambling among the crowd. Not many care for this pre-show and this little big eared creature or creation.

Now another small guy, walks toward the first ring. This one has a rough face with skin that can look as though it is rock. The ears are long also, but not as long as the first ones. He rocks on the ring the same way the first competitor did and jumps. Dod thinks the jump is too soon. With this newcomer more heavier than the last, it does not take so long for his weight to create a swing. The rock face manages to make it through by grabbing the bottom of the ring. As he starts to pull himself up Dod realizes one thing, where is a net of some sort? Maybe a very strong creation will run in and catch these guys incase they fall.

Splat! There are ooh's and aww's from the crowd after rough face lands to his death. Then they just start talking again. Dod on the other hand did not know what he paid for exactly until now. Yes some fighting, most likely to the death.

Someone else approaches, a skinny little thing with a mean looking face. He has confidence as he approaches the ring, he even pulls it toward him. An odd looking guy who has hazel fur with lines of bare spots that indicate scares. The snout is elongated and he has smaller ears that do not reach as far past his head. Dod needs to ask what is going on. He is sure these are creatures but has no idea why anyone would want to do this. Next to him is a couple who lean against the wall showing interest in only each other. Dod does not want to disturb them, but at this point his curiosity takes the best of him.

"Excuse me." Dod says behind the males back. He turns and two wide eyed creatures with fur only surrounding their face look at Dodrill. The female's fur and skin is a bit lighter but they are obviously of the same species. "This is my first time here." Dod says looking back at the arena. The skinny guy is halfway through. He stares back at the couple. "What is this?"

The two look at the arena then back at Dod. The male takes a drink from the cup he has in hand then brings it to stomach level. "The obstacle course pre-show."

"Oh, from volunteers?"

Both of the two smile letting out a laugh. "He is." The male points with his cup and looks as the creature on display jumps the rings. "Most are captured criminals. If they make it through, that is one page of a sentence gone."

Dod wonders how many pages of sentences the first long eared creature has now after he made it. "You said except for him. How come?"

The female now speaks. "That is Levrik. He already finished enough times to complete his sentences. Now it's a passion for him to jump the rings every so often. Before the creations are going to show. He gets paid buttons and can stop whenever he wants."

Understanding and nodding his head, Dod watches as Levrik finishes. Walking down the steps to freedom that he has already earned. The female puts in more. "There are different pre-shows. This is the most common. Some are not even dangerous, like pullio."

"Pullio?" Dod says and looks confused.

The male looks at Dod. "A competitor needs to have a tail for that. One very strong creature will hold two by their tails as he or she stands on both. Basically using each one as a skate. Then they race." He laughs and so does his partner.

"Yeah, and by pulling the tail that means the creature needs to go faster." Both chuckle and look back at one another.

Dod lets out a small chuckle on the side of his mouth. Letting what the couple said sink in is more than terrifying to him, about what is going on. Blinking and shaking his head he looks back at the arena. Splat again, and more ooh's and aww's. This unfortunate creature, Dod never got to see.

The time has come for Dod to go talk and find out more about the place, but not to these two creatures. Staying inside is not going to help find his friends? He hopes they are not part of the ring jumping segment. It is a terrible thing to not know about The Wide Areas. Asking about the marrows should be a common thing since they seem to be involved for these shows. Not only do they provide the parts they also make them.

No use in waiting around. Dod pursues around the back row. He examines where the door to the fence of the fighting ground is at. Maybe in some way he can sneak in. After all this entire trip, his friends and him have slipped into unfortunate areas by accident. Perhaps he can slip inside the same way. Whatever gated doors are to go in are guarded by marrows. No way is he going to get in through there. The rings above did seem like a solution but is one that Dod does not want to try.

Most of the marrows never miss an event. There are always some around, watching. One with a gashed skull stands against the wall looking upon the crowd and all their waiting anticipation. The eyeballs move side to side like a clock pendulum. What's that, a familiar green spot that draws near.

Now the entire head of the marrow turns. That green lizard creature walks among some passing creatures. The marrow does not move his head. His jaw stays a gaped opened, but not much, trying to figure out what the green lizard is doing here. The green creature is a long way from the Marrow shop. Chopping a few times all the marrow says to himself is: "I'll be damned."

CHAPTER SEVENTEEN

uzzing in each of their ears was not a problem. It was what followed. Marvin, Shrub and Clara look as they climb up from the ceiling, hoping the direction they are going towards is good enough to get away from anyone who follows behind them. They went too many directions where they knew they would get lost. Once again, they landed up in another pipe infested waste land just like where they found Shrogow. Many are rusted pipes and larger. Going up and down the walls the pipes seem like they can run forever creating another world.

There is a wide section which is it's own compartment allowing vents on the steel ground to push out air. This is where they climb towards. Pipes stream along the side walls and go inside this hallow area. At least this ventilation area is cleaner than that of the holding cell, the two creatures think. Nothing seems to bother Clara since after the operating room, anywhere else has been a lot less stressful.

"Hey, Marvin." For once Marvin and Clara hear a laugh in Shrub's voice. "We are actually travailing outside of pipes for a change. Isn't that nuts?"

"I don't think it makes the situation any different. In fact we are in more trouble than we have been the entire time. Marrows are on us, that Dr. Shrogow wants us pulled apart. Now we got to find Zeet and Dod. Hopefully they made it to Copper."

"What about, Lisa?"

Lisa, Marvin thinks. No time to help her at the moment. Not until everyone regroups. "We will have to worry about her later. She is still alive. To find out how to bring her back, we need to get ourselves together first." They start to walk down the opening.

"Of course Marvin. I meant after that." Shrub looks down the piped formed entrance. "This place goes on forever. How does it reach so high?" Shrub says now with each word copied by an echo.

"This entire facility is one of the largest places in The Wide Areas." Clara says. She should know about The Wide Areas more than Marvin and Shrub. "The doctor said this a few times. Not that I care much. But he said I should learn the area so I'm capable of surviving on my own. When I'm not in the arena."

"And why don't you care?" Marvin asks Clara.

"What for?" She looks at him and even Shrub to see his reaction. "I'm no longer going there."

A little unease. "Hopefully things go our way." Marvin has to admit. Him and Shrub realize that even Clara, and other creations, are aware of what they are going to be used for.

"Well, than that does not make me a creation." She looks at her hand and pulls one of the wired strands of hair. "Does that mean you will have to sell me. Or even use me for another purpose?"

Shrub feels he has to show the creation that they are not like the doctor or whomever was in that place they just got out of. Too bad she asks at a time like this. Shrub does not worry about that though. He worries more about Clara. Marvin sees as his friend talks to her, and leaves it alone for now. "No, Clara. You do not have to worry about that with us." Shrub says.

"I also killed a doctor. One who cut my hand." She says as if trying to figure out how to build a machine with instructions. "My fist ripped through his stomach and spilled blood everywhere."

Now shrub realizes that she has killed. That is if the marrows she helped with are still alive.

Marvin has to speak up now. "Clara. Can we talk about this later."

"Was Sharp not that important?" Marvin finds out the name but ignores this Sharp for now."

He tries his best to not tantalize what happened. "When you have to, anyone has to take matters into their own hands." No experience with kids but Marvin feels like he is talking to one. "Somone was going to take your memory. Good thing they didn't."

"But what if I did that to one of you by mistake. My hand stretched and I don't know how." Now Shrub looks at Marvin with a sour face. He taps his hand on her back. "There, no problem. That hand saved you. Thank you for telling us. Maybe we need to talk about this Marv." Shrub says just to comfort Clara.

Frustrated, Marvin looks at the two. Shrub is concerned while Clara is accepting the bulb head's comfort. "You two talk while we go on. There's little time."

Shrub rubs the creations back. More than he has to. "Look, you feel more than even other creatures. There is no need to be concerned about anything."

Clara listens to Shrub. She smiles. Marvin lets out a breadth and lets them do their thing. He continues on like he said. "We must go."

Clara leans up wiping the dust off around her. Shrub helps her even though he feels like she is fine. "Let's go. Dod and Zeet need to know about Lisa's situation as soon as possible."

CHAPTER EIGHTEEN

ack and spine tingle, Dod gets jabbed. None of the other creatures had this treatment, and they were criminals. In all honesty, the ring that he saw so far away, looks awfully closer than he thought. The poke presses again forcing him forward. Dodrill is not afraid but still does not want to put on a show for these marrows who have been giving him and his friends so much trouble their entire time here in The Wide Areas.

"Watch where you put that thing creat. Maybe we can stick it in you so you can realize how it feels." Another poke and the marrow doing the jabs has the same expression as they all do with those emotionless eyes. Zeet almost looks the same, mostly. At least he has a personality, and a strange accent of some kind to go with it. "Alright I will go. Just remember our deal. You leave me and my friends alone after this."

The rapid tapping of the teeth chatter. A creature next to the marrow's looks at Dod. He must work with them. This creature is a gray blob of a thing with small eyes. Similar to Bazook back home. "He said there was never a deal." The fat creature tells him.

Dod looks at the creature knowing there is no way out. "Yeah, I can hardly understand them also." He turns around and prepares for the jump. Dod wonders why he didn't hesitate too much to get up here. Because he knew he can clear this course with no problem perhaps.

And he thought there was a reasoning with marrows but apparently, they forgot about that. All it did is bring him to another problem. Everything him and his friends have been doing is like one huge obstacle course anyway. Just this time it deals with death looking him in the face. Ready to take the creature with any miss step. He swallows and realizes standing in front of this course. Standing on this high tower is a lot more difficult than running from threats.

His reptilian legs stretch. Tail sticks out like an arrow as he flies through the air. A perfect landing inside. The crowd does not seem interested. Yet some do. Maybe they are the ones that saw him as he was down below. That couple must be part of them or perhaps the alcohol is kicking into some of the audience. He pushes forward and back, feeling the air brush against his face and body. This is no problem, it's like on a swing, Dod thinks. Jumps again. Still no problem. Now the next ring looks further away. The jump should not be a problem, but something tells him that the marrows want the ring to be.

This time Dod makes sure to swing a little higher. Not too high, or else he will dive up and dip down. When he lands on the next ring he grabs hold of the top. No cheating in front of so many witnesses. Maybe the marrows cannot do anything out of ordinary. At least that is what Dod thinks. The next ring is a bit further but he knows he can clear it. When he jumps the ring moves up. His hand grasps the bottom. He knew they would pull a trick like that. Or perhaps they were doing this all along.

Dod should have paid more attention. He pulls himself up. There are two rings left. Now that he is in the middle, it's as intense as a high level course he has no skills in. Like the ones he would do in school. His mother always forced him to do his homework. And he did. One problem a day no matter how long the assignment took.

This next leap from Dod is higher than the rest in case anything else funny happens. The ring stays in place. What else are they going to do, lower the thing? If so, Dod would just grasp the rope. He looks down for the first time. The plane of the arena looks more terrifying than anything he has seen during the entire trip. There are two smothered dots. Oh yeah, the two criminals that fell got a proper sweep.

For this next jump, Dod goes his highest. Of course the damn thing would rise and now that Dod knows what is up these marrows sleeves, or skeleton arm he would say, most likely the ring would rise higher than where the rest are placed. This time he made sure to swing high enough for him to aim to as high as he could. His speed is all the same but he opens and brings his arms down. As the ring

gets higher, Dod starts to dip down keeping his legs aiming in the air. Once again looking at the arena's floor his face stares downward, this time in the air. Whoever is watching thinks he is going to do a flip, as if to actually make it to the other side without trying to grab on the ring. It has been done before, but not many times. Dod does not attempt this. His back now facing the direction he is going toward and his arms are still spread as if flying backwards. He looks up. Between his legs is his tail that has stayed straight the entire time. Once it touches the ring, it wraps as if it had a mind of its own. Dod knew his tail had a longer reach than his arms. All he had to do is jump his highest, and he did.

With the ring swinging Dod thrusts himself forward. The landing is no problem, but he nearly falls to his knees as he touches the ground on this other tower. He can fall on his head and not care. The reptile just cleared a death run like a professional. At least to him he thinks so. It seems there are a few more claps that are heard. Maybe because they thought he was a volunteer since he was hanging around the crowd. Some other creatures saw him get dragged away by the marrows. Not sure but maybe they have something to do with the clapping feeling bad for when the reptile was dragged away.

He climbs down the ladder only at first to see Levrik, the legend of this game supposedly. The skinny creature looks at Dod for a while then begins talking to a few other creatures. If this Levrik guy has a problem, Dod really does not care. He is tired and has been through too much. Beside Levrik, the area quickly changed into a social hangout. There is even a bar. Some creatures stand on a stage next to it. Dod is not completely sure what they are doing. A hairless peach skinned creature that can be considered a rat flares up. He drinks from a bottle. With each drink the hairless rat becomes a fat ball of skin. Once the bottle comes out of his mouth, the creature coughs and all the water comes out making him a skinny stick. Cups and other objects fly at him with a load of bo's, some creatures laugh as an object hits the hairless creature.

This is all insignificant to Dod. He did not come to Box 48 for entertainment. Even though that is what it is used for. He sees marrow guards blocking all around the small area. It is still a matter of time until one approaches him. He is no criminal but is no normal citizen either to these creatures. Sure enough, Dod can see the one with a gash walking toward him, four guards follow.

"Can I enjoy this place for a bit?" Dod asks pretending.

Another creature approaches from the side. A tall bird like with purple feathers around his eyes but the rest are all white. The gashed marrow taps his teeth. The bird creature answers. "He wants to know where the skull is. Then we can let you leave and do whatever you please."

"I don't know." Dod says now getting angry. "I took off on my own and have no idea where anyone or anything is at." His brows narrow looking at the bird, giving him all his frustration.

The bird looks down upon him with his large thick beak. "Your friends, you do not know where any of them are at? That skeleton that was seen with you after you left Shrogow's, where is he?"

"I told you I don't know!" Dod's voice rises and he looks at all five of the marrows. "Are you going to let me go or what. I passed your damn course, now get me out of here. Give me my bag also." Realizing that his friends are still not caught, he feels as though he just completely wasted time here.

All the marrows look at each other and do their teeth tapping. After seeing what the marrows have to say, the bird looks down at Dod again. "They want you to stay. You can have your things but cannot leave the Hern."

"What the hell is that? This place is called the Hern?" Dod asks.

The bird clears his throat. "Yes, this place. From this point we will figure out what to do with you." One of the marrow guards gives Dod his bag. They all walk away except for the one with the gap on his head. "How did you get that again. Was it when the skull hit you or where you the one that fell?" Dod asks. He takes out a shockla knowing that there is hardly any left. After what he has been through, the reptile does not care. "I wouldn't know. You all look the same."

The shake gets thrown up in the air and there is an impact under Dod's jaw. He sees a flash for a second and lands on the ground. The marrow bites once and walks away after hitting the reptile. Dod rubs his jaw looking at the spilled drink, more disappointed that the shake was wasted more than anything. "What a waist." Is all he can say. If not in their territory he would find away for payback.

He remembers the com that Zeet and him are using for communication. Not getting his hopes up, Dod is sure the marrows have it now. Oh no, he thinks, what if they use it to find Zeet. Still he checks as he sits on the dirt. The tellercommunicator is not where it was placed. Does not mean that the marrows put it in another spot. He scrambles around inside his bag some more. There, in the bottom of where some of the shocklas are. He still has it. He still can call. Too risky still. If he calls they might find out where it's going to. Or question him who he is calling. The marrows do not remember what pocket the com was in.

He does not care if anyone is looking. Dod smashes the com on the ground. It is solid still so he bashes it again. Finally the com loosens in his hand. Then he feels a pinch on the third smashing, now he knows it has broke. He opens the casing. A small world of wires, a yellow sheet with many lines and metal dots present themselves. All the electronics twine around each other it is hard to follow where any connect to. Of course none of the parts can move. A small wire does squirm like a small worm though. It is a worm and it has eyes? Not eyes two shaded dots that are supposed to be glasses. Other than that the creature is naked but is hard to see what kind of sex it is. Many lines that are its' legs move. The top four are thicker and actually have fingers, each with three and has gloves on. The worm shakes its head rapidly. It looks funny with those goggles on. Hard to notice but one hand does have a device of some kind. Probably to listen and send back conversations.

"What kind of create is this?" Dod asks himself. Could even be some kind of miniature creation. He tosses the com, knowing that it is broken and bugged. He shakes his head knowing that his brand new device is infected. Now not knowing what to do he looks around the place. He has nothing to do with this area called the Hern. The marrows did leave all the buttons inside the bag. Maybe he will buy a drink and think.

One thing that he does notice that's missing is their telescope. At one point it was not working but now the Marrows have it. "Damn." Is all the reptilian can say.

CHAPTER NINETEEN

Flimsy aluminum bends and pops with almost each step. This floor is very thin. Earlier, Marvin pointed out that there should be rooms under. If the walk continues any further, they best break through and take their chances. Several vents presume throughout the area. Every time the group looks inside, each seems to be meant for scrap metal, which would make a bad fall. Other vents are dark rooms that seem like a storage. Locked in one of those rooms would doubtfully help them in anyway. Other vents are hard to see through. The group figures they are there for air to come in and out of. So far all they have felt are small bursts of a breeze which smell like rotten vegetables decaying inside rusty pipes.

"I think it's time to go inside one of these vents. You know, the ones we cannot see through. Maybe those are actual rooms." Shrub walks up to one. There is no point in trying to see through the vent, but he tries pulling it up with little effort. A chill passes and the three can feel air on their skin, but the air is not from the vent.

Marvin walks closer and puts one hand under his nose so he does not have to bare the smell of what the breeze brings. He gets on his stomach. Closing one eye as he tries to peek in. Still it is hard to tell what's inside. "Maybe if you open it a bit more."

"I can't. The vent is on tight." Shrub says as he struggles with the vent.

"Let me give it a try. I can take that right off." Clara says now putting her hand on the vent. As Clara attempts to pull the vent.

Shrub goes to another incase she cannot take this one off. He attempts the same thing and still the vent is in there good. "This one won't even budge."

Marvin goes toward where Shrub is and realizes that his friend is right. Shrub, once again, goes to another vent and tries the same thing. Still, he cannot move it. He finds himself closing his nose realizing the breeze once again. He tries pulling another vent, causing him to go deeper into the area. Once again the vent barley moves out of place. The rotting stench is present, but no longer the breeze. Shrub ignores it and looks toward Marvin and Clara. "Guys, these things are not moving. Guys?" From moving from one vent to another, Shrub did not notice how far he went. The silver chrome floor with poles and pipes fades into shadow in the distance. All he has to do is go back since the area is one giant room. The entire place is just one huge maintenance walkway of some sort. Then again the bulb boy smells the stench of rot. He does not think of it too much, but there is not a breeze anymore. Who would use such a horrid smell just to keep cool. The marrows maybe? Damn things are nothing but bone, they cannot even tell a good thing from a bad thing, even when it comes to competences. No taste, I tell you no taste. Shrub finds himself, thinking to himself.

"Nasty." As Shrub starts to make his way back to his friends there is a deep sound as if water was going into a drain, but yet with the lid on. What kind of pipe can make a sound like that he wonders. The sound happens again. This time the pipe sounds more gurgled, more organic. Then he smells that smell again. Shrub turns around realizing that he never looked up. It's not a wall he sees, more like a giant stretched bag with yellow intense eyes bigger than Shrub. There are multiple welts on the dark green leathery face. No nose for the nostrils which are open and clearly seen. Folded wrinkles are on the sides touching the walls, ceiling and floor which the pipes and poles piece into. When the creature opens it's mouth the teeth are not carnivorous nor are they supporting molars. More like teeth on teeth. There are multiple struts that most likely fit in place when the thing closes its mouth.

The eyes get even more intense. The yellow is seen more and the mouth widens.

"Guys, hold on to something! Anything, fast!" Shrub yells as loud as he can just so his voice can be heard. He is not completely sure what the wall-thing is going to do. But whatever it is, it's not going to be pretty. Shrub drops and holds onto a curved handle of some sort. Again, the short temporary breeze is felt, but hot, very hot. Also very discussing like heat in a concealed plastic bag. Shrub who has not eaten a thing for the past five splits throws up. He has to lie on the floor.

Shrub thinks about getting up. He feels like it's best not to. Although there was no breeze this time, this wall-thing is the cause of the breezy air. Maybe the wall-thing did not blow but inhaled instead. "Shrub!" He hears Marvin in the distance. "What's going on!"

"Stay down!" Is all Shrub can think of saying until he figures out what the wall-thing is going to do. The eyes widen as if Shrub's yelling made the thing upset. The wideness causes the stench again and Shrub makes sure to hold his breadth. He flips, his legs hit the floor. It hurts but he makes sure to stay holding on. The wall-thing inhales, probably as best it can. Shrub would take his chances with anything else as long as he does not go inside the wall flesh and bad breadth. Once again, his legs hit the floor.

Marvin and Clara can feel air rush through their face as they hold on to the ground. It is not strong enough for them to grip tighter but they know it can cause trouble from where Shrub is at.

After the blowing of air, Clara leans up crawling a bit looking for Shrub. "Shrub. Are you alright! I am coming for you!"

"No! Stay where you are. It will only make things worse! Trust me!" Shrub holds on as best he can. The impact almost feels like it's too much for him to handle. He holds on still. Not knowing if he would rather get swallowed perhaps eaten. He holds on wanting to take his chances to be blown away. Then there is the tickle. He has shoes on but the squirm under his small feet is a bit overwhelming. That tongue is not green like the skin but red flesh that matches around the inside of the mouth. Beyond that is an abyss of shadowy blackness. The eyes frown in anger from the wall-thing, desperately trying to loosen Shrub's grip. The tongue goes on his heel and soon it will be on his back ready to pull him in.

Shrub is about to climb but knows one loose grip will cause him to lose all control. This is the end for him he thinks. He sort of knew it would happen eventually. Small bulb boy in the middle of pipe nowhere, what are the chances. Marvin's hand wraps around his wrist and he knows it's Marvin. The spring arms are not expanded too much for a stronger pull. Clara crawls her way up to the tongue misplacing her hand from the ground and onto the flesh of the thing.

The slimy red tongue whips in the air, coming down toward Clara's back. It is about to fall on her but she moves out of the way. The pound is a splash like a wet towel. "Lets go." Clara sees as Shrub gets pulled. The air dies down and this is their chance to run as fast as they can.

Since the wall-thing inhaled already it's time for it to exhale. The once rotten breezy air that touched their face is like ten pounds of blankets hitting their backs. The blow takes all of them off their feet.

They see where they once stood and lift higher from the aluminum floor. None can reach the ceiling except for Marvin. When his spring arms grab hold he presents each of his feet to each friend. Both hang on to Marvin, the pull is dreadful. He tries to bring in his legs as best he could. Having the two hold on is not too much of a problem when both reach the ceiling. Once they have a grip they let go of the legs.

Marvin brings in his legs, holding on desperately. The wind becomes intense. It stops and the three drop to the floor. Without anyone saying a word, they run. They make it almost all the way to the edge and find themselves running in the air. They get to the end quicker but go past it, finding themselves free falling the same way they climbed in through. Marvin is about to spring out his limbs again but finds out he does not have to. The three fall toward the wall of pipes. They are going to hit the clutter but the closer they get to it they feel as though they shrunk. They feel like small ants falling toward a refrigerator that is as plain as the red and green pipes in front of them. The pips do get bigger the closer they get. They realize that the pipes were a lot taller than they expected. Then they go through the gap of two pipes. The area is a giant space and the pipes on their sides are more like huge walls, one been green the other red.

At first it's as though they can grasp the pipes that make up the inside of the gap they now fall through. A new squared pathway of pipes is now created. So many pipes with bolts and poles surround them, they are not even sure which to focus on. Falling through an endless pit which leads them through the world of pipes. The three realize that no matter where they grip or where they land up, they will always be lost.

Time passes as much as the pipes do. Now noticing the bottom of the pipes is not a matter of griping something but a matter of doom. Marvin springs out like a web. Shrub grabs hold of one leg as Clara falls on his back. Marvin stretches like a trampoline would if a child be on it. His stomach goes down them propels up. Not that it launches Clara but she nearly falls off. Holding on Marvin tries not loose grip. "Guys... get off."

Clara is the first to reach the wall. She has no choice but to push down on Marvin to get to the pipes. She reaches. Marvin's body heightens and evens out, except for his leg where Shrub is holding that sinks like a line of string with a weight in the middle. Shrub works his way through the spring and gets on the other side across from Clara. Marvin brings in his legs first then his arms compact. He holds on to the wall of pipes, between the two.

Looking down and all around the piped tunnel, Shrub feels sweat trickle. "Great. We are beyond lost. How will we ever find a way to get back to The Wide Areas or any place in that matter?"

"There is nothing to worry about. One of these pipes lead to somewhere." Marvin looks at the surrounding area. "Now how do we open one of these things?"

Shrub shakes his head as if all is pointless beyond consideration. Clara looks at Marvin. "Let's get down first."

"Sounds like that is all we can do." Says Marin as they make their way down.

Standing on the floor of pipes the three still unsure where to go. Maybe with a climb to the top they will see another path. They are lost anyway and it seems as though any other path would be as good a path as any.

"There is nothing down here." Shrub says.

Clara grabs onto a pipe and pulls as if breaking one will help in some way. "It's hard to move. How about I try another." Clara does the same thing to another pipe. Nothing happens. She is sure if she keeps trying eventually one should break.

"Don't bother." Marvin says. "We should go back to the top." He sits down with a puff. "This is too much." Marvin worried and confused.

"That is ridiculous. One of these pipes should lead to another exhibit." Shrub announces as he tries to spot out the widest pipe. "Let's keep trying to break one and find our way to an exhibit."

"That is what I am trying to do." Clara says.

"We might starve in here or starve running all over the place."

"If you never went toward that wall, then we would have went through one of those vents." Clara tells Shrub not sure what to do.

Marvin indicates the two to quiet down.

"I hear something also." Shrub says knowing what caught his friends attention.

Clara looks at the ground. "There must be something around here making a noise." Behind Marvin's feet there is a hollow spot that is only shaded in shadow. Clara crawls toward it to get a better look. Marvin steps to the side and crawls as well. There's an opening. Voices are heard deeper inside.

"Sounds like creatures live down there." Marvin says. He starts to move forward.

"Marvin," Clara looking unsure by seen so many pipes. Down the path she feels a pinch of claustrophobia. "Are you sure it is safe? We are three and that path can lead to anything." "There is no choice. Whatever is down there might know someway out."

"Or maybe they are trapped in here." Shrub says.

"Fine. I will go and you two stay." Marvin keeps crawling forward.

Clara looks over her shoulder at Shrub who looks inside the path. He looks at Clara concerned.

Not knowing if it is curiosity or a sense to stay close to their friend, both follow.

***

There are the many pipes that make up the pathway. As the three go deeper in, the voices get clearer. Muffling through the pipes are felt but no one is seen. The end of the path is easy to notice. Although what is on the other side is gray like a concrete wall the path finally comes to an end. When Marvin reaches the end he sees a large wooden box, like a podium, on wheels been pushed by two headless creatures. The two creatures seem to have no necks, gray skin that is darker than the wall, and many veins run through their entire body. Fingernails are long and pointy the same way random shards of broken glass would be. Marvin ducks and looks at his friends. Both stare in suspicion.

When the pushing stops the two creatures bring their arms down to reveal their faces. They have odd pointy flat long noses. Their mouth seems to be inside their neck-less torso. The eyes are red as blood drops. They look around as if to make sure no one is looking at them, then separate. Similar to a jack in the box, but one which moves very slow, a head comes out from the top of the podium. The creature is as though their closed eyes cannot open. The lids are shut and stay that way. Why, because of the stitches that keep the lids together. The mouth looks as though its functions are opposite of the eyes. Not because the lips are shut. In fact, those stay opened at all times. The long teeth are half the size of the head of the creature. They are so big, the teeth stay in place.

As if an audience is near, the teeth creature looks to the sides and to the floor where Marvin is.

No matter how much Marvin lowers himself, it's a matter of time until these creatures see him. The tooth creature taps his fingers on the podium as if waiting for something to say. Marvin looks over his shoulder. Both Shrub and Clara stay in the same crawling position they were before. Marvin widens his eyes indicating them to lower themselves also. He is amazed that none have been seen yet. The two stay so still it's as though they do not even breathe. Clara being closer, Marvin moves his foot to tap her hand. Solid is the hand. He taps again but when he does Marvin realizes his foot does not even touch her hand. It's as though there is an invisible wall of some kind.

Leaning up in contentment Marvin pushes onto where he sees Clara and Shrub. The two stay imprinted. They are images in a wall that was just now created. Somehow a window formed with their figures imprinted inside. Marvin turns around and looks to the podium. Teeth creature stands behind the podium, still. The two gray servants stand on each side of him. All look at Marvin not moving, just like the image of his two friends.

He runs up to the window where his friends are images. There is a loud tong noise, then he falls to the ground feeling pressure on his head. Marvin walks up toward the podium and hits his head making another tong sound feeling more pain this time. He wonders how he just suddenly appeared there. The side walls are still the piped pathway, how did the glass suddenly get created?

Without thinking the spring kid runs toward where the podium area is and feels another kind of pain in his right shoulder. Glass shatters as he falls.

Now there is nowhere for him to land, nowhere for him to spread his springs out and reach for something to grab on to. No matter what he does he cannot land. Now he has lost his friends forever. It has to be one long bad dream. How did he get lost, again! What trick was it this time that separated him from Shrub and Clara? Instead of them finding Dod and Zeet, each has lost each other.

Marvin falls to a black nothingness. Once he realizes the tooth creature looks at him. He cannot tell whether the creature is smiling or not. He steps from behind the podium and looks down at Marvin.

"You came from The Wide Areas." Now that the creature talks Marvin sees the needle like teeth move up and down. He looks at the face of this strange creature. The skin is like flesh and has a dog-like look. Ears are long and point up.

"Who are you?" is all Marvin can ask.

The dog laughs. "You never know what you run into in these pipes." The dog smiles looking sinister.

The spring kid does not know what to say. He stares at the two fat guards that stand still. "What do you want with me. Why is it all black?"

"I don't want nothing with you. Maybe you want something from me?" The room is cold. "What can you offer?"

The dog creature takes out a small squared mirror. He shows it to Marvin. Even though the re- flection is not of Marvin but that of the room they were just in. "Take it and see what you can do with the mirror.

Marvin turns it and already they are back where they were. He's unsure what just happened.

"We have been able to see some of the creatures around this area. Did not know you were one that would land up here but you are. Someone told us about you."

Still this leaves Marvin confused. He starts to see a glow behind the doglike creature. Then it's a familiar face. When Lisa appears it's not the same Lisa that he saw before but one that is of her spirit. "We've been waiting for you Marvin." When she floats down she makes sure to let him know about the skull. "The Laughing Dog and his friends went looking for the skull. He has it now."

"What, he has your skull?" Marvin asks.

"Yes. And once he gives it to you he will ask you questions that not even I know what they are.

Time is short. I see that Shrub and the creation you were with are gone."

Marvin looks over his shoulder but there is just blackness. He looks back at Lisa. "What hap- pened to them?"

"The marrows took them. They are going to be part of the arena. I will follow them. You have to talk to the dog. Then we will see each other again." Just like that. Lisa floats away. Leaving Marvin with these three, creatures.

"Your friend really trusts you with this skull." The Laughing Dog takes the piece out. He looks at it through the sockets then stares at Marvin. I can give you this and take you to where you need to find your friends."

"I need to help them. Can you help me get them back?"

"No, but I can take you to them."

"Then take me to them." Marvin almost yells. The Laughing Dog who doesn't laugh but smiles all the time stares at him.

"Take the skull." He hands it to Marvin. "You will need this too." It's a flute. Looks like bone but also sand. "The spirit helped us create the instrument. It's what's left of the throat of one of the sand creatures we had to kill to get the skull back." Marvin looks at the flute with a sour face. "To transport you I will have to give you a mirror. Go ahead and use it at any time." The dog looks at Marvin still. "With that I will need something in exchange."

"What?" Is all Marvin can say.

"Your soul."

CHAPTER TWENTY

There is nothing to do but to watch. The Hern has a great spot for all the prisoners to watch the show. Sitting around worrying about his friends is not something Dod had in mind and walking around asking questions has got him nowhere so far. Are they going to keep him here forever? Never was his question answered to when he was going to be set free. Now is the time when the crowd slowly begins to get silent. Lights go out and the ones that stay on only light the fighting ground.

"Let's get the arena to a start." A voice says as a flat nosed creature with a microphone walks out. Dod can hear everyone around him talk.

"It's Porkish."

"Yes, Porkish is here." Some prisoners laugh.

The small fat creature dresses very odd. The fat creatures cloths are miscellaneous colors. "In case you are wondering why I am here and what would bring me to this occasion. There is a creature that has been misplaced." He looks to the crowd with a smile and brings the microphone closer to his face. "But apparently, she appeared. Literally! Out of nowhere." As if what the announcer said was so funny, the crowd laughs. Dod thinks it's because of the announcers talking has some kind of humor. All Dod sees a creature with a mic, and lots of cloths. Either way, Dod finds the fat creature's humor dry.

"This creation will not be the first on display. But later on, she will be here like we advertised before. After all, we did take her off and put her back on again."

The crowd cheers in excitement. Dod cannot help but wonder why. By the looks of it, to him all the creations seem to just be here to beat one another up.

"One thing has changed. The match will be, let's see. How about the creation has a creature on her back? Yes, now she needs to not only protect herself, but someone else!"

The crowd cheers in excitement once again. Porkish finishes his spew on what will be going on for the rest of the night. Dod is more curious in why this all seems so important. He looks at a furred creature who has hardly any teeth and is scared up. If an animal was to decompose, dry up and still have it's eyes, this creature is what it would look like. "What's the big deal for tonight creat?"

The creature looks down at Dod, knowing he is new. Dod now realizes he should of asked someone else instead of the prisoner standing close to him. "Everyone likes to see new creations in the arena."

Dod's face turns into a frown. What is that announcer talking about? Dod wonders and if it's something to worry about? He walks past prisoners who are all distracted by the stage. Suddenly they all yell, and cheer. Dod is not interested in the crowd or how loud they became. Then in the crowd beyond the fence of the Hern, he sees a face that is no marrow but is a skeleton. Dod knows the skeleton saw him as well. "Zeet, creat." Dod smiles as he says the words but also wishes that he did not come. He runs up toward the cage. A large guard walks up to him and sticks his hand out. This is no marrow but a gray furred creature that fits the job he is doing perfectly with a build like that.

"What are you doing?" The tall fur creature asks. His eyes narrow on Dod.

"Can I talk to someone across the fence? Heck, you can even watch me." Dod says the guard stands with a stern look. He brings his arm down letting him go. "I am glad they don't have only marrows guarding this place. Or else I would have never known what you said."

"Do you want me to throw your ass across the floor?" The guard asks.

"Hey I am just giving a compliment." When Dod reaches the fence, Zeet is already there. "So what gives, Zeet? Why did you come here?"

"Your com yost signal. Knew it broke. How did you yet in here?"

"They found me, create. Had me jump all kinds of hoops and everything. It's not safe for any of us."

"I know that." Zeet looks at the arena. "Yas long as you do not land up yin there. You should be fine."

"Yeah, no kidding." Dod did not realize as the creations walked in the arena but there are now two. One is green with a broad body. His eyes have leather patches on each with wires in the middle to see through. As tall as the creation is, that is not what frightens Dod the most. His hand is a large piece of machinery. A buzz saw spins rapidly on it. Both Dod and Zeet are intimidated, even standing on the other side of the arena where none of the creations can see them.

Coming from the side where most of the crowed is blocking the view of the two friends, a more sleek prickled blue body appears. There are many small thorns that are naturally attached to it, but needles and sharp spikes are also part of the thorned body. This one has a more reptilian face but is wide with sharp yellow eyes. There are tubes going through the body. Claws are long and sharp. Many fingers are different sizes and colors indicating the many parts attached to him. Unlike the other creation that has pants and boots on. This one has only a sash to show the long feet with sharp toenails.

Both study one another. The saw-hand creation swings the blade toward the reptilian. The blue reptilian moves and slashes at the chest of his opponent. The claws connect and cut the chest of the saw hand opponent. The crowd goes wild at the brutish attack. The creation moves back but ignores anything that happened. His blade spins faster. He charges at the reptilian who quickly moves to the side. All the tubes and such turn to a dark yellow to an even darker rusty yellow color as fluid bubbles and pushes through.

The throat of the reptile puffs up. Then compacts as the cheeks inflate. When the cheeks flatten, yellow fluid streams out of the mouth. It reminds Dod of hot soup that comes out of a pan. It also steams and is sure to do damage.

The fluid does damage as the buzz-hand creation moves to the side but not fast enough. The tip of his boot gets eaten away. He shakes it for a moment and then he lets out a small yell. When the louder yell accrues everyone knows the lethal liquid burns his toes.

There is a smile on the reptile and he drops to his hands. He runs at the buzz-hand and jumps. Without hesitation the creature with the buzz-hand stops whimpering. He smiles actually as he opens his arms, indicating all the hurt he was feeling was an act. The reptile hits the buzz-hand away with his foot but the normal arm of his opponent wraps around him. It's a strong arm. At this point everyone thinks the reptile is meeting his doom as the buzz saw gets closer to his face. If it was not for the reptile's long legs he would not be able to hit away the buzz saw arm of the creation.

The reptile's shoulders intense. The skinny bone pushes the skin showing that his arm muscles have no power to do anything at this point. His shoulder blades push up the skin also, and then break the skin. When the bone is seen Dod, Zeet and some of the crowd look confused of the shoulder blades as they rip through the skin, now revealing two actual blades on the back of the reptilian. Now he smiles again. Even his reptilian tongue licks his upper lip as he simply relaxes. The closer the buzz- hand gets, the more it pushes the legs and body of the reptile to the face of the buzz-hand creation.

Confused the buzz creation has no choice but to actually stay in the position he is in. If he drops the reptile, all the spikes and thorns will run deep into his body starting with the metal shoulder blades. Holding the buzz up will also get him tired so he moves it away. He tries bringing it down above the reptile's head but now the reptile is squirming bringing his shoulder blades into the opponents chest.

Buzz-hand has no choice so he brings the saw down some more. The reptile drops. There are two deep cuts on each side of the buzz-hand's chest. The spikes and needles do multiple scratches as well but none as bad as the shoulder-blades.

Bleeding profusely the buzz-hand swings. The reptile attacks the buzz-hand getting him weaker by the moment. Finally, another jump. The reptile is on top of buzz-hand. Working his claws and nails, he brings the creation down. Soon the face is getting torn apart. Then, no more buzz-hand.

Zeet looking at the scene, surprised never expecting to see a death, cannot move. Dod, not so surprised because of the obstacle course, just watches and sees how violent these creations can be.

Then he hears Porkish's voice.

"And there here, Larka Lava, doing his usual feast instead of glory pose at the end of the match. You can stop now Larka, we all love you." The crowd continues cheering. Some pounding on the rails wanting to see more. A group of creatures walk toward the body. They grab the feet of buzz-hand, hesitant, but they pull it away. Larka looks at the dead carcass licking and wiping his lips with his arm. He looks at the crowd and shakes his head with his mouth wide open. They all yell. "Termoil, a good opponent!" Porkish announces revealing the dead opponent's name as he gets dragged away.

"Yut should ye do? These yare all dangerous folks!"

"Time for you to move out of the way." The voice of the guard says. "I forgot you were here.

Come on move."

Dod steps back. "Keep close. Let me know if you find the others."

***

Dod gives up and sits on a bench area tucked away from the crowd, only a few criminals are around. Maybe after this event is over, he will be able to figure some way of getting to Zeet. At least he still has some shockla's. He takes one huge drink tasting blueberries with citrus and for a moment everything is normal. He looks around and sees all the criminals. Some gather to watch the event while others simply have no interest in what is going on. Dod takes another drink and looks at the arena. The next match is the one announced in the beginning with that new creation. The door opens where the dead body of Termoil was taken out of.

Without further thought, Dod knows who enters the arena. That one creation that was in the doctor's chair. Shrogow, and he was making that creation. Now why this creation is to be such a big deal is unsure. It was said by the announcer that she was gone and suddenly appeared again. Why would she be here? On her back is a round pearl white ball. One that Dod knows too well. "Shrub?" He says and realizes that this is what the sudden round is about. Shrub needs to be on the creations shoulders. Not sure how this will work but it sound like this has been done before. The real question is, who are they up against?

From a caged door what appears is a creation that is meant to kill this female. She is a tall one, that has black around the head and an odd white round face. Her teeth are large and eyes are too. The creature hunches forward with her two arms lazily hanging. Looks something amphibian like, yet the neck has no gills. Both arms have blades instead of hands that are used to hold her up at times. The creature that rides the back is one of the marrows. Not the one with the gash but one none the less. He looks out of place from the creation he's attached to. The marrow been there must have something to with the sudden change with the match. It can also do with just getting rid of Shrub and the creation. Shrub will be an easy victim at this rate. The bulb boy has no experience in any kind of fighting. That must have been the entire reason the match was changed.

Hands shaking, holding onto Clara's wired hair, Shrub manages to let words out. "Are you okay?"

"Am I okay? No, of course not! But probably more okay than you." She tells Shrub looking at her opponent who stands far away ready to kill. Shrub has a needle in one hand. The riders have a weapon of choice. Other than an axe, or some kind of shield, all the bulb boy can carry is a giant sowing needle. It's not even meant to kill. He looks at the marrows weapon which is a broad sword which has sharp bladed teeth on the back of it like a saw. "Just do not do anything. I will get us out of this mess. If you try piercing him in anyway get his eyes."

"Oh, of course." Shrub looks at the marrows weapon and swallows.

Above the crowd from the top rails most of the marrows stand and watch. Shrogow stands with them looking down at all that he has made and looks at this round as no more than a waste. "Once the both of them are dead we will be rid of these ridiculous children." He knows the female creation is not yet to her full potential.

The marrow with the gash on his head clacks his teeth at the doctor.

"No. At this point I do not feel like erasing her memory. Thinking about that creature will be a problem for her. Sharp was the only one who could do that properly anyway. I don't see any use in messing with her. Might as well make a profit with the both of them and move on. I have too many other things to do than worry about a corrupted creation." The marrow clacks his teeth some more.

"The reptile? We will keep him prisoner and maybe he will see where his other friend is if necessary. At this point, if he is looking for these two, there is no doubt he will see them." Shrogow looks at the marrow. "You will have one hell of a show with whatever creation I make with those bones. Murners are rare and can hold a kind of life in them that keeps the remains functional for short or long periods of time. I would love to see if there is a natural healing ability that can be used by attaching certain parts and machinery. Imagine having the mechanical aspects of a creation naturally functional." Shrogow looks down at the arena. "Then we can take on anyone's creation. We will be the first to create such a thing and will remain the best in all the city and around Wide Areas."

Clara fall's tasting the dry dirt get wet in her mouth. The first kick from the creation sent her to the ground. Shrub falls off right away and holds his needle waiting for the creation to get closer. The crowd boo's and yells at the poor performance. Neither two care. The blow might have been hard but it was not enough to phase Clara in anyway. "Come back on me. There is no telling in what they will do if we depart." Shrub nods and gets back on. Looking more worn than what she really is, Clara walks closer to the two attackers. The blade of the creation gets close and she is able to move quick enough, away from the swing. The other blade slides on her leg leaving a cut causing blood to come out.

Yelling in pain, Clara backs up. "Are you alright!" Shrub quickly reacts.

"Yes, just stay focused! Or we are both dead." Fighting a creation is way more different than taking out marrows. Especially one that is skilled in combat. "I need you to hide as much as you can. Poke whatever you see come at us."

"What do you think I'm trying to do."

"Just try." The bladed arm opponent comes at them again. This time Clara moves away from both swings. With her sand hand, which the arm was most likely meant for a blade of some sort, she stretches it out. The sand stretches the same way it did to kill Dr. Sharp. It's in a fist and connects with the ribs of the creation. The crowd and marrows are surprised by this. Knocking the opponent back she still manages to swing. Clara moves again but her movements are sloppy. She manages another swing which barely misses the face and she quickly moves.

The blade of the marrow comes toward her but a poke from Shrub makes the marrow lose his focus. The poke does not pierce the marrow but the skeleton turns the blade around swinging it from the end with the metal teeth. The sword manages to stick in Shrub. With a pull the bulb boy falls on the ground.

"Shrub!" Clara runs to him and picks him up.

Dod feels a sinking in his stomach. He makes his way to the cage needing to do something. He looks at Zeet who looks at him across the crowd and shrugs his shoulders not knowing what to do. "I got to go in there." Maybe a distraction. If he picks a fight with the prisoners either they or the marrows will kill him, most likely. The only way he can help Shrub and the creation is if he goes inside someway. The ring course. All of the rings are still up. They were lifted higher but they are still there. If he could somehow get to the top, then he may be able to land on the marrow and take his weapon. As Dod looks up, there is a white dot afloat. It was gone as quickly as he saw it.

Some speck must have been in his eye, Dod thinks to himself and blinks. In fact he is going to order a steak. The prisoners seem amused by this round a lot more differently than the last match. It must have something to do with the two opponents getting beat up. He hears things like, getting their butts kicked and what kind of match is this. The other prisoners may not know what kind of match it is but Dod knows exactly what kind of match it is, a slaughter. The steak will take too long to make so Dod orders a pie instead. He asks for a knife to cut it and all they have are butter knives for the pies. It is hard for prisoners to get anything sharp here. Dod starts cutting it, the crust and preserves gets everywhere on the counter. There is the sticky fruit on his hands, Dod tries to separate a piece with his fingers dropping more of it on the counter by mistake.

The cook shakes his head. "Here damn it. You're making a freaking mess." The cook says handing Dod a blade with more teeth.

"Thank you creat." Dod says as if he is actually embarrassed. He drops more buttons than necessary on the counter. The cook shakes his head and turns around. Under the counter Dod brings the knife down and snaps the blade off its handle. The blade goes into his pocket while the handle gets placed into the pie. Dod takes one hand full of the desert, shoves it into his mouth and walks off. The ladder to the top ring course is hardly been watched. The guard looks at the match that's going on in the arena and so are most of the prisoners. Except that furry one with a scare by the name of, Levrik.

Dodrill takes out one of his shocklas and starts to drink it as he approaches. "What do you think you are doing?"

No time to explain anything to this guy. As if Dod has nothing to lose he flicks the shockla in the face of Levrik partially blinding him burning his sight with florescent. Before the prisoner has anytime to think, Dod's webbed hands covers his face and pushes Leverik's head back. His head bashes the ladder and down goes Leverik. This lizard just jumped over hoops, avoiding a death drop. So this skinny furry creature has nothing on him. Not thinking about it at all Dod climbs the ladder as fast he can. Then Dod thinks he sees that white speck again. No time to care he keeps climbing. He sees that creature stepping backwards as Shrub tries to stay on her shoulders. His small friend pokes forward at the bladed hands of the opponent as if it is any help. Finally on the top Dod jumps the to the closes ring. Yes it is a little higher but the reptile manages.

He hangs with his hands gripped on the bottom of the ring. As high as they are it works to his advantage. No one can see him this high up unless they really pay attention to the ceiling. Dod is able to lift himself to where the top metal beams are that hold the roof. He places the blade in his mouth like all those spies he sees on the telescreen movies back at his home. Dod knows he is no spy but cannot help but play the part a little. Dodrill climbs to the ring that is closes to the creation trying to kill shrub. Maybe if he cuts the ring and drops it on the marrow, then the rider will be unconscious? Dod did not really think this through. Even if he is able to hit his target, what then? Everyone will see him and the match will either stop or keep going. Either way, he is a dead reptilian once he is seen.

Zeet the only one looking at Dod worries if anyone else will see him. His neck can play a part in this by finding the right spot for use. If he stretches his neck he sure will be caught.

From so high above Dod can see the creation that is with Shrub on the floor.

"Clara." Shrub grabs her by the hand. Blood shoots out from the back of her leg as one of the blades goes through.

"Aww!" One hand scratches the ground while the other grabs onto Shrub.

"Screw it man." Rapidly sawing the rope, Dod tries his fastest at dropping the ring. He hangs upside down as his legs and tail hold onto the metal beam.

The other blade goes up but the creation stops. Her eyes focus on a glowing figure flying near him. Lisa get's closer and circles around the creation causing her to search in wonder. The marrow on her back looks just as confused but quickly taps his teeth demanding the creation not to stop what she is about to do. The blade lifts. As soon as the creation's arm is about to come down, Shrub gets ready to run between the blade and Clara. A ring from the sky appears and like magic, lands on top of the creation. With the ghost flying around and the ring appearing, Shrub thinks they are all one component of mischief. He looks up as the marrow does. Not any creature would know who is above, but Shrub does even as far up the creature is. Dod hangs upside down from high up on the ceiling.

The reptile tightens his fist proud. "Got him." He takes a drink of his shockla and drops that also.

The bottle is already noticeable so the creations steps back not entirely sure what it is. It splats on the ground splashing all four fighters. It did not do anything but the creation took her blade out of Clara. She stands up limping but ready to hold her ground.

"No," Shrub says. He pulls back the needle he has in hand and thrusts it like a spear.

The long needle goes between the marrows ribs dropping him off the creation. Laying on the floor the marrow holds onto the giant needle and takes it out. This angers the creation causing him to come toward Clara and Shrub. Then the glowing figure appears. Shrub can barely see the floating white blur but yet she seems like someone he knows. The glow is a nuisance to Shrub, if it is annoying to him then it should be for the creation also. Slowly in a dreary wave the figure comes down toward Shrub like a cloth floating in water.

"Lisa?" Shrub says.

"Yes. I will try to keep this creation away as best I can."

"Okay, just distract her while we think of something." Shrub says looking at Clara's leg.

Now even the crowd is distracted wondering about the ghost flying all over the place. The marrow lies on the floor, wondering what the creation is doing. He taps those teeth rabidly commanding something that no one pays attention to either.

"I know who that is." Shrub says before looking at Clara. "Looks like we may have a chance of getting out." There is a smile on his face as if barley dodged a bullet, or anything that would lead him to his death. He helps his friend and looks about to make sure the creation and marrow do no harm. "We are still stuck in here. Looks like Dod had something to do with our luck."

Dod did have something to do with their luck But not all. The problem with his help is that it could be nothing but a temporary blow. The reptile hangs. Lisa the ghost keeps even Shrogow and the other marrows distracted.

"What is that? Out of the entire Wide city a ghost appears in our arena!" Shrogow says. The marrows look at one another chopping more rapidly than ever, creating a beat of it's own coming from so much chopping consistency. "We need to put a stop to this." The marrow with a gash on his head chops at him. "I don't know if it is hurting anything. The crowd seems to care more about that spirit than the match. We have to make it seem like she was part of the show." Shrogow looks around for answers. "I wonder if the crowd will get annoyed soon." He grabs the microphone. "Now that you see how much can be presented all at one moment. Who can actually catch the ghost? A prize is available."

Shrogow just throws the microphone down. The marrow talks some more to the doctor. "I have no clue if they will follow up on this or if that spirit can be caught. But that damn thing needs to serve a point until the match ends. Tell your skeleton down there to keep up the fight!"

The marrow does not like Shrogow's tone. He chops aggressively. Skin behind the bone sockets show anger partially covering the eyes.

"You can tell me not to get upset. Would you rather your show slow dawn and be distracted? By some unknown...ghost." He points to the top of the arena.

Shrogow cares a lot about the creations and what they do. If he did not, he would not be so good at what he does. The marrow has to respect the contribution from the doctor. He chops at him more mellow.

"But what if the ghost does cause something. Maybe the crowd will see her as a giant insect bothering rather than been a mystery above?" Shrogow looks back at Lisa. "We have to do something before that happens." The doctor looks at the top of the ceiling. "And someone get that damn lizard down."

Dod himself does not know if he should get down. The view is so enlightening especially the fact that no one cares so far that he is up there, which he wants. Strange how so many creatures can comprehend one flash of something new and ignore everything else around. Even if that something else is out of place. Time to get down and help his friends. As he focuses his attention to both sides there are faces of skeletons. They surround both parts of the obstacle course. Now Dod thinks that falling from this will be his death after all. Maybe a relief not to deal with the marrows and their annoying chopping talk. He jokes to himself.

Where is Marvin this entire time? As long as that spring kid is okay, that is at least something. After all, this was one hell of a trip, time for a Shockla. He takes one of the bottles from his backpack. You are doomed. How the marrows will get him to fall, he does not know. But they do know this place better than him.

Lisa is still afloat. She moves so fast that some of the crowd cannot make out how she actually looks like. Many creatures can. Some sights are better than others and with that better perspective and wiring in certain brains, creatures of different kinds can see better than others. She hears those ones questioning. "Never have I seen a creature like that before." Or, "What is that? There is no one like that in any Wide Areas."

Enough for the worrying about who sees her. She needs to help her friends.

"Yat, helps Dod for ya moment." Zeet says as he stares at this strange occurrence. Not caring what kind of creature it is, if it's a creature, he looks up at Dod, then down at Shrub. The neck of Zeet stretches. If it was not for the mysterious ghost then he would not have the opportunity to bite on the top of the cage. His body clinks and works its way up toward the arenas battle ground. He holds on to the top of the fence and looks at the crowd first for some kind of recognition. They are all at a frenzy. Looking at Zeet but yet looking at the ghost. Nothing to worry about them yet. He looks to where Dod is. Will his neck reach that far? Of course it will. With each bone Zeet's neck can be used as a bridge. Speed on the other hand will not be asserted because no matter how long his neck can stretch, it cannot go fast enough to follow any unpredictable falling that Dod will encounter. But he does stretch his neck upward. Across the arena.

Looking at the elongated neck there is Dod's way down and he knows it. He can walk down each bone like steps of stairs. "No point in hanging around." Dod says. He swings and wants to jump forward. Both know he cannot reach the skull.

"Yust jump!" Zeet's floating like skull says.

"I can't reach maaan!" Zeet's eyes get bigger. No they are just shooting toward Dod. Once again the skeleton pops them out. Instead of been surprised after waking up, he pops them out of his sockets on purpose. Dod swings some more. Letting go as he swings forward, he reaches for the eye balls.

Grabbing behind them the veins feel slimy and even if there is nothing there. Dod starts to fall and definitely thinks he is going to die. Now he knows how all those creatures felt as they fell. Tingling in his stomach and toes Dod free falls.

"Gaaaa!" The eyeless face of Zeet yells as his veins get pulled. He sees the top of Dod's head and starts to bring it up as the reptile holds on. The veins are almost all the way in so Dod grabs the long neck.

"Now what, creat?" Not even Dod knows what to say.

"Yeye don't know. Yust yhang on." Zeet blinks rapidly as his eyes adjust back inside the skull. The long neck is closer to the fence since Zeet started bringing it in after Dod grabbed hold of his eyes. The crowd gets amazed by the ghost and although Zeet, Dod and Lisa did not plan their distractions, everyone thinks they are in this show together. Zeet brings in Dod all in. They climb down the fence realizing some marrows getting through the crowd making to the fence. "Yot like they can't get us on this side of ya fence."

"True creat. But I'm sure they can think of something. We, need to think of something! How did you make it to the front row?"

"Yi traded my telacomunicator." Zeet says looking around the fighting ground.

"No time to worry about that." Both move themselves away from the fence. Dod looks at the arena only to notice the two creations are fighting again. "Okay. Now to approach these two is suicide."

"Is that not what ye been doing yis whole time?"

"Very true. But we might as well help." Before anything can be done that blue reptile is walking toward them from the last match. Then there are other large creations following behind him. All with various and different parts attached. "Great. They are here to finish us." Dod looks at Zeet. He has a bottle in his hand and takes a drink. "Well, this is my last one. Nice knowing you, Zeet." He drinks from the bottle knowing that trying to outrun any of the creations is pointless.

A fist hits Clara on the side of her cheek. The pressure is so intense it drops her to the ground.

Shrub who falls down beside her quickly presses close to her. Trying to get her up as best he can. "Come on Clara. We need to get rid of this creation."

"Shrub. I am..." She exhales a breadth and partially closes her eyes, knowing a defeat.

"We can still get out of here." Shrub sees the approaching creation with the marrow on his back.

There is nothing either of them can do. Shrub thinks of some kind of plead for mercy just for Clara's sake. The crowd is now attuned back to the match. The voices say, kill. The bulb boy sees the needle. He forgets about the plead and grabs the weapon.

"Shrub no!" Clara says.

The blade of the creation swipes and goes through the bulb boy. There is no better reaction from an already distracted crowd other than giving them what they want. Everyone cheers loudly. They are so loud but yet Clara hears nothing. She is next to die and she does not care.

Through the entire crowd and the upcoming attack, Dod still manages to hear the two words, "Shrub" and "no". He looks and sees his friend in two pieces. The bulb head with the upper torso and his legs separated. Clara cries on the floor, the only creation with any kind of emotion. "Shrub?" Dod asks if it really happened. He knows it did but still cannot believe his eyes.

Zeet sees where Dod is looking and although he feels the rage build up his intentions drop seen the dead bulb boy. The skeleton has no words. Then Marvin shows up out of nowhere.

The spring kid looks upon the crowd and feels like he missed many things that his friends have seen in these Wide Areas. What he manages to look at next bypasses any curiosity or amusement that he may have missed. Marvin does not say anything but runs toward Shrub. He grabs his head and looks at him wondering if he is actually dead. There is no life with the closed eyes. Marvin has seen him sleep and stay still at times but never has he seen his face with no emotion or breathing to put life in closed eyes. "I am too late." He lets go of the head. His hands clap on his temples as he shuns himself backward. "I showed up too late." There is a creation walking toward Clara ready to kill her. Marvin takes out the flute and plays the tune. He hears the crowd booing but not caring.

Lisa who know occupies the creations who are ready to kill Dod and Zeet hears the tune. She looks toward Marvin and sees Shrub dead. "I can't go. Dod and the skeleton need help." She says although Marvin cannot hear her.

Another gate opens. Marrows and Shrogow come walking toward this entire mess. There is more disappointment in the crowd as the entire match comes to a halt. The marrows spread out telling the creations to settle down. The one with the gash still stands next to Shrogow as they approach Marvin. He points at him. "You, yeah you damn kid. Why do you keep messing up everything. Where did you and this ghost come from?" He looks at the crowd who throw their food at the cage wishing it would hit every creature and creation inside. "Now look what you done. If you just gave us what we wanted none of this would be happening." Shrogow says. His arms open and not to embrace anyone.

"I don't care about any of this. Why do you want me and my friends dead so bad? Just because we are not giving you what is ours? We have every right to disturb your workings." Before Marvin says anymore the doctor snaps at him.

"You don't know what to do with those bones. In the right hands we can create creations far beyond than what we already have." Shrogow looks at the crowd disgusted. "We can take that creation elsewhere beyond fights and building inside the areas. You fool. There is more to this than fights and buttons, there is discovery. That skull is capable of withstanding water at her age. Once a murner reaches a certain maturity then it's too late. Water in pipes that none can get through. With our machines and those bones we can create a solution. Or at least try."

"Not with my friend you are. I hid the skull and can vanish somewhere else again if I want." Marvin says preferring death then to give anything these creators want. The ghost of Lisa floats down next to him.

"You do have a lot of heart. Maybe it will do good for one of my creations. How about you still give me the bones. We can revive that bulb boy if the proper amount of time has not passed. If not we can put him as a creation regardless. He will be restored and you will be safe. Just give me the skull!

The soul to the piece floats right next to you. What more do you want. She is still alive. Well, sort of." The doctor says eyeing Lisa.

Lisa looks at Marvin with sobbed eyes. She feels no emotion but thoughts are still all the same from when she died. "Give my skull to him Marvin. I do not mind been like this. I would rather live the rest of my life with you and Shrub alive other than dying for me."

Breathing out, Marvin looks at the flute. Feeling like he has the most to blame for this he shakes his head in disagreement. "No, Lisa. I brought them here and lead them all the way through this. Now they are facing death and I can still escape. I made a bargain with the mirror masters. They where going to help me find all my friends and we would teleport out of the Wide Areas. We can still do that but I wish I could save, Shrub. This will cost me my soul."

"Your soul!" Lisa says surprised. The very words now make her feel something.

Marvin holds the mirror in his hand he sees his reflection and how it takes up most of the uneven triangular shape of glass. Just drop it. Marvin remembers the Laughing Dog saying. You are the spring kid after all. Marvin's image shrinks and then there are multiple images of himself as the mirror falls from his hand. It shatters on the floor dividing new formed mirrors. Between the broken separated glass, Marvin thought the brown flat ground of the arena he stands on would still be seen. Instead it's all shadow. Marvin drops to his knees to see where the shadow came from. Shrogow and the marrows step forward curiously.

The shadow gets wider the more Marvin tries to see where it comes from as he moves the shards. He moves a piece of shattered mirror that gets bigger. He pushes the glass more and shadow stretches like black cloth on the floor. The ground below feels unsteady as if he was floating almost. He looks down now only seeing his reflection on the floor. The mirror got bigger between the broken glass, which keeps expanding into a shadow nothingness. Marvin grabs two pieces and pushes one toward Dod and Zeet while the other goes toward Clara and the body of, Shrub. Dod and Zeet run toward the piece and stay on it. Clara grabs Shrub stepping toward her piece. The creation that was so near to killing her jumps toward a piece of his own before the mirrors expand creating more shadow gaps. With his spring arms Marvin pulls the two closer to him leaving hollowness surrounding them.

Shrogow and a few marrows find pieces for themselves. The one with the gash hears panic and yelling surrounding the place. He sees as the crowd leave the building and the ground cracks like a silent earthquake of shadow. If there is a sound it's not heard by all the screaming of creatures, cups falling and chairs moving. His creations fall to their deaths along with a few of the marrows. Anger fills his mind. Not forgetting about his survival, all the doctor wants to do is kill the spring kid.

Marvin sees as everything falls. After all the creations were made and trained to kill against their own will. Each one was not brought into this and with life in them, Marvin is sure they feel something. His three other friends are now next to him. With all three mirrors touching one another each step onto Marvin's mirror which is the biggest. He looks at Shrogow and the marrows as they float away. There is now separate glass pieces floating all around in a blanket of darkness. The arena is no more. Only whoever stands on the mirrors exist now. Marvin looks to his side where Lisa gently floats.

"Do you think this is going to be able to engulf the entire city?" He asks.

"I am not sure. But we are surrounded by darkness and the arena is gone. There is no imagining what the inside of this building now looks like."

"Or how it looks like from the outside." Dod says looking at Lisa. "Your the ghost." He says recognizing her. If things were different the reptile would be more cheerful.

"Yes." Is all Lisa can say as she hears the voice of the doctor yell in the distance.

"I will get you and when I do it will have nothing to do with those bones! I will twist your mind and make you kill for me and to kill all your friends!" The marrow with the gash grabs Shrogow by the shoulder and moves him with a thrust to look at him. There is chopping at the doctor with anger in his eyes. "Do not blame me for this. I have no idea how that spring kid managed to...to make this. It has to do with that spirit girl. It has to." The shard is now far away sailing as if it was in water. Shrogow and the marrows look toward where Marvin and his friends were, which is now a dot in the distance. "This has to end at some point. He would not just place everything in nowhere and not have a plan to get out."

"Creat, how do we get out of here?" Dod asks looking around the rim as if to find land or some kind of solution for a way out.

"I'm not sure. The dog that gave me the mirror just told me to use my abilities." "What dog?" Dod asks. "Never mind. Then that should mean a way out."

"The flute!" Lisa says surprised.

Not knowing what good the instrument would do, Marvin takes it out. He plays a tune and shrugs his shoulders.

She looks at him confused. "Well those other pieces seem to be stuck on. That's not normal." "None of this is normal." Marvin says. He wants to look at Shrub but cannot. Clara has not said

a word as she holds the upper body on her lap, embracing the large bulb head. "Ya mirrors. Have yem make yother mirrors."

"What?" Dod asks.

"Have yhem reflect yon one yanother. Why would yey just stay close together like yat?" Zeet says. "What else you want to do? Float all course?"

"Good point and it is worth a try." Marvin sees how they all are together. He grabs one from the side and brings it forward making a side wall. Dod does the same as he grabs the top of one end.

Having them attached almost makes the group in a triangular cup of many of the same images of each other. With three mirrors reflecting each other, it looks as though the friends many reflections stand on mirror stairways. The visual is quite overwhelming for them all. Even Clara needs to shake her head a bit from getting bombarded with so much reflections. They all close and open their eyes the vision of them in the mirrors gets distorted. They see thousands of each other and feel as though they are now falling. Not down the shadow nothingness for they see their many reflections imprinted everywhere looking the same then moving to the side creating new sections in a thousand areas. When the mirrors turn something comes from between each reflection as it shifts. Pipes and more pipes they add up and overcome the reflections. Like wire twining together then creating a single pipe path mirror a round tunnel is made.

They slide. The laughing dog's face appears in this new tunnel which can be a mirror. Yet the dog's giant face is all that multiplies and it continues down this sliding tunnel moving his jaw up and down with the same motion. Not blinking an eye or twitching his nose the dog laughs and disappears and there is darkness except for the end of the tunnel. Moist air is suddenly felt. One by one they fall out and drop to solid brick. It's not a long drop but Marvin is the first, then Clara, embracing Shurb. Both quickly move. Dod falls no more than one foot with Zeet suddenly dropping on him. Lisa flies down and joins them without the harsh drop. Green grimy metal walls surround the group. The smell of wet seaweed is strongly potent in the place. They are back at their exhibit.

Getting up with familiarity, Marvin knows the place and so does Lisa.

Dod gets up holding the side of his head feeling pain. "I could not even think of what was happening to us at all exactly. I am surprised I did not throw up on the way."

All look around and Lisa remembers this is where she and Marvin first met. She was playing a flute she made long ago. Not the same flute they have now, that she newly made. But one that she used, until it broke, long ago. Marvin kneels next to Clara. He looks at Shrub. A young boy, too young for what happened to him. What will his parents think. How will Marvin go on with memories of his best friend for the rest of his life?

"Shrub you got to wake up." Marvin looks at Clara.

Clara takes away her tears still looking at the bulb boy. "You two gave me something that no creation ever can get. Shrub named me. From there he meant so much to me. Now he is gone." She hugs his head tighter.

"You can stay with us. I will tell his parents everything. With you maybe they will see the smallest one from their kids did so much."

Clara sniffles. "We can do that. I'm sure they will not be so enlightened. I mean, look." She presents Shrub's body without any arm or hand gestures.

Marvin brings his head down. Dod kneels next to them and puts his hand on Shrub's forehead.

New emotions seem to introduce old feeling to the ghost. Zeet himself feels saddens. Even though he did not know Shrub too well, he still was his friend.

CHAPTER TWENTY-ONE

Talking with Shrub's parents was the most overwhelming thing Marvin has ever done. The entire Wide Area trip was like a day in school after seeing Shrub's parents worried if he is alive or not. The bulb boy is with a local doctor now. Did they blame Marvin, they were angry of course. Marvin even brought his parents to come by, to face the situation. As the time passed Shrub's parents came to the conclusion that he had a mind of his own to go that far. Anytime he was in trouble, Marvin has always been there for him. This time, the situation just went too far. Marvin and his parents had to leave. At least when they did, Shrub's family had no blame on Marvin.

***

Marvin forgot about two things. His soul and Lisa. Maybe the mirror masters forgot about him. Perhaps they are letting him enjoy what little time he has left to be with his friends and family. The time for the Laughing Dog's appearance remains a mystery. Him and Lisa go back to that spot they first met.

"Bulb-Heads usually let their dead flow down a water filled pipe. I hope it does not lead to that.

Maybe they will let Clara take him with her." Marvin looks at the spirit of Lisa flowing next to him. "I wonder where she wants to go.

Maybe somewhere she remembered before she was a creation?" Lisa says.

"Perhaps." The slight glow of Lisa is hard for Marvin to ignore. Especially walking so close. "How are we going to figure out what to do with you? The exhibit will now know you as a ghost and will not be happy about it. The silent girl who can now go everywhere. We need you back to how you use to be." Marvin says and holds the skull. "Had it the entire time. There are places in The Wide Areas that might know something."

Lisa stops. "No. Before we ever have to go back we have to try other things first. I wonder if all the areas got swallowed like the arena." She looks at her own skull in Marvin's hands. "Let's try the skull. Maybe then we can figure something out." Lisa stops. "Place it in my face."

Marvin faces her examining his friend wondering if it will work. He holds it close to her. Lisa's eyes are where the sockets are and it seems like the skull should belong there. The jaw chops. She looks at Marvin surprised. If he never knew her, he would be a frightened creature. Spiritual face over a murner skull, frightening to see in any area. Since that is not the case, a sense of joy substitutes.

"Nothing else is happening?" He asks.

Her spirit hands move around the skull but nothing else takes place. "Not at all."

"Play the flute." Marvin hands her the instrument. He thinks if nothing works then he might ask the mirror masters before they take him away. That would be a laugh for the Dog.

She closes her eyes tighter as she exhales. Marvin holds the flute next to her since she cannot do it herself. She blows. The tune is sweet. Marvin's eyes widen. Something actually happened, how energy, oxygen from a ghost? She must remember how to play from when she had her last flute. She takes hold of the instrument. Now it almost turns into the same tune that Marvin heard when he first found her. The ghostly fog starts to turn pale. Like milk into a glass of water. Then her face appears exactly how it use to. Her small cheeks a little puffed out and eyes closed as she plays. When her black hair gets painted the natural color, then Marvin knows she is becoming complete. He does not say anything not wanting to disturb the process in anyway. When her whole body is fulfilled she stops playing to feel her dress, then her face. She opens her eyes and looks at Marvin.

"Your back." He says.

A smile that he has never seen on her appears. Her large pupils expand, the gills on her neck raise. "Let me see. Give me a mirror."

Marvin looks at her stern. "I don't have one."

She is back and she sees the drape she had on and her hands that now have skin. There seems to be another presence so the clapping from whoever it is does not surprise them. Both turn to see. The Laughing Dog. He has his regular face again. This time it is more tame and clean. Marvin thinks it's a new skin completely.

"Now that you have solved all your problems and see that your murner now has her body. Care to talk about what we mentioned before?" The Dog asks.

"Do I have a choice." Is all Marvin asks.

Lisa steps forward. "Take my soul."

A laugh comes out of the Dog. "You just got it back." He slaps his leg laughing still. "Sorry. A good trade. A possible one also." He smiles with that large grin.

"What are you saying, Lisa? I'm going I made the deal."

"No, Marvin. It is my burden to bare. You came for me. My soul was lost then found. Now Shrub is nearly dead. Take care of him. I may feel complete but still cannot bare going on just thinking that he died for my mistake."

"Exactly, a mistake. There is no need for you to leave. I'm going to go..." Before he says anymore Lisa holds one hand in front of him and places her other in Marvin's really quickly. Lisa cups Marvin's hand with both of hers. She lets them slide off like water and follows the Laughing Dog.

"No Marvin. This is good-bye." As if there was not a chance of saying anything, the two are already at a pipe entrance that has never been noticed before. She follows the Dog down the path which begins to shrink.

The path disappears and there is nothing but silence. Marvin looks down and opens his hand.

He looks at the flute.

THE END

www.ingramcontent.com/pod-product-compliance
Lightning Source LLC
Chambersburg PA
CBHW040900010826

48978CB00013BA/1092